P9-CFR-377

. . . That morning, sitting on her flowered spread in her small, frame house in Glendale, Kit's mother had raised her wavering head to ask, to demand, "And what was she to you, anyhow?"

And not to say. Not to answer that rightful question with its rightful answer now, after all the years of silence and discretion. Not to say, We lay in each other's arms for eight years. We felt passion. To tell her that her daughter, Katherine, had been a mountain climber with careful hands moving with Juno toward a precipice, ledge by ledge, deftly. That they had held each other, trembling, tight together. That they lived inside each other, body and soul, for eight years. That they had planted flowers and baked bread and built bookcases. To say their lives were the same as everybody else's; to say their lives had been different. . . .

Spring Forward/Fall Back

a novel by

Sheila Ortiz Taylor

Spring Forward/Fall Back

the NAIAD PRESS inc.

1985

Copyright © 1985 by Sheila Ortiz Taylor

All rights reserved. No part of this book may be reproduced
or transmitted in any form or by any means electronic or
mechanical without permission in writing from the publisher.

Printed in the United States of America
First Edition

Cover design by Tee A. Corinne
Typesetting by Sandi Stancil

Library of Congress Cataloging in Publication Data

Taylor, Sheila Ortiz, 1939–
    Spring forward/fall back.

    I. Title.
PS3570.A9544S67   1985   813′.54   85-15526
ISBN 0-930044-70-3

Sheila Taylor was born in Los Angeles in 1939 and by the age of eleven had decided to become a novelist. Her quest for narrative content led her into early marriage, travel to the midwest, the east, England, the continent, and eventually divorce court. She attended graduate school at UCLA, often flanked on either side by a small daughter. She tried her hand also at raising rabbits and compiling a bibliography on Emily Dickinson, both of which enterprises flourished. The bibliography was ultimately published by the Kent State University Press in 1962 and the rabbit saga by Naiad Press twenty years later. She teaches literature and writing at Florida State University and lives a quiet, rustic life in the country, surrounded by her partner, an occasional daughter, a small poodle, and a Sheltie who chases airplanes.

This novel is a work of fiction. Names, characters, incidents, and locales are either used fictitiously or are a product of the author's imagination.

For Margie, with love.

I wish to thank my daughters, Andrea and Jessica, for their advice, trust, and enthusiasm; to Marjorie Craig for her wise criticism and gentle support; to Florida State University for a year's sabbatical.

Spring Forward / Fall Back

CONTENTS

BOOK ONE

SPRING FORWARD

CHAPTER 1: THE SEA GULL CAFE

Olive Rivers balanced precariously two nearly empty ketchup bottles on top one another, then watched through cat's eye glasses at the Baron climbing his lifeguard tower. Now there was a man.

She wiped the turquoise formica counter of the Sea Gull Cafe, then slipped into the back booth for a late morning cigarette. Lighting a Kool, she edged *The New Avalon Times* out from under the glass ash tray. Nobody around, just old Loomis on a stool watching the saltwater taffy machine in the window. She read carefully, her mouth shaping the words, her glasses glinting opaquely, tilting opaquely, tilting twin spots of sunlight onto the walls, onto old Loomis's back as he watched protectively the chrome arms swimming through sea green taffy.

Tomorrow Sunday. Day of rest, thank you Jesus. Worked her fingers to the bone, day in and day out. Body and soul together. And for what, she wanted to know? Not a thank you. Elizabeth thinking money grew on trees.

Time she woke up, Elizabeth. Time she thought about things. Seventeen was time enough. Seventeen meant helping your own, asked to or not.

Time enough and more. Some folks were married by seventeen, having a baby even, and then up and left alone and no way to keep body and soul together.

Olive Rivers stubbed her cigarette into faceted, clear glass, where a red sea gull was inscribed on the ashtray's bottom. Almost 11:30. She jerked her head up, aiming her eyes at the clock shaped like a coffee pot, shaking the tabloid into obedience. She ran her thumb down page two, making the crease, and reached for another Kool.

Time enough. The phosphorus flared strangely, a double head, probably, that Olive had not noticed because her eye had come to rest on the photograph of a giant tuna hanging slack-jawed from a hook like a scythe that poked through his upper lip. Underneath the tuna were two men, one of them the Baron, wearing his tiny life-saving trunks, the other some society man—from the look of him—one of those Wrigleys, most likely. "Tuna Club Hosts Distinguished Guest," it said. The distinguished guest looked small under his tuna. The Baron did not look small.

They said he was a millionaire, the Baron. Twice over, World's most famous lifeguard. And then his suntan oil business. You would not think there was so much money in suntan oil, but there he was, living proof. And Bill Wrigley with all that chewing gum. Showed what could be done with a little good sense and a lot of hard work.

Even in the picture you could see the suntan oil. Smell it, almost. Like fresh-baked macaroons. His arms shone, his muscles looking like greased birthday balloons straining to bust his little t-shirt wide open. Sitting in his lifeguard tower, millionaire or not, doing the job the city paid him to do.

Leon said the Baron inherited his money from his rich

relatives and had not earned it at all. Then in the same breath Leon would say the Baron was a phony through and through, not really royalty at all. From this Olive could tell that Leon was just jealous.

Probably royalty was in the eye of the beholder. And Olive Rivers was glad she could appreciate it when she saw it. She peered again through her glasses. Over fifty they said he was, and all those girls with nothing better to do hanging from his lifeguard tower in transparent bathing suits, morning till night, hanging from his arms when he left for home at six o'clock. Could have any one of them he wanted.

She shook the paper into its original shape and started to fold it in half when she saw, "Daylight Savings Starts Sunday Set Your Clocks."

But which way? It never made a lick of sense to her. Always she had to set clocks quickly, trying not to think what the change meant, or whether she got another hour of sleep or lost one. Somebody made money off it, you could bet. And the government was not about to ask Olive Rivers what she thought or what she wanted. Still, she was a person too. Worked hard and paid her taxes and raised her daughter to do the same.

Abruptly she stood. 11:45. The bell tower on the west hill had given one quick warning peal. Lunch trade would start arriving in the next quarter hour. She eased the empty ketchup bottle down and tossed it into the open trash, then wiped carefully the lip of the newly-created bottle, and screwed the white lid down tight. Heinz.

Eight sugar dispensers and they all needed filling. Damp contours of sugar reached around inside the glass as if trying to escape. Sea air did that. Made the salt stick together too, even with rice mixed in. No time now to fix anything. Steamer would be on the horizon in another fifteen minutes, if it was on time, and the morning boatload of tourists ordering sacks of hamburgers and fries, not to mention the regulars from as far away as Marilla Street wanting and expecting the lunch special—stuffed bell peppers Saturdays—by rights, on time, and with a smile.

Hurriedly she filled the twin glass coffee carafes with water, ripped open with her teeth brown foil envelopes of measured coffee, shook them over the filters, and flipped twin switches.

Chimes from the bell tower began their song: "I left my love in Avalon." Eddie did. Eddie left his love in Avalon. And his baby too. That's dreamers for you. And where was she now, Elizabeth? Olive Rivers wiped her hands on her apron, gauging the time remaining, gauging the distance to the bathroom.

Here she was day in and day out working her own fingers to the bone just to put meat on the table, and that Elizabeth gone off into the hills God alone knew where, and never so much as washing a dish or lifting a broom.

There was time, but only just. She stuck the Kool into her mouth and drew heavily, walking toward the bathrooms: Buoys and Gulls. She smacked open the Gulls' door just right of the limp knob, not breaking stride, and passed through the tiny outer room where she and Grace hung their street clothes, and into the toilet.

Cautiously she sat. In her daughter's hand, scrawled across the door, she read the words slowly, sounding them out, "Amazing Grace." And where was she now — that Elizabeth?—thought Olive Rivers as she dropped her cigarette between her thighs and watched it spin down the toilet like some drowning steamer.

CHAPTER 2: DIVER

Elizabeth Austen Rivers sat on the steamer dock eating her second hamburger. Sometimes she felt like she would never be full. She felt sometimes an army of people inside her demanding to be fed. For a moment she half-considered a third hamburger, but saw now on the horizon a fleck of white, the steamer, bearing toward her. She got up from her perch on the Harbor Master's steps and stretched in the sunshine, and then turned instinctively in the direction of the bell tower on the hillside, just as it began to toll the hour.

Once there had been two steamers. Things change, Mr. Loomis had said, and not for the better. Two steamers was a luxury, her mother had said, that nobody needed, much less wanted. Elizabeth could remember, though, the twin white steamers, one leaving, the other coming, always an arrival or a departure, the two ships sailing toward each other and then away from each other, attracted and repelled like those little scottie dogs on magnets or like the arms on the taffy machine in the Sea Gull Cafe.

Noon. As the twelfth tone struck, the band began straggling down the Pleasure Pier toward the steamer gangplank with their glinting instruments. Elizabeth spotted Leon Feeney, fingering his saxophone and sucking in an awful way on his reed.

"Hello, Beautiful." He tipped his white yachting hat with "Five Corsairs" embroidered in gold and showed the matching gold caps on his teeth, under what must be a very prickly mustache.

Expertly Elizabeth spit into her diving mask and ran her fingers around slowly inside hoping that Leon, watching, would want to throw up. Chicken-hearted Leon. Harmless, she guessed, but very ugly.

There was hair all over him. Curly black hairs grew even on his fat white fingers. Musicians were supposed to have delicate fingers. Leon's fingers looked like uncooked sausage links. She watched them move up and down the curve of his saxophone just as she had seen them move up and down her mother's freckled arm. Elizabeth shuddered. Then she snapped her mask over her eyes and nose, inhaling sharply. The glass sucked in on her face like a sea anemone to the dock.

"Ten dollars, for that!" Her mother had been incredulous. It was the best mask made, Elizabeth had explained. Her mother knew somebody else who always had to have the best, but out of sight, out of mind. Her mouth snapped closed like the lid on the coffee cannister.

"This mask represents an investment. A business investment."

"Monkey business is what."

"I mean real business that I can earn money at."

"What doing?"

"Diving for coins at the pier."

"Boys do that, and not the best kind either."

No, they were not the best kind, Elizabeth supposed, watching them now scuffing along the dock toward her, cut-off Levis riding low on slim brown hips, fins and masks dangling carelessly from their careless fingers, as they laughed and talked in voices that knocked and squeaked like oars in rusty oarlocks. What were they, she wondered, these creatures that seemed to saunter forth from some remote crevice to breathe up all the air?

She pulled the diving mask from her face, letting it dangle around her neck. The steamer was making the curve of its approach now. Backwash sloshed under the pilings and yanked small boats at their moorings. The band was playing "I Left My Love in Avalon." Hilo Hattie swayed in the light April breeze, while Elizabeth struggled into her swim fins and flapped toward the pilings.

Passengers leaned out over the rail, waving and taking snapshots of the Baron, Head Lifeguard, in tight blue denims, his arm around Hilo Hattie, barking a welcome over the PA system, and the Five Corsairs below on the dock flashing their instruments.

Elizabeth, poised on a piling with the other divers, looked up expectantly at the line of tourists crowding the rail. Then it came, the first coin, like a splinter of sun. Three boys knifed the water.

Let them. Elizabeth had other business. Always she waited for the coin that was hers. The one intended for her alone. Then she would bend her legs lightly and spring through air into water, scarcely feeling an impact, through the silence, down toward where the coin fluttered just out of reach until, with three strong fin strokes, she took it. Hers. Then the breathless rising through shafts of light and explosion onto the surface, where—bobbing and smiling—she would nod a ceremonial thank-you toward the coin-giver.

CHAPTER 3: JUNO

By stretching far out over the railing Juno Reed could just see Kit parking the jeep in front of the Sea Gull Cafe. Katherine, bless her, was always late, and when Juno chided, Kit would pull her face into Emersonian seriousness and say, "Time is just the stream I go afishin in."

Juno picked up the bundles from her mainland shopping expedition and, finding herself unable to move in the crush of tourists, set them down again. The gangplank was not even in place yet. Island life, she reminded herself. There really was no place for haste. She reached for a straying hairpin and tucked it back into place, leaned her elbow on the rail. The band swung into "Twenty-six miles and an isle of blue, Santa Catalina is waiting for you."

Waiting, yes, she thought, feeling the need of Kit beside her, feeling excited and calm all at once, permitting the sun its warm hand on her back, dropping her gaze down the crevice to the wash of water between steamer and dock.

Divers! She had told Richard a thousand times that as Harbor Master it was his duty to put a stop to this dangerous pagan custom, or somebody, one day, would drift into those screws. She clamped her eyes tight shut and curled her hand into a fist that soundlessly but emphatically beat warning on the railing.

The first casualty might even be one of her own students. She peered closer at the bobbing heads, then ran her teacher's eye up the wooden ladder the divers climbed hand over hand, then onto the pilings where others waited, most of them familiar, of course, in a town this size, and then she saw—she was quite sure—yes, Elizabeth Rivers, a senior, her pride. Elizabeth, poised for the dive.

Suddenly, though Juno had not spoken aloud, could not speak, Elizabeth looked directly up, apparently straight into her teacher's eyes, when, as if in a single related movement, a fat woman at the rail next to Juno flung wide into the air a coin that seemed somehow propelled by Juno's own hand. Elizabeth dove.

Something like anger ran up Juno's legs, unsteadying her, as if springs had unlocked in her knees. She could not look. Except in memory at a cake she'd seen as a child at a birthday party, a cake celebrating a neighbor's new swimming pool, where the mother ran the knife through swimmers made of pink icing and spread the stain of blood the length of the pool-shaped cake. She remembered next Alan Ladd floating face down in a swimming pool with his blood spreading out from him like ribbons from a Maypole. Someone—was it Gloria Swanson?—had screamed, covering her movie star eyes in horror.

She would look, must look, finally, down into the clear dark water, where at last a shining, seal-dark head broke surface, smiled, nodded its thank you.

Juno stepped abruptly back, pausing only to gather her parcels. Katherine would be waiting.

CHAPTER 4: HOMECOMING

Old Loomis stood blinking outside the Sea Gull Cafe, like a dozing cat suddenly scooped off the sofa and deposited onto the front porch.

Katherine Tebolt waved in his direction as she tossed packages into the rear of the jeep. "Olive throw you out, Mr. Loomis?" He smiled, as if glad for an explanation. "There's always the library," she reminded. He crossed the street toward the two women.

"Now we're in for it," groaned Juno, scrunching down into the passenger's seat.

With a sideways smile of apology Kitty slid the key into the ignition and rested her hands on the wheel.

"You look like a gangster," said Juno, "driving the getaway car."

"I *am* a gangster. I steal hearts."

Mr. Loomis was murmuring toward them. "Lunch trade, lunch trade, lunch trade." He shook his leonine head in time to his lamentations. "Tell me this, if you can. It's what I want to know."

"What's that?" asked Juno, leaning forward.

He turned in the direction of the taffy machine glinting in the window of the Sea Gull. "Where have Olive Rivers' values gone to?" He took a clean, old-man's hanky from his pants pocket and unfolded it square by square, as if her values might be concealed in its recesses, then passed it twice under his nose. "It ain't exactly like I didn't know her since she was pigtails. 'Lunch trade,' " he grumbled. "Friends first; lunch trade after, is what I think."

"That's what I think too, Mr. Loomis," Katherine assured him, "but I'd better feed Juno in the next five minutes or she'll start questioning *my* values. She's just back from shopping over town."

"Well, curse me for a thoughtless old man. I've been keeping you like you had nothing to do with your time except waste it, same as me."

"Mr. Loomis," said Kit, with a robust pat for his bony hand, "you can always go around to the library."

"Thank you, no, Miss Tebolt. I don't hardly go there since you retired. That Helen Valentine is the meanest part of Sunday. Acts like the library is her own living room. Besides, she wouldn't know a good book if it bit her legs clean off." He looked longingly at the taffy machine's bright arms revolving like a perpetual motion machine. "Olive'll let me in after these tourists go off. Meantime, sun'll do me some good. Won't keep you two ladies another minute."

The jeep lurched off down Crescent, past the St. Catherine Hotel, and onto Sumner, away from the bay, past Cycle Town rentals and the Island Wash, toward the hills and home.

"Poor Kit," said Juno, leaning across the gearshift to plant a kiss.

"Why 'poor Kit?' "

"You must miss them, your wards."

"Well, sometimes," she admitted with a shrug. "But I haven't gone anywhere and neither have they. We're all marooned on the same island. As you were just painfully reminded."

"Oh I don't mind old Loomis," she smiled. "Or the others from the library. Besides, I have my own collection of strays from school for whom you have shown a truly saintly patience."

"Truly saintly, truly saintly." Kit reared her head back and snorted. Juno watched the bowl of gray hair swirl in the wind and put her hand out in wonder, to touch.

Then they were turning at last down the asphalt drive that led to their house, passing through a grid of sunlight cast by a stand of eucalyptus stretching away into the hills.

Katherine wheeled the Jeep up to the house and turned off the ignition. "Welcome, love."

CHAPTER 5: STILL LIFE

Really it was nice sometimes to be alone, Olive Rivers thought, as her freckled fingers in their freshly lacquered nails curled around her rum and Coke. She clutched her chenille robe at the throat, then leaned her head back, guiding the La-Z-Boy into its reclining position, feet elevated, waitress feet. Rubbing her soles and ankles together made a whistling sound from her knee high hose.

It was six fifteen. Plenty of time. Leon would not pick her up for an hour or so. Olive wondered mildly where Elizabeth was, but she liked having the house to herself with nobody to tend or feed or see to. Just herself.

She trickled some rum and Coke through pink lips and thought of Paul Newman in *Cat on a Hot Tin Roof* when he was always drinking too much and telling people he was waiting for it to hit that blue line. It was real, that blue line. You did not need to be a movie star to know that, much less an alcoholic.

Olive had too much self-respect ever to be an alcoholic. One cocktail in the evening for the purposes of relaxation did not make you an alcoholic. Leon said drinking by yourself did. He had read it in a magazine. People who drank alone were alcoholics. Leon knew a lot of facts and was always improving his mind. Still, Leon did not know everything. It was not Olive's fault if nobody was home when she wanted to have a simple drink or two.

She shook a Kool out of the white pack, the last, she noted, crumpling the wrapper into a reminder to buy some more when she went out. And there was something else she must remember too, but what was it? She snapped on the table lamp as if the light might help her remember, and drew in powerfully on her cigarette.

No use, to save her life she could not remember. Olive took off her glasses and set them next to the lamp, thoughtfully caressing the painful crescents formed during the day on either side of her nose. Leon had bought her a book called *Thirty Days to a More Powerful Memory*. It was around here somewhere.

The book had said that contrary to popular opinion you did not have to be old to lose your memory. That people started losing their memories in their mid-thirties and did not quit until they were fifty. If that was true she had been losing hers for a good year now and would go on for another fifteen. If that was true, then what a pitiful thing life must be. But Olive was a Christian and liked to think God had better sense than that.

She emptied her glass down to the line of blue daisies and wondered about Paul Newman's memory. Or the Baron's, for that matter. With all his forgetting nearly over, the Baron could concentrate now on his sun tan oil business. But was there hope for Olive Rivers, only a year into the forgetting stage and miles from concentration of any kind? God was merciful.

She wanted another cigarette. She was not drunk, yet she felt strangely heavy, as if she could not get up, put on her shoes, and walk the three blocks to the drugstore and get some more. Even though she was known for energy like that, on her feet as she was, morning till night, day after day, walking as much as seventy-five miles (even housewives walked as much as fifty, she had read somewhere), working her fingers to the bone, just to put meat on the table for Elizabeth, now she had none of that energy left for herself. Did not have the memory of a cat.

Elizabeth paused on the wooden steps for a last look seaward. Fog was blowing in. She strained up onto her toes and tried for a look west. The sunset shed an orange glow everywhere. But of course she could not ever see from her house the sun setting, living in the flats as they did. Always the glow and never the thing itself.

Not that she wanted to be rich. She just wanted to live in the hills and see the sun set. To see all of the sky at one time.

She tossed her fins into a cluttered corner of the sleeping porch as the screen door banged behind. Starving. It must be seven o'clock. Then she saw through the failing light of the living room her mother asleep in her chair with a nearly empty glass tipping perilously. A circle of pink light from the lamp shade shone down one cheek. Elizabeth approached on bare feet and took the glass carefully out of the sleeping woman's hand.

This woman, her mother, wrapped in an ugly lilac bathrobe, Gypsy Rose polish on her nails. On a hanger over the door hung the pink pantsuit she had sewed on all day last Sunday, for Leon, while smells of pot roast slicked the walls.

Sometimes it seemed this woman could not possibly be her mother. This woman who was so unlike anybody she had ever admired: Juno Reed, Eleanor Roosevelt, Florence Chadwick. Elizabeth tried to imagine her mother smeared like Florence Chadwick from head to toe with bear grease, walking into the surf before the television cameras, beginning her twenty-six mile channel swim through shark-infested waters, from the mainland to Catalina Island. The truth was, Olive Rivers swam like a dog, head held high out of the water to keep her hair from the salt.

Elizabeth ran her hand over her own salty hank: her hair felt like seaweed. In the small, darkened kitchen she pulled the light chain, and set her mother's glass in the sink. Sweaty highball glasses made her want to throw up. She squirted a stream of Joy across the yellowed, eroding ice cubes and filled up the glass with foamy scalding water, shuddered, turned to the refrigerator and stood before the open door.

Meat loaf! How she despised meat loaf. Contemptible meat loaf. Unable to commit itself to being one thing or another. Meat loaf lacked . . . conviction. *Conviction*—the word satisfied her.

"Elizabeth!"

The girl slammed shut the refrigerator. Mothers could not stand refrigerator doors being open. They could tell in their sleep.

"Yes, Mama." Elizabeth rolled her hair up and fished in her Levi pocket for a bobby pin, as she walked into the dim living room. Her mother's hand stretched out toward her. It felt cold.

"What time is it, dear?"

"You going out with Leon?"

"How long was I asleep?"

"It's after seven." Elizabeth held her Benrus under the pink glow. "Seven ten, to be exact."

"That's it, that's what I was trying to remember all this time. It's about the clocks. The paper said tonight we set them back. Or was it forward? There's a way to remember.

Spring forward, fall back. That's it." She swung her chair up-right, gathered up her glasses and the crumpled cigarette package, then paused, as if looking for a missing object.

"I got it, Mother."

But her mother was already disappearing into the tiny hallway, half-hearing, reminding, "You'll do that, won't you, Elizabeth, while I'm out with Leon, set the clocks?"

CHAPTER 6: THE WORLD BENEATH

Elizabeth looked past Larry Sutton's head, studying the brass clock on Mary Broadwin's mantle. The face had lean, spread-out Roman numerals. There was a bell jar over the whole thing, but no back. Every gear and spring was visible, as if nothing was concealed.

She would pretend to Larry that her mother had told her to be home from Mary Broadwin's party by twelve. She and Larry would ride their bicycles down Sumner Boulevard through the dark and stillness toward her house on Clarissa Street. Their gears would make a twicking sound. Larry would be thinking about how to maneuver her away from the porch light so he could lunge at her invisibly. She would be planning how to make this impossible.

She did not know why she had agreed to come with Larry Sutton except that she wanted to see Mary Broadwin's house in the hills and because she always thought something important, something *significant* might happen at a party, but it never did.

Larry's lips were too fat. He would look like a button perch coming toward her through waves of night.

In fact he was mouthing something at her now. She could not hear over the thumping music. He gave a never mind shake to his head and took slippery hold of her hand, leading her through the dancing couples, out the front door and into the street.

"Old Larry thinks of everything," he said, as if speaking of a beloved comrade and nodded in the direction of their bicycles, leaning like lovers against a solitary eucalyptus tree.

Elizabeth doubted he did. While he dug through his bicycle basket Elizabeth looked up into clear sky and sharp stars. Across the bay a nearly full moon trembled over the dark water. "Mother, I will," she murmured, moon-ward.

"Whuzat?" said Larry, suddenly straightening, a rolled up, white t-shirt protectively clutched to his not very firm belly. "You say something?" He tenderly unwrapped a Jim Beam bottle from its swaddling.

"That's what Jane Eyre says to the moon when the moon tells her to flee Mr. Rochester and not marry him after all."

"Who?" asked Larry.

"Jane Eyre."

"Jenn-Air?"

"*Jane Eyre.* It's a book."

"You like to read, don't you?" He produced two plastic glasses from a dingy beach towel in his bike basket and poured generously. "That enough?"

She nodded, taking the glass, watching him pour his own until it washed up over the lip and dripped down onto the carpet of pine needles at their feet. He licked whiskey from his hand.

"Well, I like to drink, Liz." Half-way through his attempt

to down the whole glassful he began choking, eyes filling with tears.

Elizabeth slammed him hard on the back. "You don't have to do that on my account, Larry."

"My own," he gasped. He finished the glass and wiped his mouth with the t-shirt.

While he stooped to replenish his own drink, Elizabeth trickled some of hers onto the ground, and looked about her. She loved Mary's house. It followed down the hill without cutting into it. A bridge-like walkway from the street to the front door seemed the only contact with the world. Windows were everywhere, natural wood blended into surrounding oaks and pines. It looked like a tree house. Or like a ship.

Elizabeth could see the dancers in the bright living room light. From this perspective they seemed to be having more fun than they really were. Or maybe they were having fun, and she, Elizabeth Austen Rivers, was the true outcast, the alien spirit. Just there, in the room where light shone out, directly under the living room, was where she wanted to be.

Always at a party Elizabeth would feel that there was somewhere else in the house she would rather be, with people other than her date, that there was a life going on underneath the one everybody thought was the only real life, and that this underground life offered a freedom, a richness, that the other lacked. But how could she know what it offered when she had never received an invitation, had no assurances that it even existed outside her own ravenous imagination?

Absently she gulped whiskey, as if it were water, not thinking, but suddenly feeling it sear its way across her tongue and down her throat. She coughed.

"Way to go!" Larry approved, patting her experimentally on the back. Then he slid his arm around her.

"You know, I really need some Coke with this." She moved out of range and toward the lighted house, not with a plan but unconsciously staying beyond his range. Then, when she reached the walkway she knew abruptly that she did not want to go in, found herself sliding through fresh peat moss down the far slope, out of sight. She was breathing hard, not from the exertion but from the fact of escape. She heard a surge of music, then the front door slam behind Larry Sutton as he rejoined the party. She emptied the rest of her whiskey into the peat moss, careful to avoid the tender new strawberry plants that sprang up at patterned intervals. She would look into that window now, the one beneath.

Voyeurism they had called this in Grace Medina's sex book. Maybe it was true, that she really was a voyeur. Elizabeth loved to wind just after dusk through the tiny alleys that ran behind the houses in the flats. Lights came on and people moved through rooms or sat in chairs or lay on couches watching the news on television. Silver clinked and scraped in kitchens. Dogs barked. Cats winked on window ledges. Old women and old men sat in canvas chairs on screened porches and breathed stories, waiting for dinner. And who were they, what did they know? What did they have that she, Elizabeth Rivers in her seventeenth year, incurable voyeur, what did they have that she needed?

Through the window, she saw a woman sitting, her back to Elizabeth, on a tall blue metal stool. The woman leaned down over a plywood sheet where a toy house had been set out. Then she straightened up and ran her hand through ragged blonde hair, as if she were tired or as if she might be trying to think her way through something difficult.

She adjusted a lamp clamped to the plywood, turning it this way and that, loosening some nuts and tightening others until she had it at just the tilt she wanted. Then she fell into a crouch over the toy house again and stayed that way, as if she had forgotten her body, as if she had become the lamp, while Elizabeth herself felt cramped by her own efforts to see and not be seen.

When the woman straightened back up, Elizabeth cautiously eased her own body and, intent on finding a new position, was surprised to find the woman suddenly looking her full in the face. And even more surprised to see her smile. Then she was opening the window—this strange, angular woman—and motioning her in as if she were a guest paying a call. Elizabeth had never climbed through a window before.

Luckily the screens were not on yet, the woman told her, because the house was not done yet and might never be at this rate. She thought for a minute: "Maybe screens are a big mistake. Without them windows and doors could become interchangeable and people might see less difference between outside and inside because getting from one to the other would cost less effort. But sit down," she concluded, as if people were constantly reminding her not to confuse them by whirling around in her mind like a private helicopter. "I'm Chris Broadwin. But who are you? I thought you were a tree." She stopped abruptly, lit a cigarette, offered Elizabeth one, and waited in an attitude of politeness.

Elizabeth declined the offer. The lamp felt hot. She studied the window, still open. "I'm Elizabeth Rivers, Mary's friend, from the party, upstairs."

"Oh, you've escaped, then. I used to do that when I was your age. Hated parties. Purely hated them. I would leave and walk through a graveyard—if one was handy—and recite Edna St. Vincent Millay into the night. It's important to walk out on parties. I still do it, matter of fact, just to keep in practice. Last week I walked out on a cocktail party at my boss's house. Strolled in the front door, shook hands, and strolled out the back."

Elizabeth said she thought she would have one of those cigarettes after all. They smoked together in silence. Chris wandered back to her blue stool and perched as before, looking intently at the cardboard house. Then she picked up a knife shaped like a razor and carefully cut away a wall. "All wrong. Should have known better. They'll go crazy in there. Step that wall out a good three feet, and open the whole thing up with windows, ones that open out. Like little doors. 'Oh, come to the window. Sweet is the night air!' Four tall windows." She cut the other three walls away with evident satisfaction. Nothing was left now but a half dozen paper pine trees glued at intervals across the property.

"I like your house," Elizabeth said.

Chris looked up, the three walls spread in her hand like playing cards. "You mean this?"

"No, *this* one," Elizabeth swept the room with her hand.

Chris laughed her appreciation. "I made that one too. Or rather, I didn't pound the nails in, but I designed it. I like it too. It's small, but you don't feel that so much. Big enough for just Mary and me. And she's off to college in the fall. Being able to see the ocean is the big thing for me. That's why the house doesn't really look toward the street. It looks out." She dropped the four cardboard walls into the waste-basket.

"I live in the flats," Elizabeth admitted.

"Now don't say it like that. If I couldn't live here in the hills in my tree house, the flats would be the next best thing." She slid off her stool and opened a wide, shallow drawer in a small cabinet on wheels. Then she rummaged through sheets of poster board until she found one to her liking. "I enjoy the history of it." She drew lines quickly along hinged rulers that bent and flexed under her small, square fingers.

"History of what?"

"Those houses."

"I wouldn't call it *history*."

"What would you call it?"

"Why do *you* call it history?"

"Because it helps me feel what it was like to summer in

a beach cottage sixty years ago."

"A lot of rich people is all, from over town. I like the people that live in them now, winter and summer alike. Islanders."

Chris opened a glue pot and inserted a tiny brush. Fumes caught in Elizabeth's throat. She tried not to cough and snuffed out her cigarette so she would not look unpracticed.

"I see your point." Chris ran her brush thoughtfully down the edge of one of the new walls. "But still, they were real people after all. That's what you have to feel. That their lives were real to them and rubbed off onto your walls where you inhale them even in your sleep. You've got ghosts. A rare privilege."

She pressed two walls together and nodded toward her ceiling, the beams on which Mary Broadwin's friends must be dancing at this very moment. "My house, unfortunately, has no ghosts. It hasn't even got screens yet. So the advantage is really all on your side. Oh, here, hold this a moment, will you?"

Elizabeth took from her hands the two joined walls while Chris Broadwin leaped to answer the phone that was ringing in a muffled sort of way. She crossed the room to a narrow bed neatly made with a bright blue Indian blanket, sat down lightly, and pulled open the bottom drawer of the bedside table from which she extracted a telephone receiver.

"Oh, Kit. Well, yes, I'm surviving it. I just hide out here where it's safe." She smiled at Elizabeth. "I suppose for a little while I could. Okay with you if I bring a refugee? Elizabeth Rivers. Yes, I thought you might. Fine. See you in a minute."

Chris closed the drawer on the telephone and retrieved the walls from Elizabeth. "That was Katherine Tebolt. From the library. She wants us to come have homemade bread with her and Juno."

Elizabeth hesitated.

"But you may want to rejoin the party, of course."

"Oh no. It isn't that, not exactly."

"Well, I have too much experience with teenagers to ask you just what it is *exactly*. I'll check in with Mary and make sure everything's okay upstairs. If you like, you can exit your window and meet me outside in front of the house. It isn't far, and we've got a wonderful night for a stroll." Picking up her cigarettes, she shot Elizabeth a smile and headed for the stairs.

CHAPTER 7: CLARISSA STREET

"If she was my daughter I'd know where she was every minute." Leon Feeney held his rum and Coke up to his forehead and lowered his eyelids in exasperation.

"That's what you think." Olive Rivers spoke through pins, gesturing her daughter to turn, so that she might finish adjusting the hem of her graduation dress. "That's what everybody thinks who hasn't got a daughter they've tried to raise alone. How do I know where she goes and what she does? Am I supposed to lock her up?"

"I was just saying, honey, that a little more discipline and you'd have a fine young lady there." He winked at Elizabeth over Olive's bent form.

That's what Leon did, switched sides, pretended his anger was really affection. Elizabeth held herself motionless, like a department store dummy. She would turn for her mother.

Her back to the kitchen, Elizabeth could hear Leon

rooting around, could reconstruct in her mind his search for the Ron Rico, match sounds to the upturned Coke, his assault on the ice cube tray. She always felt as if he were about to blow the house out at every corner and leave it flattened like a hurricane had been through.

Not that Leon was big. Actually he was kind of short for a man and, when he was not wearing his Five Corsairs topsiders, wore shoes with thick soles that looked like gum erasers. If her mother wore heels she stood half an inch taller than Leon. Elizabeth liked to think that Leon did not know this.

He was saying something from the kitchen, but since the water was running you could not hear him. Her mother tugged her another six inches in the circle.

"Course it's different with boys," Leon, suddenly audible, crossed the small room on his erasers and eased himself into her mother's La-Z-Boy.

"What's different?" Elizabeth asked in a flattened out voice.

"You got to let them run loose all to hell and gone. Makes men of them." He crossed his thick shoes at his ankles, stuck a sausage finger into his drink, and whirled the ice around. "Not safe for girls, though. Girls are different."

"Look, are we almost through here?" Elizabeth twitched the skirt of her graduation dress. "Because I've got someplace I'm supposed to be."

Leon rocketed forward in the La-Z-Boy. "Now you see Olive, that's just exactly what I mean."

Olive crooned into her pin box words Elizabeth and Leon could not hear. An ancient chant that slowly gathered momentum until the words became distinct: "Have to be, always having to be somewhere, some people, with their always having to be eternally going somewhere that other people are not supposed to be asked about or even told about, not able to sit still for one living instant."

On the last word she threw her head back and looked Elizabeth dead in the eyes. "And you know what I mean and what I'm talking about." Then the moment of control spent itself, broken by Olive's own lapse into the lighter lament: "Here I am trying to make a home for you and you aren't even in it half the time. Running from one end of this island to the other like a heathen Indian, like you had never been taught how to act like regular folks, and me working eight, nine hours a day, six days a week just to keep meat on the table."

The meat Elizabeth saw on the table when her mother used this image was always raw meat. When she grew up Elizabeth would be a vegetarian and live in her own little house on a steep hill somewhere in San Francisco. A yellow house. She would not share that house with anybody on God's earth.

Olive snapped her pin case shut. "You'd think I was doing this for myself. I'm not the one that's graduating high school in two weeks."

Elizabeth stalked off to her bedroom, ignoring the straight pins that scraped across her shins. A moment later she emerged in Levis and t-shirt, the blue dotted Swiss dress suspended inside out on her arm, held away from her body. "Where does this go?"

Olive nodded in the direction of the portable Singer that perpetually sat on a card table in the darkest corner of the living room. Elizabeth slid the dress onto the table, plucked her wind breaker from the hook by the door, and was gone.

CHAPTER 8: VOYEUR

Elizabeth turned off the asphalt road and pedalled hard a few yards into a stand of pine. She stopped, listening. Fog was blowing in, but light from the almost full moon sent a glow through the woods like a path. A small animal thrashed suddenly through the shrub, a fox perhaps, or a wild pig. Quietly she leaned her bicycle against a tree and lifted her gym bag from the front basket. She extracted carefully a large pair of binoculars and hung them around her neck, the excitement she had tried to keep down on the long ride from home springing into her blood, sounding in her ears. Her legs felt weak and strong, all at once. She turned toward Juno's house, her father's binoculars heavy on her breast.

She would circle around toward the patio. Juno had said they sat there, she and Kit, every evening. When she said it, she had touched the older woman lightly on the arm. Elizabeth had shot a glance over to Chris Broadwin to check out her face, but she was simply smiling in that good-humored way that seemed to make no judgments. So they had all gone with Juno out onto the patio, a broad brick semicircle, with flower beds terraced up toward the house on three sides. The house followed around the contours of the patio, as if the builder had begun there, with the patio, and built the rest, perhaps piece by piece, as the people living in the house discovered their needs. She knew why Juno and Kit were drawn here every evening; it simply *was* the center.

They had sat that evening of Mary Broadwin's party in chairs made of bent eucalyptus and could see each other only in the faint glow from the French doors and in the flickering light of citronella candles placed on each of three small tables. Then Juno brought Mexican coffee in blue ceramic mugs. Elizabeth could remember the feel of the mug in her hands, the aromatic bite of the coffee, the talk of the three women, their words on the night, the night as thick as water.

Elizabeth parted a bough now and crouched down at some distance from the patio's edge. The moon faced her like a lover denied, pulling at the tide in her.

She raised her binoculars and swept the darkness. The two women were still inside. Lights shone in the kitchen just left of the French doors and in a room upstairs. She settled herself more comfortably, voyeur that she was.

Chris Broadwin had told the two women that night how she had found Elizabeth looking through her window instead of joining the party upstairs.

"Oh, a voyeur!" Miss Tebolt had exclaimed. Elizabeth felt her blood rush its answer up her neck and spread across her cheeks.

"Not at all," Chris had defended. "An island historian."

Elizabeth had felt foolish and angry. Miss Tebolt excused herself and went through the French doors and into the kitchen. She returned holding aloft a loaf of bread fresh from the oven. Then she served it around with butter and honey that smelled of flowers and said how since Elizabeth was interested in history she really should go to the Island Museum and meet her dear friend, Mr. Gem, if she had not done so already.

But Elizabeth was not a child, to be bought off with bread and butter. Maybe Miss Tebolt had meant nothing, but then again maybe she had.

Elizabeth fitted the binoculars to her eyes and trained them on the upstairs window. They brought the window ledge into such sudden clear focus she almost spoke out in surprise. The shade was pulled down tight. But she could see straight into the kitchen, sharply, as if it were a lighted aquarium. There were a few dishes in the sink and two wine glasses on the white and blue tile counter, empty except for slender maroon disks at their bottoms. Against a wall Elizabeth saw a green mesh basket hanging with purple onions inside.

A door shut somewhere in the house, then a laugh swept through the house like a light wind across water. Juno's laugh.

Kit came into the kitchen alone, took a copper kettle from the stove and held it under the tap. From where she crouched Elizabeth could barely hear the thrumming. Then Kit set the tea kettle on the glowing burner and took down two ceramic mugs, the same ones they had used that night. She could almost feel in her hands the weight of blue clay.

Juno came in. She had on a worn work shirt with sleeves rolled carelessly half-way up her forearms and some Mexican-looking pants that tied in front. Her arms looked intensely brown. Kit was reaching high for something on a shelf. Juno came up behind her, the taller of the two, and reached down a cannister of coffee with one hand and slid her other around Kit's waist; then, still with the coffee in one hand, Juno gently turned her lover, sought her mouth, while Elizabeth stood, too suddenly, staggered with the blood suddenness, and made her way back through the night toward the road.

CHAPTER 9: CHANNEL DRIFT

The first thing you noticed was that enormous mouth, then the sheer mass of her, the broad but flat belly in black jersey swimsuit, the strong thighs. Then, squinting eyes, goggles resting on the wide forehead, hand upraised, waving at the cameramen, one of whom had captured her in this very photo, *Newsweek*, August 21, 1950. Florence Chadwick. Florence Chadwick smeared thick with sheep's grease, triumphant, saying to the newsmen, "I guess I look a wreck." That was her first channel swim, France to Dover. Elizabeth remembered it only through these scrapbooks Mr. Gem had put together for the Island History section of the Archives.

But she remembered on her own Chadwick's channel crossing from Avalon to San Pedro, had watched on Louise Sampson's seven inch Magnavox the entire fourteen hours, wrapped in quilts on the floor. The whole country had watched, Mr. Gem said, and now, say "Florence Chadwick" out loud anywhere on the Mainland and you were sure to be answered, he said, with a glazed eye.

Still, island people remembered her. Elizabeth had only been eight years old, yet if she shut her eyes today she could still see that white bathing cap glowing on the horizon, small against the channel chop, the longboat keeping its distance, Chadwick's mother in the bow, snuggled into a vast Navy coat out of which she kept watch, while the oarsman stood, sculling, silent.

How did the world look through those steamed goggles, the sea and horizon through rivulets? How did the warm bouillon taste as she hovered near the boat, careful not to touch, her mother ladling soup into her frozen mouth?

Elizabeth turned the page. A photograph from the Dover to France crossing; the "hard way," they called it, because of the powerful opposing tides. You could just see her bathing cap as she swam through an artillery range, caught in channel drift. They had almost fired on her, the British soldiers. And to her they must have seemed little more than boys at play. Through their range she continued, swimming hard, muscles feeling for the clue, for the correct angle, and at last understanding the power of the channel drift, she let the current carry her away from the boy soldiers and far out beyond the fastest swimmer in the race.

Elizabeth, bending over *The Florence Chadwick Notebook* at the Catalina Island Museum, felt a shiver start somewhere deep inside, sending fingers through her body until the sun bleached hair on her arms stood up and she thought she might cry. This woman moved her so, with her squinty eyes and her big mouth, this Florence Chadwick, this stenographer who in five weeks broke four channel records and then said: "I don't know yet exactly how far I can swim."

It was a way of thinking her mother hated. She hated striving and danger. Her mother wanted everybody to hold still. Her mother, only three years older than Florence

Chadwick, had sat in her La-Z-Boy recliner drinking tea while the other woman swam in the dark through shark-infested waters. Elizabeth stood so suddenly her chair fell over backward, sending echoes through the tiny, deserted reading room.

Mr. Gem appeared in the doorway, smiling quizzically, wearing a carefully ironed work shirt, with a paisley tie of melon and pale blue. His cords bagged softly at the knee. "Into the Florence Chadwick again?" he smiled. Elizabeth made a helpless gesture. "Well, come give me a hand in the kitchen. I want to tell you about somebody I met last week."

Elizabeth half expected to find someone waiting in the small kitchen. But she and Charles Gem were alone. He rolled up his sleeves and playfully flipped his tie over his shoulder. Then he dealt out slices of bread like a deck of cards across the counter. "Cucumber sandwiches. Take my advice and always serve cucumber sandwiches if you want something." He handed her a knife and a jar of mayonnaise.

"What is it you want?" Elizabeth asked, smearing the first slice.

"I want the Museum Board to finance a new room to house the artifacts from the Indian dig near Little Harbor."

"Think they'll go for it?"

"If we cut off the crusts fine enough." Charles leaned over the trash can, shaving off dark curls of cucumber rind. "But let me tell you who I found last week. I went down to the Isthmus for a conference with some ornithologists from Los Angeles. They're doing some work at the cove with eagles. Anyway, one of them was talking with this old guy out on the dock. Turns out he's Karl Jorgenson, the man who rowed for Chadwick in the island crossing. You probably saw him on television."

"The guy who rowed standing up?"

"The very same."

"Would he talk to me?"

"Apparently he talks to anybody and everybody. Always about Chadwick. He cries when he talks about Chadwick. The ornithologists can't bear it when he cries. Tender hearted lot."

"I want to go see him."

"It'd be good training for your career in archaeology."

"I'm going to be a writer. I told you that."

"It amounts to the same thing." He sliced the last cucumber and began arranging lids. "You can cut the crusts off now."

"Seems silly."

"It is silly, but we certainly can't get our money for the new wing if these crusts stay on. You'll never grow up to be Jane Austen if you don't grasp the subtleties of manners."

"I'd rather grow up to be George Eliot." Elizabeth sacrificed the first file of crust.

"People would think George was a funny name for a girl."

Elizabeth laughed and popped half a sandwich in her mouth. "I'm ravenous."

"Yes, but what about my Indians? They'll never get their wing if you keep eating up the Board's sandwiches. Manners again, Elizabeth. Writers merely observe; archaeologists eat." He snatched up a sandwich and popped it whole into his mouth. "And what are you doing, anyway, loitering around here. I thought you'd graduated and sailed away to college without troubling to say good-by to an old friend."

"I graduate in ten days, but I'm not sailing away to college. I'm staying here to eat your sandwiches."

"Seriously, Elizabeth, you're not going to college? Why not?"

"Mother says it's time I earned my keep?"

"Nonsense. Who ever heard of a writer earning her keep? Writer's are the jewel in the public crown. They were never meant to do anything merely useful. They are meant only to *be*. Nobody ever expected Jane Austen to do anything so vulgar as to "earn her keep," as your mother so picturesquely puts it." He gave a small shudder, and the door swung suddenly open, catching Elizabeth on the right shoulder.

"Did someone mention Jane Austen?" It was Katherine Tebolt, sliding an angel food cake onto the counter and giving Elizabeth a quick pat of apology.

Mr. Gem and Miss Tebolt squeezed each other and pecked cheeks, making Elizabeth feel the kitchen was too small to hold them all.

"Elizabeth, do you know Miss Tebolt?"

"Kit," Miss Tebolt corrected. "Call me 'Kit.' Now that Elizabeth is about to graduate and now that I'm no longer her librarian, but her friend, I think we should be on a first-name basis.

"But what is this about Jane Austen? Austen is the love of my life."

She was pulling down milky green sandwich plates, as if, Elizabeth thought, she were in her own kitchen and they—Elizabeth and Charles—were her hungry children. People who said they were not going to treat you like a child always did.

"Well, it had to do with Elizabeth's wanting to be a writer and saying she wasn't going to college."

Miss Tebolt paused with six plates in her hand and fixed Elizabeth with her blue, eagle eyes.

"Just not right away I'm not. Of course, later I will. Listen, Charles . . . Mr. Gem . . . I've got to get moving or I'll miss the steamer docking."

Smiling, Mr. Gem handed her a parting sandwich.

CHAPTER 10: THE VOYAGE OUT

Elizabeth looked through the crack of the door at her mother lying asleep on her back in the neat bed. She slept quietly, always, not disturbing the covers. A row of pink curlers lay across her pale and freckled forehead. She breathed easily, her arms spread wide in both directions as if she were holding something back. On the wall over her bed hung a small, pale Christ, his face half-turned away, as if some things were better left unnoticed.

Her mother would sleep another hour at least. Elizabeth scrawled a note and stuck it to the refrigerator with a magnet in the shape of a ketchup bottle. Quietly she eased the front door past its customary squeak, turned the dead bolt and took a deep breath of morning air. Clarissa Street slept its Sunday dreams. Elizabeth turned left at the corner, then followed Catalina Avenue toward the harbor.

Yeasty warm smells from the Island Bakery reminded her she had not eaten. She was starved. Through the pane glass she could see Tula whacking a huge aluminum sheet and sliding hamburger buns onto a tray. Elizabeth tapped lightly on the window.

"And have I got to feed this starving Elizabeth again?" Tula opened the door. "This island rover. Where are you off to, you heathen, while good Christians are asleep and only the devil's servants labor?" She nodded toward the ovens, tucking a wisp of gray hair back into its hair net. "No bear claws yet, but the blueberry muffins are just out."

"Better give me half a dozen. I'm going down to the Isthmus for the day, crewing for Sally Bates on the *Island Queen.*"

"You better take some of these sourdough rolls too, then." Tula began filling a white bag with provisions while Elizabeth dug in her pockets. She placed a string of quarters along the top of the glass counter. "Now what's all this?" asked Tula, handing the bakery sack across.

"Sea coins," said Elizabeth. "Sunken treasure brought up from the bottom of the ocean."

"Four and no more. You keep that treasure, Elizabeth Rivers. You're going to need it and sooner than you think. Now get along. And tell Sally hello." She waved Elizabeth out the door.

The Westminster chimes were tolling the quarter hour. She would hurry. Sally had wanted to leave by seven-thirty. No one on the beach this early. Only Jake Hicks spearing papers, moving like a sandpiper across the littered sand.

She started up the pier. A fine, perfectly clear morning, sailboats rocking gently on their mooring lines. Sally's broad back she could just see. An upraised arm, directing the placement of cartons and crates. A tangle of dark, curly hair shot with gray, nodding the cargo into place. Captain Sally.

At the gangplank Elizabeth stooped to pick up a box filled with the Sunday edition of the *Los Angeles Times.* "You can stow that crate in the cabin and then go forward to handle the bow line," Sally said, turning in Elizabeth's direction.

From her vantage point, Elizabeth watched two men carry aboard boxes of vegetables and crates of eggs. Elizabeth recognized one. Roy Tripper. Grace had told her his name late one afternoon when he had come into the Sea Gull for lunch at the counter. He was tall and thin, with sunken-in jaws. Not an islander.

He passed by Sally Bates now, carrying lettuce. She made a mark on her clipboard and called to Elizabeth, "You about ready, Elizabeth?" Roy Tripper turned and stared at her.

Elizabeth moved forward and unwound the bowline from its cleat. Then she tossed the coiled line onto the dock and moved aft, ready with the stern line.

"Cast off the stern line," called Sally.

The dock, from here, was a long way off. Elizabeth could see Roy Tripper standing next to the rusty cleat, looking skeptical, fishing a cigarette out of a crumpled pack.

Elizabeth coiled the line in her right hand and sailed it out over the water. It fell with a thump next to the cleat, almost at Roy Tripper's feet. She could read the surprise in his eyes when he looked up at her, then a hardening as his lips formed the words, "Want to fuck?"

She turned away, the breath sucked out of her. Then she turned back toward the dock and shot him an emphatic bird. Where had those words come from anyway? Was she supposed to feel honored? Instead she felt assaulted. She glanced toward the wheel house. Sally shrugged, then motioned her over, as the *Island Queen* pulled away from the dock.

"One thing my old mother told me I never forgot. 'Sally,' she told me, 'boys is different.' Jesus but she was right. More than that I can't tell you. Get me a beer, love. Get yourself one too."

Elizabeth, who had never drunk beer in the morning,

popped the lids on two Hamms and handed one to her captain.

"And here's to the Casino." They were cruising past the round ballroom, with its arched portico, tile roof, and on the far side—Elizabeth knew—the statue of Venus, her red hair streaming out around her glowing, naked body. Sally stood, beer can hoisted reverently in the direction of the Casino, "Here's to the Casino, without whose existence I would not be here at all."

"Why not?"

"In 1937 I came over on the big white steamer to dance to Tommy Dorsey's orchestra. He left and I stayed. Simple as that. Simple case of love at first sight. You want to take the wheel, Elizabeth? Just follow along the coastline and don't run her aground."

Sally stretched out flat on a wooden bench, crossed her hands on her chest, and said, "Wake me up when we get to Goat Harbor."

"How'll I know we're there?"

"On account of the goats," she said, and fell asleep.

CHAPTER 11: DESERTED VILLAGE

They found the Isthmus's Harbor Master squatting in a dingy, bailing with a rusty coffee can. He was wearing a white bowling shirt with a blue marlin embroidered over the pocket. He squinted up at them, where they stood on the dock.

"My guess is you're in luck. Boy Scouts won't be landing for another week or so. Most likely old Karl is still bedding down in one of their cabins round to White's Landing. Might still be out hunting abalone this morning, though. That's another thing old Karl does that I'm not supposed to know about."

"Thanks for the info, Dan." Sally Bates and Elizabeth started down the pier toward the tiny settlement. "As my old mother used to say, the sooner you're gone, the quicker you're back. How does four o'clock sound? Got a watch on you?"

Elizabeth held up her waterproof Benrus calendar watch

for inspection. "Ask a silly question," said Sally, as she gave Elizabeth a sudden hug.

Elizabeth loved this beach even more than the one at Avalon. In tourist season Avalon was covered with hundreds of reclining tourists roasting themselves in the sun. They littered the beach with their beer cans and hamburger wrappers and had long since plundered the sand of all shells. She could see the Baron strolling among them, with girls her own age clinging to his hairy arms. His bathing suit bulged obscenely. Elizabeth gave an involuntary shudder.

But on this beach there was no one. No one but Elizabeth, striding along with her topsiders slung over her shoulder, her feet cool in the sand. She felt glad to be alone, to have a destination toward which she could bend her muscles and her determination. She would find Karl and he would tell her.

She started up the trail. Rocky cliffs jutting out into the sea on either side of the Isthmus made following the water impossible. So she would climb high and then dip down again toward the water when she found herself directly over the scout camp. She stopped to put on her shoes. Here the shrub was low and brightened by scattered patches of wild roses and berries. Ten minutes walk brought her into the shadows of pines and eucalyptus with their warm and magic fragrances. She loved this moment, this sun on her head and shoulders, this island where she could move as freely as the buffalo, the fox.

She had reached the highest point on the cliff. The Pacific spread out below, the glass sea leading away toward the invisible mainland, and beyond. She stood for a time watching, listening to the light surf surge in, then retreat through eons of shell and smooth stone. Tightening the arms of her sweatshirt around her hips, she started down the winding path toward the cabins.

There were eight of them, staggered up the hillside, and

another long, low building which obviously housed the kitchen and dining hall. Down by the water was an aluminum flagpole, a boat house, and an open pavilion with a weathered stage and peeling benches for the audience. The place seemed on the verge of exploding into activity—as it really would in a week or two—but it also felt to Elizabeth as if it were a tiny, failed world and she, a time traveller, an archaeologist of space, come to observe, to record.

Her topsiders crunched on the shell-strewn pathway as she passed between cabins, rounded the dining hall, and paused beneath the vacant flagpole. Nothing but lapping water and the cry of gulls.

"Sweet smiling village, loveliest of the lawn, Thy sports are fled, and all thy charms withdrawn," murmured Elizabeth, seeing Miss Reed, the thick blue English book balanced in her left hand, hearing her warm voice, feeling it move through her like a finger of sun. Juno. Juno, who lived in her mind now like a part of her own sane self.

She crunched back up the walk. One of the cabin doors stood ajar. Karl might be inside. But no one answered her call. Slowly she opened the door and went in.

The air was rank as fox. Eight stained mattresses hung at random angles off the bunks. In the corners were relics of clothes: stray socks, jockey shorts, t-shirts, a baseball cap, a pair of bathing trunks. Elizabeth turned to go, her foot kicking something bright across the floor. She stooped to pick it up. A foil packet: Trojan, lubricated, seamless. She sailed the packet into the far corner, flung the door open, and strode into sunlight and sea air.

CHAPTER 12:
FLORENCE CHADWICK'S BATHING SUIT

Karl stood still, his thick hand resting on the sculling oar. His thick eyes tried hard to be sure of what he thought he saw; his little darling, swimming again, darting her arms in arcs through the water like bright fish, stopless. His chest clutched in on him; his hoof of a foot sought out the sack of abalone, to touch back down on what he could be sure of.

She stopped, treading water, looking at him as surely as he was looking at her, then made for the shore, at that same quick pace, steady, easy. She had no clothes on, he thought. Or if she did, they were pink. Florence always wore black. A black jersey bathing suit, she said, brought good luck. Then who was she, this other?

His leathery hand circled the oar again, and his arm fell into the looping rhythm, the double swooping arcs that sent his boat and his life forward together. The girl who was not Florence disappeared into the holly bushes, a dark bundle in her hand. His heart felt wide and on its own. Still, he did not require that she be there when his skiff slid against the dock. Things happened or they did not.

But there she was, starting up the dock toward him, a thin sort of girl, but with a strong walk, wet hair hanging straight down and an ear poking through each side.

"Karl?" she called, hurrying forward.

He nodded. She went down on one knee at his skiff's approach and took the painter from the bow, making the line fast to the dock cleat in two quick motions. He reached for his sack of shellfish and handed them up to her, feeling for a moment as if surely he was the old man and this was the old man's daughter, who met the old man every afternoon to help him with the day's catch and to walk with him in companionship up the path to their cottage.

She took the sack in one hand and reached out with the other to steady him. Usually words came to him and he said them. He talked and people listened or they went away. Now he felt that talking would not say it. He listened simply to their feet on the gravel walk. At the door to the kitchen he took off the padlock that always hung open, like a question.

"We'll need a bucket of water," he said, gesturing toward an aluminum pail beside the door. Sea water." She went out, and he took his knife out of its leather sheath and began cutting the pale meat out of the bright shells. By the time she returned, the abalone steaks were ready to wash. She held the shells up to the light of the kitchen window. She looked as if she held jewels.

With his wooden mallet he pounded the abalone steaks thin, careful as always not to tear the tender flesh. Then he knelt before the stone fireplace and blew alive the morning coals, feeding the fire with dried twigs. While he did this, the girl walked about the room, peered through windows, studied his iron bed with his dead mother's quilt tucked in all around, the photograph of his little darling smiling behind cracked glass. He did not mind. He watched the fire.

"You knew her," the girl said, holding the frame.

He dropped the last of his butter out of its waxy wrapper into his pan, where it sizzled. He nodded to the girl, but could not tell her now, because if he cooked the steaks too long they would be tough and have no flavor. People cooked abalone too long. Over and over he explained to the people on their sailboats how to cook his abalone. Still they cooked them too long and without concentration. After a few minutes he shook the four steaks onto the thick blue plates his mother had left him and carried them over to the table. His table. Then he brought the wine and a little French bread.

The girl ate as if she had never eaten in all her life. She must still be growing, to eat like that. He was himself not very hungry, so he shared his second abalone with her. Afterward he wanted a cigarette. They went outside and sat on the front steps. She watched carefully while he rolled tobacco in the white paper. It could be that she wanted one but was too polite to ask.

She took the cigarette he offered and he rolled another for himself.

"They'll be back soon, the Boy Scouts," she said, nodding in the direction of the empty cabins.

"Yes, and then I'll move into the hills and live with the goats again. I have two homes. One for summer and one for winter. Like Mr. Wrigley." He smiled and she smiled back at him.

"Tell me what it was like, rowing for her."

"A long time to stand up." He rubbed his thick hands together, so his hands would do the remembering for him. "And cold. The night was cold. But when the sharks came, we forgot to be cold. So close you could touch them. Sailors firing over our heads from the cutter. Almost rather have the sharks. But she kept swimming all this time like there was nothing to do but that.

"I couldn't stop if she didn't. I knew that. Twenty-six miles." He shook his head. "How did I know if I could scull twenty-six miles?" He puffed the strong tobacco. "And that mother of hers. Every time she came in close for her broth, her mother saying to get in the boat, to not be crazy, but feeding her anyway, promising to buy her a hotel if she would only quit; and Florence would just move away from the lights back into the dark. Then you would hear her start in again, like that's all there was to do.

"Did you see it?" he turned to Elizabeth suddenly.

"Only on television."

"You can't *see* on television."

"No," she said, "that's why I came."

Then she was picking up her little wet bundle and looking at the big watch strapped to her wrist and tying her sweater around her waist, with only just enough time to put her arms around him, to hold him tight, before she started up the trail into the late afternoon, the softening light.

CHAPTER 13: TIME OUT

Olive Rivers sat in her green aluminum porch chair, bending over the brand new July issue of *Mademoiselle:* "The ABC's of Luscious Nails." Leon, thank goodness, was asleep. She would like to do the Sunday dishes now and get them out of the way, but she couldn't risk waking him. Carrying on as he had about Elizabeth missing Sunday dinner. And he was right, too. Olive set her right hand to soaking in a ceramic ashtray filled with warm soapy water. This was for her cuticles. "Pamper yourself," the magazine had said.

Well just you try. Olive rested her head back on the chair's hard rim and sighed. Then she leaned around to see Leon, feet up in her La-Z-Boy. Honest to goodness sometimes she did not feel this house belonged to her at all, with those two—Elizabeth and Leon—grabbing this way and grabbing that way. Peace, a little peace, was all she asked. Leon saying things had to be just so, that Elizabeth needed disciplining and she, Olive, must do it now before it was too late or her daughter would grow up spoiled and a bitch. Olive did not know what discipline meant. She'd had a little dog named Chiquita, almost pure blooded Chihuahua, that Eddie had brought her from Tiajuana, when he was stationed in San Diego. How she had loved Chiquita, had bathed her every Sunday in her own Halo shampoo, and fed her Mrs. See's best chocolates. But Chiquita always did exactly as she pleased. There was no discipline to it. And then Chiquita in her wildness had run under the laundry truck wheels when Elizabeth was just a baby. Perhaps with more discipline Chiquita would be alive today, lying at her feet asleep.

Olive took her right hand out of the ashtray and placed it, fingers up, on her towel-covered lap. There seemed no difference in the two hands yet, except the fingertips of the one were wrinkled. She blew her nose on a Kleenex and placed her left hand experimentally into the cool, green water.

It seemed to Olive that life grew around you and did not consult with you about your wishes. Had Eddie? No, Eddie had simply left one day saying, "I'm a sailor." What did that mean? Where was the discipline in that?

If anyone had discipline, she thought, jerking her left hand out of the ashtray, it was herself. Every day she went to work and fed thirty or forty people, walked miles doing it, probably (Olive had read about an experiment where housewives walked all day with speedometers on their ankles), kept a roof over Elizabeth's head, put meat on the table, paid her bills, and all her taxes. Whatever life asked of her she gave.

Olive Rivers seized her orange stick and began pressing her cuticles back up where they belonged, disciplining them.

But dearie it was hard to see. She slipped off her glasses, breathed on the lenses, and wiped them carefully with a fresh Kleenex. Sun was around to the back of the house.

Must be past five. Daylight savings kept her mixed up all summer. She must listen for the chimes and wake Leon up at six so he would not be late for the Sunday evening steamer. He had brought his saxophone and Corsair cap so he would not have to stop at home first.

Why Leon had been so mad she could not say. It was true Elizabeth had gone off for the day leaving only a note ("Gone to the Isthmus with Sally Bates. Back about six-thirty. Kiss, smack"), that she had missed dinner, but Elizabeth did such things. Went off. A wanderer like her father. Why should Leon mind more than she, Olive, minded? Olive had read about teenagers in *Good Housekeeping* and in *Ladies Home Journal*. Teenagers wandered, played loud music, and were rude to their elders. This was normal. You only had to wait and it would go away.

Still, there was something about Elizabeth that the magazines never seemed to get at. It was like she was listening to something far away, something Olive couldn't hear. Like when Chiquita pricked her ears at thunder on the mainland.

Around the rim of each nail Olive worked in a little cuticle cream, then shook a Kool out of the package and lit it. Pamper yourself. Olive blew the smoke out and, straining around the chair, looked at Leon. His mouth had fallen open. Peace.

Sometimes she wished there were no Leon and no Elizabeth (God forgive her), and that she lived here alone, doing for herself, washing a dish that she knew would stay clean until the next meal, putting food in the icebox that she could count on eating herself, sweeping that everlasting sand out the front door once and for all; the trespassers on her life gone and everything simple.

She wiped the cream off and buffed each nail fast and hard. Her father had once cautioned her against hasty wishes: all wishes came true, eventually, he said.

There was a creak of naugahyde and the sound of springs

popping in the next room, and Leon calling foggily, "Hon, get me a cup of coffee. Almost time to mosey."

Olive Rivers screwed down tight the lid to the cuticle cream and got to her feet. Polish would have to wait.

CHAPTER 14: GEOMETRY

An isosceles triangle! It came to Elizabeth all at once, this particular Monday morning, though she had ridden her bicycle to school past the hospital every day since grade school. Practically a lifetime. But she could see now she had for years been traveling a triangle. The school itself was one angle and the hospital the other, forming the base, from which the two equal sides extended upward until they met in the hills at the third angle: Juno's house.

She stared in hard through the hospital windows, trying to remember what she once knew about triangles. It was hard remembering all those shapes and axioms they carried along with them. (Elizabeth steadied her bike through ruts chewed into the hospital driveway.) They had always seemed unreal, parallelograms and all the rest. Not just invisible; *unreal.* As if all of tenth grade geometry might be a figment of Mr. Cochran's imagination.

Not that she had anything against imagination. In fact

she rode her own like it was the roller coaster at Lick Pier. But figments were so often incommunicable. Take pi. Every time Mr. Cochran said pi, Elizabeth smelled blueberry pie, even saw it, resting, freshly baked, on a window ledge of a yellow house, the house in San Francisco she sometimes imagined, the one she knew would be hers. One day people might say, "Elizabeth's house" with the same wonder and satisfaction that she always thought, "Juno's house." She would live in this house, this small yellow house, with her books, and her cat, and a tree at the window.

A eucalyptus tree, like these, she thought, wheeling her bicycle into the rack beneath three large, peeling, fragrant ones. Sometimes she had to struggle against an impulse to embrace them and listen to their great tree hearts.

"Umbellate," she said out loud.

"Umbrella?" asked Larry Sutton, wheeling his bike abruptly into the space next to hers.

"Umbellate," corrected Elizabeth. "Eucalyptus trees have umbellate blossoms."

"So, Friday's the big day, speaking of flowers and all. You doing anything after graduation?"

"Dinner at the St. Catherine Hotel with my mother."

"And afterwards? Louis Heydon's having a grad night party, and I thought maybe . . ."

"Then we're going to a movie," she lied. Larry drove people to strategies. She tried another; with a wave she bore straight for the girls' rest room.

But she did not stay long. She ran her hand through her hair, counted to ten, checked her watch, and emerged, carefully searching the walkway for Larry Sutton. She would have to hurry. In two minutes Juno Reed would pull her jeep into faculty parking. Elizabeth took up her station on a bench under an oak, opened a disheveled copy of *Middlemarch*, and pretended to read.

She heard in a moment tires on gravel. The thwunk of

door. She slowly floated her eyes up to the top of the book so that she could trace Miss Reed's progress across the left page, up the stairs and into her classroom. But this morning she stepped over the geometric lines she traveled every morning to her classroom and was in fact coming across the grass, with her easy, long-legged stride, the wind playing her hair loose from where—standing in her bathroom in front of the medicine cabinet—she must have swept it up, toward Elizabeth. How many times in her imagination Elizabeth had cracked her free of the usual pattern and seen her turn suddenly in Elizabeth's direction, as if following an energy field. She was so close now that Elizabeth could feel the air waves about her alter and zing around in random directions. She locked her eyes onto George Eliot's careful sentences and did not look up until Juno sat on the heaving bench beside her.

"Where are you?"

Elizabeth stared.

"I mean in *Middlemarch*?"

"Oh. Casaubon has just asked Dorothea to promise not to remarry after his death, which I hope is going to happen any minute. His death, I mean."

"But will she promise?"

"Not if *I* was George Eliot, she wouldn't."

"What would she do?"

"Leave Casaubon shut up in his gloomy old house and go build sunny cottages for the laborers and their families, just like she said she would in the first chapter."

"People hardly ever end up doing what they say they will in the first chapter. That's generally what novels are about. The middle shows people coming around to doing what it is they actually will do instead of what they said they would in chapter one. If you follow."

Juno laughed, and looked out along the invisible line that led to her house. "This is all probably an awkward way of leading up to what I really want to talk with you about. You may think this is none of my business, and you could be right. But if George Eliot is to be believed, then we are all part of the web of humanity, connected by fragile lines of relationship." She laughed again, and in the voice of a newscaster announced, "George Eliot has authorized this intrusion into your life."

"I trust you," said Elizabeth quietly.

"Thank you. Kit tells me you're not going to college. She knows how highly I regard you. Otherwise she would never repeat a conversation. Is it true, Elizabeth? You're really not going to college?"

"Dorothea Brook never went to college," said Elizabeth in a thin voice.

"Neither did George Eliot. But if she were your age, today, I think she would. I feel sure. And so would Dorothea, even if those cottages had to wait a few years."

"My mother wants me to stay."

"Is she ill?"

"No, it isn't that. She just doesn't see any point in going to college. Nobody in her family ever did. And my father, well, he left before I was born. She's had to raise me alone."

"I see," Miss Reed said softly, her hose whispering as she uncrossed her legs, as if to stand. But she did not stand. Instead she looked seaward, the morning breeze freeing a few more strands of hair. Then, finally rising, looking Elizabeth straight in the eye, she said, "You may find, Elizabeth, that you will have to rescue your own life more than once from the Casaubons of this world."

CHAPTER 15: DINNER OUT

Elizabeth Rivers' fingers closed about the crystal stem of her champagne glass. Certainly champagne could not make her stomach feel worse, and it might make it feel better. When she had tried to explain this feeling in her stomach, her mother had said, "Graduation butterflies." Well, graduation was over, but the butterflies had not gone.

"Wait a minute, now." Leon put a damp, restraining hand on Elizabeth's. "Let's have a toast to our graduate."

Her mother smiled and tilted her head back until light from the St. Catherine Hotel's chandeliers reflected off her glasses. Elizabeth had asked her a hundred times to get a new pair of glasses. Cat's eye glasses had been out of style for ten years. She had other things to spend her money on, she would say. Money did not grow on trees, though she knew some who thought it did. If she mentioned money tonight, Elizabeth would run screaming from the room. If she said anything whatever about meat on the table Elizabeth's stomach would take its own revenge.

Leon was raising his glass: "Through the teeth and over the gums, look out stomach, here she comes." He laughed and champagne trickled over the black hairs on his hand. "No, seriously, Elizabeth, good luck on the road of life."

Then Elizabeth touched wine glasses with her mother and saw that tears stood in her eyes.

Large, gilt menus intruded between them. Her mother would have the Red Snapper Almondine; Leon, the Surf 'N Turf. Elizabeth imagined Butterflies en Brochette. She swallowed more champagne. Her mother reminded her this was a celebration. Elizabeth set the clumsy menu aside, almost knocking over the thick amber water goblet. She would have Sauteed Abalone. She would think of Karl and their shared meal, the two of them in the Boy Scouts' dining hall, sunlight falling in bars across the tables, their cooking fire crackling from time to time. Of Karl's neatly made bed in the corner, the picture of Chadwick behind broken glass.

She sipped her champagne and studied the back of a woman about to sit down, seeing something of Juno about a perfect stranger. As she did several times every day.

But this time she was right. It *was* Juno Reed. Along with Mary Broadwin, and her mother, Chris Broadwin, Kit Tebolt, and Charles Gem, her friend. Charles saw her first and tipped an imaginary hat in her direction. Then the others turned, smiling and nodding their congratulations at the graduate.

"Well, ain't we grand," muttered Leon into his champagne glass. Elizabeth stared down into her watercress salad.

"Elizabeth, you aren't eating," her mother observed, testing the outer perimeter of her teased curls. She had spent the afternoon at the Stay Rite Beauty Parlour, taking time off from work.

"Only one thing could stop a healthy girl her age from eating," remarked Leon, stretching back in his chair. "Olive,

I believe this girl's in love."

"No she's not," snapped Olive. "She's smarter than that by a yard and a half."

"Olive, the fact is you've got a young woman on your hands. Time she *was* in love. I like her better for it. And say, I've got to have a rum and Coke. Champagne's for ladies. And fags." He looked meaningfully in the direction of Charles Gem. "Where's our waiter at? And get him to take away this pile of grass too. No wonder Elizabeth won't eat it. Fit for rabbits."

"It's watercress, and the waiter's been hanging around our table so much I feel like he's having dinner with us. You don't need anything more to drink, either."

"You our waiter?" Leon asked the busboy. "I need a rum and Coke."

"No sir. But I'll tell him."

Elizabeth gazed across the room at the other table. Mary Broadwin looked bored. How could she be bored in such company? Probably they were talking about books. Mary Broadwin had no right to them, these special people. She did not belong there. How did she get a mother like Chris Broadwin, who built houses? Mary Broadwin was a tiresome wimp who would marry Larry Sutton and spend her life doing her nails, the kind of daughter her own mother would find inspiring.

"Well this is more like it," said Leon, rubbing together blimpy hands over his new drink.

"I said you've had enough, Leon Feeney," Olive murmured.

The waiter set their plates before them. At each sound of plate touching table, Elizabeth's mother bobbed her head in professional syncopation.

The abalone was tough. Probably cooked too long. Elizabeth, from where she sat, could just see the outline of Juno Reed's jaw and the tip of her left ear where her hair had wisped down. It must be like silk, the way it floated down. Elizabeth touched her own thick hair, absently. "It's your own fault," remarked her mother, a silver square of red snapper suspended on her fork.

Elizabeth raised dark eyebrows in inquiry.

"I told you to get a perm at the Stay Rite. Just on the ends there so you could do something with it. Instead of just having it hang down like there was no plan about you."

"I like it this way," said Elizabeth, sawing at her abalone.

"Quit picking at her, Olive."

"And what would you know about it, Mr. Bachelor? Mr. Free Spirit." Olive glowered at her snapper.

"Well, she looks fine the way she is. That waiter over there's been gawking at her ever since we came in. And no wonder too. He'll have to wait in line, though."

Elizabeth looked in the direction indicated by Leon's chin. Roy Tripper, in a tuxedo, leaned against the wall, staring, just the way he had that day she sailed for the Isthmus on the *Island Queen* with Sally Bates. His big mouth forming the ugly words. What was it Sally had said? Boys are different?

Yes they were. Fox smells and Trojan rubbers.

CHAPTER 16: FIREWORKS

"There he goes now," said Grace, observing through the rotating arms of the saltwater taffy machine the figure of Leon Feeney crossing Crescent Avenue toward the Pleasure Pier. "That's him, alright."

"Thanks, Grace," said Elizabeth, sliding out of the front booth.

"Listen, what's all this secrecy? I feel like I'm in a Nancy Drew Mystery. A supporting character, of course. You're Nancy Drew." Grace took out a twenty-five pound bag of sugar and thumped it down heavily on the counter. "Got to fill all these fucking dispensers before I get to go home."

"Look, I just don't want to run into Leon right now. Let's leave it at that."

"We've been friends a long time, Elizabeth Rivers." She led Elizabeth to a booth, where they both sat down. They were alone, except for Mr. Loomis keeping his vigil at the taffy machine.

"He kissed me last night."

"Leon?"

"I don't mean a fatherly, graduation kiss. I mean a slidy, wet kiss when my mother was out of the room."

"Well, what did you do?"

"That bastard! I shoved him into the sewing machine. Then my mom came in, otherwise . . . . But I don't want to see him ever again, and I don't really even want to see her for awhile. That house is getting too small, this island, maybe."

"Then come with me. Come with me to Irvine. You know you want to. You know you have five times the brains and talent I have. You can't stay here. Neither of us can. We'd turn out like the Munchkins in *The Wizard of Oz.*" Grace blew out her cheeks and wagged her head in pantomime.

"I always liked the Munchkins," said Elizabeth, giving Grace's hand a squeeze across the formica table.

"What you really are," said Grace rising and straightening her stained apron, "is a horse of another color."

"A late horse," qualified Elizabeth, checking the time in the Chase and Sanborn clock. "I've got to meet Miss Reed and Miss Tebolt at the Pleasure Pier for a Fourth of July picnic out on Casino Point."

"But you haven't answered my question," objected Grace. "Don't just brush it off."

"I promise an answer in one week, at . . ." she consulted her watch, "seven fifteen. Now push me out the door, dear Grace, amazing Grace, or Miss Reed will mark me tardy."

Grace unlocked the door of the Sea Gull Cafe and pushed Elizabeth playfully in the direction of the Pleasure Pier, where Miss Tebolt, Miss Reed, Mr. Gem, and Chris Broadwin were already assembled and peering into each other's picnic baskets and laughing.

"Oh, and here's Elizabeth now," said Kit Tebolt.

"Am I late?"

"Not as late as that blasted Harbor Master," said Charles Gem, flipping down the lid of his basket. "And don't think you're going to get a look in here just because you're Florence Chadwick." "Mary couldn't come," explained Chris Broadwin. "She had a date at the last minute with an ugly young man named Larry Sutton." Elizabeth laughed. "Better Mary than me." "Mary hadn't noticed his bad manners or his hopeless grammar, or his weak mind by the time I left. I pray she will start noticing such details. When does adolescence lift, anyway? Juno, you should know things like that."

"Mary will be alright," said Juno.

"Mary already is alright, but I'm half dead of hunger. Ah, here he comes," said Charles.

Richard Cross, the Harbor Master, approached, his white cap under one arm and a huge Tupperware container under the other. "Sorry I'm late, but I had to get things squared away with the fireworks people so they wouldn't burn up the pier tonight." He shook the container. "These are token vegetables. The real food is in Charley's basket. We don't want to fill up on vegetables and have no room left for cake."

"Who brought a blanket?" asked Kit. "Nobody, apparently."

"I'll get one out of the jeep," offered Juno.

"That's right," said Richard, taking Chris by the arm and leading off toward the Casino. "Juno will be the mother today and the rest of us can be irresponsible."

"My Pleasure Peer," said Charles Gem to Richard amorously. Then, "I don't suppose any of you is quick enough to recognize humor when it accosts you. Pleasure PEER, for Christ's sake. Come on Kit," he took his friend by the elbow, "we've got the cake."

Elizabeth found herself standing alone. Her arms felt

too long for her body. Around the palm she could just see Juno bending into the back of the jeep, searching.

"Well, I have one loyal friend," said Juno, walking energetically toward Elizabeth, an old blue and white quilt draped over one shoulder.

"Can I carry something?" asked Elizabeth, holding out empty hands.

Juno filled them with the quilt. "Thanks," she said, settling her remaining burdens more comfortably. "Oh, smell that?"

"What?" asked Elizabeth, securing the blanket under her arm. "Smell what?"

"Sun tan oil. Warm sun tan oil. It makes me think of fresh baked macaroons." She led off, following their friends toward the point.

"It makes my mother think of the Baron. You know, that bulgy old lifeguard who made his fortune in sun tan oil?"

Juno shuddered. "I'd rather be reminded of macaroons."

"To my mother it probably amounts to the same thing."

Juno smiled. "Yes, mothers are funny things. I know I never could quite believe my mother was really my mother. I was sure I was adopted, probably from royalty. Then she got very sick. This was when I was away in Michigan, going to graduate school. It was Thanksgiving, I remember, and I thought nobody would let me on a plane and that I wouldn't get to see her before she died. Somehow I did get on a plane, and all I could think of was what if she died before I got to find out who she really was."

"And who was she?" asked Elizabeth.

"Ah, who knows?" said Juno. "All I know is when I walked into her hospital room she was sitting cross-legged on the bed plaiting her hair. And I thought, 'That is courage.' She died next day in surgery. But she really was royalty. I did know that much.

"Your mother works at the Sea Gull, doesn't she?"

"I was raised by Indians," said Elizabeth.

"Stolen from the wagon train?"

"Yes. And now that I've been returned to my mother she wants me to eat with a knife and fork. And to admire the Baron in his disgusting swim suit. But I never will."

"No, you never will," Juno agreed, stopping to look across Crescent Bay. The odor of kerosene wafted toward them, mingled with cooking from the moored sailboats.

"I love that smell." Elizabeth gulped air. "And I like to stare into portholes when the lamps are lit below and see the people moving around. You can hear all kinds of things too, sometimes a knife on a plate, part of a sentence, music across the water."

"And the man with the bagpipes. Have you seen him? He wears old Levis with holes in the knees and he marches up and down the decks piping the sun down.

"Oh," she said, suddenly noticing the others, already passing the Chevron dock. "Are we walking too slowly? I love to poke along when I'm not at work. Kit keeps to a schedule even now, when she's retired. When we first met I made the mistake of quoting Emerson to her. You remember the line, 'Time is just the stream I go a-fishing in?' I think that's it."

Elizabeth nodded.

"Well, she hasn't let me forget that one in eight years." Juno laughed. "She pulls a long face, like this, and says it with a Boston accent. She's horrible.

"But I've been running on while you've been very quiet. You don't like Kit, do you?"

"I don't really know her," said Elizabeth, trying to penetrate the shuttered windows of the Tuna Club. "She doesn't know me either."

"She knows that she likes you. I think she has a secret fantasy of your going away to school, then sailing home again

as the librarian-redeemer, to wrest the public library out of
the hands of Helen Valentine, whom she abhors. Helen, she
says, believes it her sacred duty to protect the books from
people."

"I know. I don't like to go there anymore. Even Mr.
Loomis doesn't like to go there anymore. He's happier
sitting in the Sea Gull drinking coffee all day and watching
the taffy machine, even though my mother throws him out
twice a day when she sweeps."

"Speaking of your mother," said Juno. "Have you
thought any more about our conversation?"

"You mean about going to college? Grace Medina and I
were just talking about it. She's going to Irvine in September
and wants me to come too. We've been friends since we were
babies. I don't know though."

They stopped, leaning against the rough railing, listening
to the tide sucking at the spaces between the jumbled rocks,
feeling the ocean breezes playing their hair free.

"Hallooo," came Charles Gem's voice. He was waving his
arm in the direction of the Casino's rear lawn, marking for
Juno and Elizabeth the wandering course of their party.

"Be right there," called Juno with a wave of dismissal.
Then she turned again to Elizabeth. "Tell me, please. Is it
just your mother, or is it something else too?"

Elizabeth smiled. "It's always something else too. Isn't
it?"

They walked on. "I'm very glad you know that already.
I was thirty, at least, before I did."

"Is that Emerson's fault?" Elizabeth asked.

"And is it my fate always to be taught by my students?"
asked her teacher.

They made their way now onto the grass and joined the
others, busily setting out paper plates of food at the clay feet
of Venus, Elizabeth's favorite statue in the world.

"You see now what pagan rites you have driven us to by

not hurrying up with that blanket," Charles Gem said, taking the quilt from Elizabeth and casting it wide.

Chris Broadwin handed her an icy plastic glass.

"What's this?" Elizabeth asked. There was a slice of orange floating in it whose center had turned a brilliant purple.

"Sangria," said Chris, counting the strokes from the bell tower above them.

"Eight," Elizabeth pronounced. "What's sangria?"

"Oh, Burgundy, oranges, strawberries, lemons, soda, and just a thought of brandy."

"A thought of brandy," echoed Elizabeth, looking at her Venus, the shining plaster hair sculpting her naked body.

"Who wants broccoli? Who wants Quiche Lorraine?" Kit was slicing through the circles.

Quiche Lorraine, thought Elizabeth, tasting the stream of sangria take the plunge down her throat. Quiche Lorraine. It sounded like a sunlit village in the south of France. Or a movie star with large eyes fringed in lashes the length of a lawn rake. Kit put a sliver of each on her plastic plate and handed her a frail, translucent fork. Elizabeth did not feel hungry. Just thirsty. She cut off a triangle of quiche Lorraine and balanced it on the blunt tines of her plastic fork. Somehow it did not seem like food.

"Eat up," advised Charles Gem, "or you'll never grow up to be Jane Austen."

"Did someone mention Jane Austen?" asked Kit, turning around to face Elizabeth.

Elizabeth swallowed the quiche whole.

"If you grow up to be Jane Austen, then you won't have to marry Larry Sutton," mused Chris Broadwin, her mind on her absent daughter.

"No," agreed Charles, "she could marry Darcy instead. I always thought Darcy had a certain something."

"Boots," said Richard, "it's the boots. They were ebony

and came up to here." He marked a place on his leg just below the knee and poured himself another glass of sangria. "Anybody like more?" He raised the picnic jug in invitation.

"Here's to a well-turned leg," said Charles Gem, glass uplifted. "Somebody should write an ode to Darcy's leg."

"And a companion piece called "Elizabeth's Leg," suggested Richard amiably.

"Nobody ever saw Elizabeth Bennet's leg," said Chris Broadwin, shaking off her lethargy. "Not even Darcy. For she always undressed in the dark."

"So much the better," said Charles. "The unseen is far more erotic than the seen. I remember once . . ."

"And I remember," interrupted Katherine Tebolt, "that we have a young lady in our midst."

Elizabeth flushed and snapped a carrot in two with her teeth. Juno and Charles stared at Katherine. In the silence an outboard motor choked itself off twice, then coughed into a steady mosquito hum.

"Elizabeth is an historian," Chris said quietly. "We musn't stand in her line of vision."

"Oh hell," said Richard, "let's eat the cake." He dug a stack of blue paper plates out of a rumpled bag, while Kit roused herself in a search for more forks.

Charles carefully reached into his hamper and lifted out a rectangular sheet cake decorated like an American flag.

Richard let out a moan of pleasure.

"Anybody remember to bring coffee?" Juno asked. "No? Then we each get two fingers more of sangria and that's that."

"So let's hear it for the pastry chef. You never saw a cake like that before," Charles said, sticking an experimental finger into clustered stars and licking it thoughtfully.

"It's beautiful," admired Elizabeth, holding her glass for Juno.

"Poetry in motion, poetry in motion," Richard agreed,

handing Charles his Swiss army knife. "Now let's have it. Let them eat cake, for God's sake."

"None for me," said Kit, leaning back on her elbow, crossing her feet at the ankles.

Juno stroked her friend's gray swirl of hair. "Tired darling?"

"Tired or not she's got to eat this cake. Otherwise I get temperamental. Artists are like that," Charles Gem warned, licking the knife and handing the first slice around the circle.

"I hate it when you do that, Charley," said Richard with a shudder.

"You mean when I get temperamental?"

"I mean when you lick knives."

"I seek danger. I hurl myself against its sharp edges to define myself."

"That's why you're a museum curator."

"That's why I'm a sword swallower impersonating a museum curator." Charles held the Swiss army knife poised over his open mouth.

"For Christ's sake, just pass the cake. It's nearly dark. Those fools from Red Devil will be burning down my pier in another ten minutes, and I want to eat my cake first."

Elizabeth stared down at the improbable piece of cake resting in her lap. Chimes struck the half hour.

People had been straggling out of the promenade for the last half hour, tourists and islanders, opening out lawn chairs, floating old blankets out onto the grass.

Riding lights winked on in sailboats tugging gently at their mooring lines, and families arranged themselves on boat cushions in cockpits. Sometimes a dog barked or a child cried out. Sound walked on water.

Suddenly overhead the sky was split by a cascade of greens and blues, a shrill scream, followed by a dull cannon bang. Charles picked up the cake plates, stooping to kiss Elizabeth on the head. At last they all settled down to watch the fireworks, Richard and Charles next to the glowing Venus, then Chris, Kit and Juno, with Elizabeth on the far end.

Elizabeth swallowed her last two fingers of sangria. A curious moving line of relaxation began at the top of her spine and followed the sangria downward, tripping off an electric light display at the intersection of each vertebra. She lay on her back and watched an enormous red zinnia grow across the sky, dragging with it an uuuuuuuuuuuuuu from the line of spectators at the railing. Then, just as it began to fade into yellow streaks, from a dying spear came another zinnia, and from it, another.

Elizabeth Rivers sat up abruptly, overcome by these zinnias and the shared uuuuuuuuuuuuuuu of strangers. A window was sent up that fell into shards over Crescent Bay. In the shattering light Elizabeth glanced quickly at Juno, to see her face, but instead saw Kit, saw the plumpness of her kind face fall inward, revealing only a glowing skull in the sharp and empty night. Uuuuuuuuuuuuuuu. The breath sank out of Elizabeth. She edged closer to Juno until their shoulders touched.

CHAPTER 17: CARETAKER

Juno's cat sat on the top step of the patio and washed her face. Morning sunlight falling through jacaranda leaves shaped bright shifting triangles on her white fur. Elizabeth, leaning on the ledge of the kitchen window, smiled, rubbed her eyes sleepily and remembered coffee. She held the tea-kettle under the thrumming faucet, then set it on the burner. The August breeze through the kitchen window made the blue flames dance. Bare feet padding across earthen tiles, she opened the French doors onto the patio, stooped to stroke Diana's ears and cheeks, put on a Beatles album.

In the kitchen, humming now, she reached up high for the coffee cannister and the box of filters, took out a circle of paper, folded it into a triangle that fit neatly into the glass coffee pot shaped like an hourglass, and spooned in four measures. Her mother would say anybody'd have to be out of their minds making coffee this way. Kit had showed her how the morning they left, she and Juno, ten days ago.

How to shake just enough little stars into Diana's bowl, how to run water into the disposal so it would not back up into the shower, when to water the plants, where to put the mail and the newspapers. All this Kit had attended to, gray hair spilling over her forehead like a small haystack, her pants cinched in on her thinning waist, breathing so that you could almost hear, could almost see the skull beneath the skin.

Juno had simply moved about silently, washing dishes, sweeping the kitchen floor, carrying their suitcases out to the jeep. Then, when Kit went into the bathroom, Juno had taken Elizabeth quickly aside. To thank her, to say Kit's mind would be at rest knowing Elizabeth would be caring for the house, to say she could not know when they would return, to say the cancer was already in her lymph system, to say that she would write or call.

Elizabeth had stood on the drive, waving as they entered into parallel lines of eucalyptus and disappeared at their intersection. Four days later came a scrawled postcard from a Houston Travelodge, Juno's hand unmistakable, yet with an exaggerated up and down slash like a seismograph reading. They had arrived. And that was all.

Elizabeth poured her coffee into one of the blue ceramic mugs and made her way out to the patio, the newspaper tucked under her arm. Diana yawned in one of the bentwood chairs. Remembering the flowers, Elizabeth put her coffee and paper down on the table next to Diana, then set the hose trickling into the snapdragon bed.

Pools of clear water rushed circling around the roots. Elizabeth straightened, feeling the morning sun on the top of her head, across her cheeks, wondering about Juno, about Katherine Tebolt, about the cancer that grew inside her like invisible fireworks, like fields of deadly wild poppies.

She drank her coffee, the paper in her lap, her hand on the sleeping cat.

CHAPTER 18: STILL LIFE IN LEO

Olive Rivers stared into the kitchen sink. Radishes bobbed about, colliding with green onions, celery stalks, heads of floating iceberg lettuce, a bun of parsley tied in the middle with a slim string of jute. Pretty, really, when you thought about it.

Olive remembered the parakeet that loved to play in the sink among the vegetables when Elizabeth was little. It would circle overhead, screeching, then dive down, flutter in the water, bite the lettuce, and rise screaming in delight. What was his name? Pretty Boy, that was it.

Dead now. She had slammed him herself in the bedroom door. It didn't pay to have pets. Everything she had ever loved either died or left her (Eddie running off like a tom cat before Elizabeth was born). Pretty Boy had only been wanting to look in her bedroom mirror (Chiquita going squash under the tires of Ted Banion's laundry truck one morning).

Olive bent down to get the big colander from under the sink, then lifted the dripping lettuce, piling everything up to dry nicely before dinner. Sandy water ran down the drain. Elizabeth had said, No meat. Leon would say, A man needs meat. Elizabeth wanting this, Leon wanting that. No agreement. No harmony.

Libras needed harmony. She had read that in a magazine somewhere. They needed peace like others needed air. But could she get it? There had been in the article a little drawing of a woman in her nightgown with a blindfold over her eyes holding up an old fashioned scale. Libras, the drawing showed, loved balance. They loved justice and tended to be artistic.

Leon was a Scorpio. No one would take the trouble to get along with a Scorpio, except a Libra. Everybody else had more sense. Olive reached the avocado off the window sill. Gently she squeezed it in her freckled, curled hand. Ripe. She scored it lengthwise and split it neatly.

The pit. A tiny root stuck out the bottom. She had been fooled before by such pits, promising they would live if she, Olive, would only give them a chance. She had skirted them with toothpicks and placed them in jars of water on this very shelf. They sent up a single tiny, bright green shoot. Up, up it would climb. Then it would turn brown and the water in the jar turn to slime and then, out with the garbage. No, she had seen enough of avocado pits.

The skin came off easily, a sure sign of ripeness. Elizabeth would be pleased. She loved avocados. Olive looked up at the round pink cake on top the refrigerator. Eighteen, her Elizabeth. Grown really.

And what would she do now? Olive swung the netted potatoes onto the counter, selected five good ones from the sack, and swung it back under the sink. Now that she was eighteen. It was two months since graduation and she had made no move to get a regular job. Olive set the peeler flying over the muddy potato skins.

She did not want to believe Elizabeth had no gumption. Of course, there was the diving. Olive shuddered, the peeler poised in her hand. She did not like to think of Elizabeth diving for those coins when the steamer docked (her only daughter crushed against a piling). That's how boys earned pocket money and welcome.

But you could never tell a Leo no. That's what the article had said. And besides it was too late to start up on something she had never done before. *No* was a word that caught sideways in her throat, like a hook. Since she was a baby, Elizabeth Rivers had had a mind of her own. Maybe, thought Olive, scratching the end of her nose with her forearm, that's gumption. She had always gone straight ahead with whatever it was.

Olive reached her largest Pyrex casserole down from the top shelf and wiped it out with a dish towel. Where was the margerine? She peered through glasses into the dim recesses of the small refrigerator. She saw the green perspiring bottle of André extra dry pink champagne, a surprise for Elizabeth. But the Blue Bonnet. Where? Ah! Behind the strawberry jam. The jam jar was empty. Why did Elizabeth always put empty jars and bottles back into the icebox? Sometimes she moved like a sleepwalker, her daughter. Olive smeared the casserole with the margerine and sliced the first layer of potato circles into the bottom.

Still, Mr. Smallwood at the bank was willing to take a chance on her, had told Olive at lunch yesterday that Elizabeth was a responsible young lady, made her deposits regularly (did coins thrown from a boat by tourists amount to bank deposits?), that he was looking for just such a young lady to make into a bank teller. And Mr. Smallwood was a kind, successful businessman who had eaten his lunch every day at the Sea Gull for as long as Olive could remember, even though he did not like the Thursday lunch special:

calves liver with smothered onions.

Olive took out a new package of Cheddar cheese and began grating orange streamers onto a paper towel. Elizabeth had never liked liver either. After dinner tonight Olive would tell her daughter what Mr. Smallwood had said. A bank was a clean place to work. Grace Medina's mother used to work at the bank until she got too fat to walk anymore. You could wear nice clothes, working in a bank, and eat your lunch next door at the Descanso Gardens at a little table under the trees, the way Grace's mother always had. Elizabeth could not object to a job like that.

The chimes struck five times. It was alright to have a drink now. People who drank before five might be alcoholic. Olive took down her favorite glass and poured in rum up to the line of blue flowers. Then Coke. Three ice cubes. Rum and Coke fizzed up her nose and down her throat.

In a minute she would relax and have a cigarette while the scalloped potatoes cooked. Quickly she layered the remaining cheese and potatoes into the dish, poured in some milk, and set the oven for 350 degrees. On top of the potatoes she dashed some paprika. Touches like this, *Family Circle* had said, cost nothing, but provided meal appeal. She slid the casserole into the oven, picked up her ashtray, cigarettes, and glass, and headed for her La-Z-Boy.

Elizabeth would be here, and Leon, in another half hour. She swung her feet up and lit a match, drawing heavily on her Kool. The house had seemed strangely quiet without Elizabeth, gone now nearly two weeks, or was it longer? Even though she came by every day when Olive got off work and they would sit out on the porch and talk. Still she would never stay to dinner, except on Sunday, saying she liked fixing her own meals up there in that big house on the hill. Olive did not like to think of her daughter alone there at night, did not like being alone at night herself the few times when Leon had not slept over.

When someone was sick, though, you had to do what you could do for them, even if it meant being afraid sometimes on your own account. Miss Tebolt, they said, was very sick with cancer. That sometimes happened to people when they retired, she had read somewhere. The illness you had fended off by running yourself ragged, day in and day out, lunged at you the moment you had earned your rest, like a hungry tiger.

She saw Miss Tebolt now with her throat torn open simply because she had wanted a little rest. It was up to the well to take care of those who fell. And so she was proud Elizabeth had said she would look after their house and pets and their garden. It showed she might someday know how to look after people. But she had not known then her own house would feel so still, that she would feel, waiting for Elizabeth now on her eighteenth birthday, a sense of excitement, of something about to happen.

CHAPTER 19: A QUICK ONE

When Estelle Nolin brought Leon Feeney his second rum and Coke he caught hold of her hand and squeezed a dollar bill into it. Women appreciated gestures like that. Any little kindness, in fact. Like dogs in that respect.

He studied his Timex waterproof under the cuff of his new dress shirt. Plenty of time. Elizabeth's birthday celebration would start at six and he felt the need of a drink before. Something to relax him.

Elizabeth might still be mad. Not that he had meant anything. A fatherly kiss, that was all. A simple graduation kiss to which he was—after all—entitled. Hadn't he been like a father to her these past three years? He threw the drink back so abruptly that the ice clunked against his front teeth. Quickly he checked the caps on his incisors with his tongue. Gold was a soft metal, the dentist had warned.

Leon's hand closed over the small, square box that held

Elizabeth's birthday present in a nest of white cotton. Women appreciated jewelry. Leon studied the back of his hand, noted the black manly hairs that spread even down his fingers. The velvet box felt small, easily crushed in these strong hands of his.

Many powerful men were not tall. Take Alan Ladd. Alan Ladd stood on a box to make love to the long-legged women in the movies. And nobody had ever complained about Alan Ladd. Leon drew his breath in and stretched his spine up and up.

There was time for another drink, but where was Estelle Nolin? Jawing at the bar with Tula from the bakery next door. Tula stood on one foot, the other crossed casually behind. Her feet were in white nurse's shoes and looked gigantic. A bakers apron wound around her broad waist. Very definitely unfeminine.

You would never catch Olive Rivers alone in a bar. She might have her faults—forgetfulness, to name one—but say what you would, Olive Rivers was a lady. She kept herself up and read magazines so as not to get left at the starting post.

Leon raised his finger to catch Estelle's eye when she threw her head back to laugh, but she only fell straight into close formation with that freak baker, Tula.

Leon stood, screaking the legs of his captain's chair against the wood floor. He would have a quick one at the bar, since that seemed to be the only place you could get any service, then off to Clarissa Street and his two lovely ladies.

CHAPTER 20: KRYPTON

"I'd rather hear your news when Leon gets here," said Olive Rivers, placing the cut glass bowl of carrot sticks dead center on the birthday table. "And get that chair at the sewing machine. Rickety as it is. I'll sit on it."

"This doesn't concern Leon, Mother. It's between you and me," said Elizabeth, seizing the chair as if it were an adversary and plunking it down beside the steaming scalloped potatoes.

"As much as you don't like to admit it, Elizabeth Austen Rivers, Leon Feeney is a member of this family. He cares about you like you were his own. Worries and frets. All the time worrying about Elizabeth this, Elizabeth that. Aren't many men in this world would take the time. There," she said, untying her apron, "ready."

"Worrying doesn't necessarily mean caring. It might mean somebody wants something, something for themselves. I think somebody who really loves you and knows you've got trouble will keep their hands off. I mean, figuratively speaking, will keep their hands off."

Olive stared at her daughter. Sometimes she purely did not know this young person confronting her at every turn. Sometimes she thought Elizabeth had arrived like Superman from some faraway planet where people behaved in unaccountable ways. And who had entrusted her, Olive Rivers, with that tiny stranger eighteen years ago? And when would they come for her?

"At it again?" asked Leon, banging through the screen door. "Seems like two such beautiful ladies would have better things to do than argue."

"I'm not a lady," Elizabeth said.

"Nearly," said Leon.

"I'm a woman, Leon, and I see through you."

"Dinner's ready," interjected Olive.

"Seems like we could have a drink first, hon. What's the rush?"

"Just sit down, Leon. Elizabeth, get the surprise—you know the one—out of the icebox. Sit down, Leon." Olive patted the chair next to her.

In the kitchen Elizabeth ran x-ray eyes through the packed refrigerator. At the back, behind the Philadelphia cream cheese, rested a bottle of André pink champagne. She pulled it carefully through random spaces on the shelf and into kitchen air. Pink champagne. Her mother had bought this for her.

"Bring it here," said Leon, craning his neck to see.

"I'll do it," said Elizabeth.

"You need a man with a corkscrew."

"It's plastic," said Elizabeth, winding pink foil from the neck of the bottle and easing the cork gently, evenly, with her two thumbs.

"Didn't even pop," complained Leon.

"It's not supposed to," said Elizabeth, striding into the

living room, bottle in one hand and three wine glasses in the other.

"Thank you, Elizabeth," said her mother, emphasizing each word.

"Who in hell told you that?" said Leon, feeling in his jacket pocket for the black velvet box.

"Charles Gem at the museum told me that."

"Gem. That fairy."

"I prefer fairies to pigs," said Elizabeth.

"And I prefer decent manners to almost anything," said Olive rising to her feet. "And this is *my* house."

"That's right," said Leon, standing now next to Olive and lifting his glass. "What we are first and last is a loving family. To Elizabeth."

Leon's glass collided with Elizabeth's, then Olive's. He set his glass down and brought out the black velvet box, held it toward her.

"Shall we eat first?" asked Olive, sitting down heavily.

Leon refilled their glasses, sitting on the edge of his chair, knees bouncing. "Presents first," he said. "Go ahead. Open it."

Elizabeth lifted the lid. The gold word, "Elisabeth," glittered. Elizabeth with an "s."

"Hold it up," said Leon. "Show your mother."

She held the name up to her neck. Her mother opened her mouth to speak, then shut it.

"Go ahead. Put it on," said Leon, reaching for the necklace.

"Later," said Olive in the indisputable voice she reserved for Mr. Loomis when it was time for him to yield his place by the taffy machine. "Dinner's getting cold."

Elizabeth dug the serving spoon deep into the scalloped potatoes and made two mounds on her plate. Olive held the salad bowl for Leon. He picked his way around the slivers of avocado. Then he peered into the dish of potatoes and wanted to know where the meat was. Olive said there would be no meat tonight, that three million people every day survived without meat and so could he for one night out of the year. It would not kill him. Elizabeth made her way through salad like a foraging moose. Leon said, A man needs meat. At last Olive carried in the pink cake. It had one large candle in the shape of a question mark and said her name, Elizabeth with a "z." "I love pink cakes," said Elizabeth. "They're so improbable."

Olive felt strong arms around her, stronger than she could have guessed, and a phantom kiss on her cheek. Her daughter. Her daughter with the news, this superdaughter.

Later, when the table was cleared and Leon was asleep in the La-Z-Boy, his feet, his intentions afloat, the two women carried thick cups of coffee out to the porch and sat down together.

"You're grown now," said Olive.

"Yes," said Elizabeth.

"You'll be wanting to go."

"Yes. To college, with Grace."

"I like Grace," said Olive, nodding. "She counts her change and keeps the salt shakers filled. You can count on a person like that."

"Yes."

"But I can't think what her mother will do now. She can't do much but sit on that porch. What with the weight."

"She'll manage."

"I guess so. But where's all the money to come from? It's not like it grows on trees. Of course, if I had it to give . . ."

"I know Mother. You would. But I've saved some, almost eight hundred dollars. And Mr. Smallwood at the bank says he'll give me a student loan."

"Borrowing, Elizabeth?"

"And I'll get a job there."

"You never seemed to be paying attention to money, all that time, with your wandering and your reading and your dreaming. I must have done something right."

"Yes, dear," said Elizabeth, rising from the green porch chair to encircle her mother in her arms.

CHAPTER 21: TEMPEST

Olive Rivers could see storm warnings flapping from the mast of the Pleasure Pier. Six-thirty by the Chase and Sanborn clock; you could not hear the chimes above the wind. So dark it looked like midnight. She screwed down the lid on the last sugar dispenser. Grace was giving a new batch of saltwater taffy a final punch or two before she set it to pulling on the machine for the night. Old Loomis would stand by the door wringing his hands while Grace did this. Like creation itself had stopped. Throw him out, was Olive's advice, but Grace had a heart that was too soft for her own good.

Olive lit a Kool and rested her bones for the first time in five hours. The lunch crowd had been bad enough, then there had been the new Businessman's Early Dinner. Olive did not care what Leon said, Victor Early was a fool. Constantly changing things around when people liked them the way they were just fine. Victor Early said she had no forward

vision and no sense of humor (Early Dinner, ha!). Olive
sometimes wished she owned the Sea Gull Cafe and not
Victor Early. Then just see. She would call it Olive's Place.
She would throw out that taffy machine and Mr. Loomis
right along with it. If they wanted improvements, they would
get them. She would throw out the Businessmen's Early
Dinner. She would throw out the businessmen.

Olive Rivers looked up to see Grace Medina setting the
chrome arms in motion, to see old Loomis' face relax again,
to see the Baron, clutching his sky blue terrycloth robe,
chase his yachting cap past the plate glass window of the
Sea Gull Cafe, like a boat under heavy sail, heeling dangerously.

Grace was urging Mr. Loomis to leave. Olive liked Grace.
She would turn now, Olive knew, now that old Loomis was
out the door, off her hands, off her mind; she would turn
now and start filling the salt cellars without being told.
Olive snubbed her cigarette into the glass ashtray and started
in on the ketchup bottles. She was glad to work with Grace,
but now she would go, she and Elizabeth together. They
would go over town and sink out of sight like coins flung
from the steamer.

She watched Grace, wisps of dark hair escaping the net
just in front of her ears, bending over the stream of salt
flowing like sand from an hourglass. Beautiful girl. Leon
said her strong jaw made her look like a prize-fighter. Olive
liked strong-looking girls; then she did not have to feel so
afraid for them. Besides, Leon did not know everything.
Grace counted her change and minded her own business.
She looked after her mother, which was more than Leon
Feeney ever did.

Good Housekeeping said if you wanted to know how
a man would treat you after you married him, look at how
he treated his mother now. Leon sent belated birthday cards
that said in more ways than you would think possible that

Bertha Feeney was old and did not deserve a real present. Leon said these cards would hand her a laugh. She imagined Leon extending his hand toward his mother, smiling red lips cupped in the palm. Bertha Feeney lived over town in a rest home and he visited her once a year if she was lucky. Bertha Feeney would one day die of all that rest and greeting cards that came too late.

And how could she, Olive Rivers, think of marrying such a man? She wiped a pool of ketchup off the counter and smiled absently at Grace. Still, to give him his due—for Libras must always see both sides to anything—he did know what kindness was, took her out once a week to someplace nice, loved, truly loved, her daughter, though try to convince Elizabeth of that. And it hurt him, Elizabeth holding him always at arm's length that way.

He had sat after her birthday party on the top step of the porch, after Elizabeth had gone back to Miss Reed's house that night, had sat there drinking out of the champagne bottle, looking like a little boy then and not a man at all. Disappointed, sulking.

Disappointed in what, she had asked him? In his life, that was what. In his own miserable goddamned life. One day, he said, he would end up like Jake Hicks, spearing up trash from the beach and putting it in black plastic bags for the city. A useless, failed person (what was failure?).

She had been afraid he might cry (why should she fear that?). And then he had gone on about Ned Carter, and how Ned Carter would take him into Island Realty if Leon would study and get his license. Leon would just die if finally he did not get a piece of the action (as if success was a pink birthday cake to be shared up).

But he needed help, it seemed. He could not do this thing alone. He could only do it, get his piece of the action, if she, Olive Rivers, would agree to help him, would be his wife and stand behind him, as a wife does. His eyes swam in misery. She had put her hand on his shoulder. But she had not said yes.

And now, tonight, she would have to say yes or no. She had used up her week of thinking things over. Through her mind all week thoughts had run like water through a tap that would not shut off. She had practiced saying no in the shower each morning. She had not told Elizabeth.

Still, she could not go on forever living her life for Elizabeth. If Elizabeth was to be her own separate person, then she, Olive Rivers, had a right to be that also. But would she have that right if she became Mrs. Leon Feeney instead of just plain Olive Rivers? And did she really, at her age (thirty-six come October), want this thing that Elizabeth counted so high? Maybe it was a thing for girls to want and not for grown women who had already had their own true love (never a card from Eddie, only the divorce papers served by that sad-eyed Sergeant Alton one morning while she was handing Mr. Smallwood from the bank his eggs over easy with crisp bacon) and had borne and then raised single-handed a child into this world.

Well, she did not know. Really it was too much for her, and getting darker, too, while she mooned about over the ketchup bottles. It would be a fierce one, alright. One of those tropical storms. She wiped off the counter, one last time. Grace had changed into her street clothes and was snapping her slicker closed up to her chin.

"Want me to walk you?" Grace asked.

"No thanks, hon. I don't mind a storm." Olive closed the door behind Grace, then walked quickly back toward the Gulls sign, smacked the door open. Her clothes hung, looking like a drowned person, from an iron hook. No use putting them on. She would only have to change again for Leon, who would pick her up at eight. She snatched her clothes down and stuffed them into an Island Emporium bag (the plastic would keep them dry), put on her yellow slicker, pulled the light chain overhead. Dark, but she knew her way like Audrey Hepburn in—what was that movie where she was blind?—*Wait Until Dark.* Audrey Hepburn's big mistake was when she opened the icebox door. Or had the murderer opened it?

At the front door Olive paused, watching the saltwater taffy machine in the glow from the street lamp, the glint as one shining arm rose and the other obediently fell, feeling for just a moment perhaps what Mr. Loomis sometimes felt as he watched these circling chrome sharks, the sense that their being there might not depend after all on your watching them. Olive Rivers locked the front door of the Sea Gull Cafe and made her way toward Clarissa Street, a yellow spot on the wet, black night.

CHAPTER 22: PASSAGE

Juno lay her hot cheek on the rail of the heaving ship, felt the tremulous plunge down, her wet fingers tightening, her body bracing itself, riding the storm. She might be half way now. Off the bow she could see no lights, nor off the stern. Against her hip pressed the outline of the box that weighed nothing. And against the night pressed this ship that weighed everything, its lights streaming over her head and into gullies and mountains of heavy, cold water toward Avalon.

She reached into the deep pocket of her trench coat and folded her fingers around the dry box. Trash, Kit's mother had said that morning sitting on her flowered spread in her small, frame house in Glendale, asking Juno what right she had to burn Kit up, to burn up her only daughter like she was so much trash? Her finger had traced rapidly, again and again, the contours of one blue chenille flower on the spread. Then she had raised her wavering head to ask, to demand, "And what was she to you, anyhow?"

And not to say. Not to answer that rightful question with its rightful answer now, after all the years of silence and discretion. Not to say, We lay in each other's arms for eight years. We felt passion. To tell her that her daughter, Katherine, had been a mountain climber with careful hands moving with Juno toward a precipice, ledge by ledge, deftly. That they had held each other, trembling, tight together. That they lived inside each other, body and soul, for eight years. That they had planted flowers and baked bread and built bookcases. To say their lives were the same as everybody else's; to say their lives had been different. That they had known joy.

Discretion; it was no passive virtue. It was a perpetual self-monitoring, self-denial, denying you wanted to reach out and hold the hand of your love, unconsciously and in public, to lean forward in a restaurant and take the hand lying palm up on the tablecloth.

For eight years she had loved this woman, Katherine Tebolt, body and soul; had gone when it was time to ease her dying and read her books into the night until she could no longer comprehend their frivolous windings, had held her head as she vomited out the chemicals, the pain, the discretion, gone, all gone now, turned to ash, like her dear body, her dear loved body.

The ship lurched suddenly, as if it had struck something in the dark. Juno grabbed the rail with both hands, watching the waves running unbroken past the bow, the pain behind her eyes hovering like the orange, incomplete moon over the incomplete horizon.

She was trying, trying to think of fish, fathoms beneath, turning and feeding in silence. The earth was seven-eighths water, she reminded herself, and she the smallest fish of all. But still the fear of death singled her out, called her mammal, cut through the tossed water toward her like a submarine on a locked course.

Time is just the stream, she hazarded against this fear, saying it first to herself, then aloud. Time is just the stream, her hand closing around the dry box in her dark pocket.

A dim light appeared at last off the starboard bow: Avalon. Now she would do it. One numb hand drew the box out of its hiding place, this cheap porcelain thing (she would not call it an urn), container, envelope, body, trash you burned.

What remained? What could stand for something? The black thing in her hand. The ash inside. Ash, the perfect loss of ego, the ultimate refinement. She held aloft this thing; then, as the bow sank deeper, hurled it across the hollow wave like a star plummeting, her Kit, dropping into the sheer of sinking wave.

CHAPTER 23: REFERENCE

Elizabeth Rivers threw a eucalyptus log onto the coals, then stepped back quickly from the cascade of snapping sparks. She thought she heard a sound against the French door, the kind Diana made when she wanted to come in. But it was Chris Broadwin in a yellow slicker, her hand rapping the glass almost soundlessly, the storm behind lighting her angular face.

"I couldn't phone," she said as Elizabeth helped her out of the dripping coat. "I had to come."

"You never phone anybody. You hate phones. Besides, I'd much rather see you." She hung the slicker from a peg in the kitchen. "Coffee?" she asked.

"A drink," said Chris. "One for you too. Juno called."

"Bad news?" asked Elizabeth. She bent over the low cabinet, searching blindly through the bottles. Then she felt Chris standing beside her, heard a low groan go through her like a sound rushing out of some ancient cave. Elizabeth rose in ancient reply, held Chris tight against her until the pain diffused, held her still against the wind and rain.

The fire cracked. Elizabeth stepped back. "Ah," said Chris. "Better now."

Elizabeth jabbed the smoking end of the log with a poker. It flared up. "We could have wine," she said. "I've finished off the gin."

"Yes, wine." Chris sat on the couch and ran a lank hand through her damp hair. "I'm really sorry, Elizabeth. I meant to tell you in a way that would command your respect. But I always cry when my heart breaks. I should have remembered that. And now I've lost my cigarettes," she declared, patting her pockets.

Elizabeth slid open a drawer in the coffee table. "You left this the last time you were here. I smoked a couple."

"My pleasure," said Chris, offering one to Elizabeth before taking her own. Elizabeth held the table lighter for Chris. The flame moved in the currents of air.

"I guess the storm leaks in through the windows and doors," said Elizabeth, drawing a bottle out of the wine rack and studying the label. "How's this look? I don't really understand about wine."

"A little sweet," said Chris. "Let's have that Yugoslavian stuff. Yes, that's it."

Elizabeth carefully twisted the corkscrew into the cork. "How's Juno?" she asked.

Chris thought. "Alright, I guess. She says she is, but then Juno would say that." She drew in quickly on her cigarette. "We used to be lovers. Did she tell you?"

Elizabeth shook her head.

"I probably shouldn't have mentioned it then." Elizabeth handed her a glass of wine. "But I always babble when my heart is breaking. Also, you have a way of eliciting the truth from people, as if it's your right to have it."

"Well," said Elizabeth, "I do stare in windows, as you know."

"Yes," laughed Chris. "Otherwise we might never have met. But you do it with such style. Also—and this is rarer— with such responsibility. As if the truth is safe with you." She sipped her wine.

"So you had an . . . affair . . . with Juno?"

"Now here's an example," said Chris, reaching for another cigarette, "of why we must come entirely clean with our historians. You've concluded Kit and Juno were the given and I was the interloper. Actually Juno and I were together first. We arrived here together, with Mary, who was just a baby then. A pioneer family. Thinking we were the only homosexuals on the island. Sin of pride. We always imagine we are unique."

"But there were others," prompted Elizabeth.

"Oh yes, a whole society of them, moving right through the mainstream of people, but having as well their own separate community, like a party going on beneath the main one, a smaller party but one where the people seemed to be having more fun."

"But what happened?"

"What do you mean?"

"I mean to the pioneer family."

"Probably just time. Time and change."

"It sounds like what happened was Katherine Tebolt," said Elizabeth.

"I don't see it that way. At least, now I don't. Juno and Kit took me in when I felt broken. They insisted I get back into school so I could get my degree. And they were right. For three years they kept Mary, while I rode the steamer back and forth across the channel. They were caretakers: those who take care. Maybe what we did was just expand the pioneer family. It doesn't need to be exclusive. Or even stable, for that matter. What I'm trying to say is you never really lose anybody."

Elizabeth stared into her wine glass.

"You're wondering how I could possibly believe that and still be weeping all over this perfectly beautiful couch. Well, I've perhaps said more than I believe. But that doesn't mean it's not the truth, my dear historian." She got to her feet.

"It's still raining," said Elizabeth.

"Yes, but I promised Charles Gem a sketch of the new museum wing long ago, and I'm afraid it's due tomorrow for his board presentation. He's going to ask them to name the wing for Kit."

"And when will Juno be back?"

"She'll call tomorrow or the next day to let us know. Right now she's visiting Kit's mother, heaven help her. I'd rather visit Lady Macbeth, from what I've heard. Anyway, I'll let you know as soon as I do."

Elizabeth helped Chris into her slicker. "Take care."

"You too," said Chris, giving Elizabeth a quick hug and slipping out the French door as Diana darted in, dry except for a bedraggled tail.

Elizabeth watched Chris spring down the brick stairs and disappear into the trees. Diana rubbed hard against Elizabeth's ankles, purring, but still Elizabeth stood, watching through the rivulets, until finally she said out loud, "Equanimity."

Yes, equanimity. That was the word she wanted. How could Chris have such equanimity about Katherine Tebolt snatching Juno away from her? Or maybe it was not so much Chris who was to be wondered over, but Katherine herself.

Who was she, this plump, gray woman? Who had she been that she could command the lives of two beautiful and brilliant women, women for whom Elizabeth was ready, should they ask it, to lay down her very life?

She moved abruptly toward the kitchen—Diana breaking into a padded gallop before her—yanked open the utensil drawer, and plied the opener to a flat, silver can. Then she bent over Diana's bowl and thunked down half a circle of tuna into her bowl. She would find out.

She had already looked at her clothes, librarian clothes, then house clothes, shapeless cotton pants with drawstrings for people whose waists edged forward day by day. A pair of gardening shoes with muddy soles resting on a newspaper. And under her bathroom sink, hemorrhoid suppositories, an Ace bandage for the ankle (varicose veins?), and a rubber douche bag. Only the debris of age. She would look in the library for this Katherine Tebolt.

She made her way down the hallway, objects jumping out at her in their clarity, as if she looked thrugh a diving mask: the umbrella stand, the Klee prints the length of the hall, Diana's catnip mouse flung against the baseboard.

The library was a small room opening onto the patio, Kit's own, for Juno loved to read in bed, she had said, or before the fire, if there was one, or even in the bathtub, anywhere at all. But this was Kit's room, the librarian's room, with books lining three walls, even up over the door where nobody could see or reach.

And her plants, everywhere. Tiny pots spaced on shelves between books, large baskets by the French doors where philodendra drooped (had Elizabeth overwatered them?), and planters of cactus wherever the light shone strongest.

Elizabeth sat at Kit's desk in her old office chair with the stuffing poking out, swiveled left, then right, stopped, drew toward her a blown-up photograph in a heavy gilt and glass frame. It was Kit down on her knees under the jacaranda tree, holding her hand out to a child in red corduroy pants who was laughing and reaching back. Their movement toward each other had such momentum that you could not believe they had not fallen yet, laughing, into one another's arms. It was as if the picture suggested its own completion, as if the time in it moved backward, or perhaps forward.

The small figure in corduroy must be Mary Broadwin when she lived here with Kit and Juno as if she were their own child. The pioneer family. She felt this idea now as the strongest reality of her life, as if she had been part of that family in some other life, on some other planet.

She sat, listening to the storm, listening so intently to the sound of rushing in her ears that when a key turned in the lock, Elizabeth rose, knowing without having to think that this was Juno Reed, that she was home at last.

BOOK TWO

FALL BACK

CHAPTER 24: MAINLAND

Mrs. Arthur B. Stetwiler angled the rear view mirror in the direction of her mouth. As she suspected, powdered sugar dusted her lower lip. She ran her tongue the length, then toured her mouth with her new tube of Periwinkle Pink. It was not that Mrs. Stetwiler even liked sweets, but business was business. The morning's Calvacade of Homes had ended up at Chez Diane's for a mid-morning snack and she could not very well say no. People took it as snootiness if you said no to an eclair right in front of them. And real estate people, she was bound to admit, were more sensitive than most and took offense quicker. So she had selected from the tray a simple slice of pound cake dusted with powdered sugar and sprinkled with toasted almond slivers. Not what you could really call deviating from her grapefruit diet.

She kissed her lips together, then slipped a tissue between, and impressed a pink O on the folded sheet. The clock on the dash wore a startled expression: 11:00. Time she was

off for her first appointment. She turned the key in her
Buick Riviera and felt its subtle lunge left, then right. Deftly
she gunned the engine, at the same time levering into Drive.
The car leapt.

Before changing lanes she glanced into the mirror and saw
her own pink lips careening toward her like a speeding road-
ster. She adjusted the mirror, smiling at her own forgetfulness, and stole an exploratory hand up the inclines of
Tuesday morning's shampoo and set. Nothing had changed.

Mr. Charles, easing a lavender rat-tail comb from behind
her left ear, had declared it "structurally sound," a "geo-
desic dome." Mr. Stetwiler had said later, with a shake of
his evening paper, that Charles was making fun of her. Mrs.
Stetwiler knew better. She respected Charles and he
respected her. It did not matter to her in the slightest that
he was a homosexual. In fact, if anything, she felt safer, as
if she were chatting with another woman, almost. Except
that sometimes he seemed to be flirting with her.

Mr. Stetwiler said if he was a queer he should act like a
queer, and cut the fooling with other men's wives. Mr.
Stetwiler inclined to be jealous and did not like his wife to
work. While not inquisitive about the people she met on her
daily rounds of business or housekeeping, still, if she mentioned someone, he sat suddenly straight like a hunting dog
sniffing the air, aquiver, as if he scented an infidelity.

Mrs. Stetwiler gave a small laugh, half aloud, at the idea,
and stopped the car more gently than usual at the red light
in front of Vons. She had not looked at another man in
nearly thirty years of marriage. Not that she claimed any
credit, not for being just what she was: a loyal person. Mrs.
Stetwiler was not one of those people who made a promise
and then broke it.

Honest in her marriage; honest in her work. When Mabel
Burnside gave her five dollars too much Monday afternoon at
California Security, Mrs. Stetwiler had handed it proudly

back. That was how she liked to do things, and that's what made her a success both in her marriage and at Red Castle Realty, where she was named September's Top Producer. She liked her job and was good at it, but that did not mean she neglected Mr. Stetwiler, who was the light of her life. No, marriage first; job second. And if she quit her job tomorrow—she laughed at the very idea—why, then Mr. Stetwiler might find her a boring companion. Work kept her young.

She edged her red engagement book toward her from the passenger's seat, and scanned Wednesday while negotiating with one hand a particularly sharp curve around the Self-Realization Fellowship Society. Gravel flew. Just as she thought, Wednesday's page said Marcie and Buck Tyson. They were perfect for the old Simon place, which out of consideration for the Simon children she was committed to selling quickly and quietly, before any unpleasant litigation could begin and tie up the property forever and a day. Mrs. Stetwiler could not believe for a moment that May Simon really intended leaving her house to that woman. What good was a note scrawled on the back of a grocery list anyway? And the poor woman half out of her mind at the time with pain.

Certainly May would have wanted her own children to have the house they had grown up in. Not that it was a particularly valuable piece of property. The house was the last on a dead-end street where the neighbors had long ago given up on watering, mowing, trimming, keeping things nice. No curb appeal whatsoever, but then sentiment has its own reasons.

Mrs. Stetwiler eased to a stop at the three-way light at the end of Sunset Boulevard. She was glad to see, though, that May's children had some business sense, unlike their mother, who had frittered away whatever Mr. Simon had left her when he died these ten years ago. You could not keep a house as a memento, the way you could keep a pair of earrings or even a pet. No, houses took constant care. You could not manage a rental from Utah or Wyoming or wherever it was they had settled. And besides, they had lives of their own, everybody did, she acknowledged, steering carefully past a white cat that blinked in indecision from the curb.

White cats tended to be deaf, she had read somewhere. And suddenly she remembered May Simon blinking from her front porch last winter, before her illness began, May Simon holding one hand out in greeting, the other resting in strange intimacy on the shoulder of this woman, this not-so-practical nurse who now wanted to snatch the family house away from May's own flesh and blood.

She would sell that house, if it was the last thing she ever did.

CHAPTER 25: LEGACY

It's not like I'm going to live forever," said Bucky Tyson's mother, leaning heavily back in her porch chair and propping herself with one black lace-up shoe wedged against the deck railing.

Marcie looked out toward the bay, winking along Will Rogers State Beach and tried to imagine Mrs. Tyson through the wrong end of the telescope she kept permanently set up in her jumbled living room, a memento of her dead husband.

"All you got to do is wait and all this will be yours." She swept her arm in an ample gesture, displaying for Marcie's approval Tyson's Bait Shop, Bill Rose's cottage, and the wooden bungalow on whose deck they now sat.

"Oh I know a bait shop hasn't got much in the glamour department. But Harry Blue runs the whole sheebang same as he's done ever since Mr. Tyson passed on. And you don't have to do anything but laugh all the way to the bank."

She reached down vaguely to hoist one by one the nylons held just below her doughy knees by bands of elastic. Her legs looked sectioned, like a doll's. Sometimes she wore her dead husband's thick wool socks over the hose, when her "chillblades" were troubling her. But today, in honor of the realtor's visit, Margaret Tyson had dressed with extra care, exchanging her usual Sears house dress for a black nylon dress with white polka-dots, that clung to the outlines of her 24-hour girdle.

Marcie pulled in discomfort at her own blouse. Her breasts had swelled almost immediately, even before she really knew she was pregnant, and now, in her fourth month, her waistband had begun to squeeze.

"That'll get a whole lot worse before it gets any better. If it ever does," qualified Mrs. Tyson cheerfully. "Course you being nearly thirty's going to make it a whole lot harder. I see you're starting to show already, honey." She lifted Marcie's blouse. "That'd be the muscles starting to give out. Well, what's to be done? Life is life, that's my philosophy."

Both women turned at the sound of Lu Stetwiler's brand new Mandarin Red 1966 Buick Riviera turning off the highway and into Mrs. Tyson's compound. Mrs. Stetwiler's car shuddered twice after she turned off the ignition. Waves of automobile sounds swept in from Pacific Coast Highway. At last the Mandarin Red door swung open and September's Top Producer stood up from her car, one hand balancing her hair as if steadying a basket of fruit, the other clutching her red blazer with the Red Castle emblem on the breast pocket.

"Oh, fiddle, Lu, hot as it is for October you can leave that red jacket of yours in the car. Mrs. Tyson struggled out of her chair to lean over the railing for emphasis, her nylon dress sticking to the back of her legs and riding high enough to reveal her garters from behind. "I hope we are all friends here."

"It might be better, Margaret, if Buck and his wife just came on down," said Luwanda Stetwiler, struggling into her red blazer. "I'm running a little late on account of the Calvacade of Homes this morning."

"Call me Peg and come on up here for some lemonade. It's at least two years since you paid me a visit. You got time for lemonade." Mrs. Tyson's mouth puckered toward a smile.

"I don't remember these many steps being here." Mrs. Stetwiler put one tentative, patent leather Red Cross pump on the bottom step.

"That's it," Mrs. Tyson waved a plump hand in encouragement. "I'll just go on in to the kitchen and get the lemonade started. My daughter-in-law, Marcie, here will see you up. She's pregnant, would you believe it!" Mrs. Tyson gave a cosmic laugh, flapped her hands, and disappeared inside.

Mrs. Stetwiler, not halfway up, paused to examine a potted lime and catch her breath. Marcie could hear soft little rasps emanating from beneath the Red Castle emblem. The realtor bore on, her shoes making a slow, rhythmic scrape on the wooden steps.

She removed her red jacket. She tucked an escaping strand into her glinting beehive.

Two steps away from the summit she felt her Red Castle jacket snatched from her crooked arm and her gray leather handbag lifted from her limply curled fingers. "It does keep you young," boomed Peg Tyson, bearing her trophies away into the dark interior of the bungalow. Mrs. Stetwiler followed her belongings into the gloom.

She stepped on a cat and fell into the recesses of a couch whose softness would not let you sit straight. Askew, she reached blindly for her hemline, gave a yank, and fell over the other direction.

"So what's all this, Lu, about you wanting to sell these

two young people not dry behind the ears a piece of property they can't afford and don't need?"

"Bucky called me, I didn't call him," corrected Mrs. Stetwiler, fighting for an upright position. "Where is he anyhow? He said he'd be here."

"Sugar?" inquired her hostess.

"Plain," replied the Top Producer.

Marcie cleared her throat. "Well, I would like to see the house today, even if Buck can't make it. It's been over six months, Peg. We really shouldn't have stayed that long."

"Nonsense, Marcie. You and Buck always have a home with me. You know that." She beckoned an old white cat with extra toes on each foot toward her ample lap, but it leaped into Mrs. Stetwiler's lap instead. "Cats always know who hates them," said Mrs. Tyson with a snort.

"I don't hate them, I'm allergic." Mrs. Stetwiler balanced her lemonade over the cat's head.

"We need just a small house," said Marcie, lifting the big white cat out of Mrs. Stetwiler's lap, "two bedrooms, a yard, maybe a . . ."

"Swimming pool," concluded Marcie's mother-in-law. "Bucky's got to have a swimming pool, on account of that's his business. Why that's where he's at right now, cleaning Mrs. Tanholt's swimming pool for this impromptu party she didn't know she was going to have until last night. He gets these emergency calls, you know. So if there's got to be a move there's got to be a swimming pool for Bucky, but ask me, I say it's plain and outright craziness to walk away from what I'm ready to give him. This house, the bait shop, the cottage. It's not like I'm going to live forever."

"Isn't that the truth," said Mrs. Stetwiler in sudden accord. "That's just what May Simon was so recently forced to remember."

"What in the name of our sovereign Lord are you talking about, Luwanda Stetwiler?" Mrs. Tyson tried several times in her irritation to cross her plump doll legs but was obliged to abandon the gesture.

"I'm talking," said September's Top Producer with slow deliberation, biting off each word as if from a slice of pound cake, "about the death of May Simon early in August and the subsequent pending sale of her desirable property."

"Desirable!" exploded Mrs. Tyson. "Why that house is hid behind a regular Viet Nam jungle."

Mrs. Stetwiler sank sideways in the shooting gallery of Mrs. Tyson's contempt. She thought fleetingly of retreat, but a second cat, an enormous orange cat with an eye swollen shut, dozed on her red blazer. "If the young couple want privacy"—her eyes skirted Mrs. Tyson's and fastened gratefully on the wide ones of the daughter-in-law—"they certainly can't do better than the Simon place."

"Privacy," said Mrs. Tyson to the orange cat working its claws rhythmically on Mrs. Tyson's blazer. "Privacy! We'll all have privacy quick enough. None of us going to live forever."

"My point exactly," Mrs. Stetwiler observed, smoothing her white perma-prest skirt across her knees.

Mrs. Tyson drew in her breath at this and thought. At last she narrowed down her gaze to the little spot between Mrs. Stetwiler's arched eyebrows and inquired softly, "And why the Simon place?"

"Because it meets their needs," Mrs. Stetwiler said brightly. "Because it's got two bedrooms, and because it's got a pool, and because it's priced to sell."

"I heard things about that house," said Mrs. Tyson in the direction of a stuffed fox crouching on top of a leaning bookcase.

"What kind of things?" asked the realtor.

"Just things." Mrs. Tyson quirked her head abruptly in the direction of Mrs. Stetwiler.

"How truly sad, how unbelievably sad it is to think there

are always people to keep false rumors flying," observed Mrs. Stetwiler, conspicuously consulting the gold watch that hung around her neck from a chain. "Oh my, that late, is it?" With a deep sigh she thrust herself onto her red pumps, tugging tentatively at her coat under the cat like an apprentice magician with a loaded tablecloth.

The cat's good eye snapped open and fixed Mrs. Stetwiler midpoint in his shining lens. In the instant before the cat could uncoil itself in the direction of Mrs. Stetwiler's liver-spotted wrists, Marcie sprang out of the rocker and grabbed it by the haunches.

"We won't be long," said Marcie, dangling the squirming cat before her mother-in-law.

"Bucky should be with you." Her daughter-in-law dropped the cat onto the coffee table, where it began lapping margarine off of Mrs. Tyson's cold morning toast. "You don't do anything without Bucky. Nothing. You hear?"

But Marcie was out the screen door, following the red jacket of her realtor.

CHAPTER 26:
THE LAST SUNDAY IN OCTOBER

Marcie startled awake as if she had heard some sound through the open window, but it was really emptiness that had wakened her. Bucky was not home yet. She could not feel him pressed against her all the length of her body. The first three months of their marriage, after lovemaking, she could not sleep, lying in his narrow childhood bed with him, his knees pressed into the backs of hers, his warm breath stirring the fine hairs on her neck. She had not been able to sleep, being still like that. Now, on the nights he stayed away so long, if she slept at all it was tucked tight against the wall, not turning, leaving him the space he would not claim.

She looked at the luminous hands on Buck's baseball clock: almost two thirty. Earlier that evening she and Bucky's mother had argued over the time. The paper had said that night they would go off Daylight Savings Time.

Bucky's mother had said that it would be a relief to be back on God's time where they belonged, that they would set the clocks all ahead an hour. Marcie had said she thought it was back. Bucky's mother said that no, it had to do with farmers and crops and school children wandering around in the dark. "You catch up to God's time, you don't lag around and wait on it."

Marcie didn't see any point in arguing, so she had shrugged, then set the living room and kitchen clocks ahead an hour. The baseball clock she had set back an hour.

What time did Buck think it was? What would he say this time? Maybe nothing. He got quiet and angry when she asked lately. He would bang out the screen door and drive off in his truck.

A glass of milk might help her sleep. She swung her legs over the side and reached for Mr. Tyson's old flannel bathrobe. Marcie had noticed it one day hanging behind the bathroom door, as if he meant at any moment to pick it up, though he had passed away in his bed five years ago, reading James Fenimore Cooper. How had Mr. Tyson lived amicably with the irascible Mrs. Tyson? Maybe reading Cooper had taught him patience. Maybe things had been different five years ago.

She pulled open the door of the old round Cold Spot and reached out the carton of milk. Jamie came in, wailing. She splashed some milk onto the mount of rejected Savory Stew that remained in his bowl. He hesitated, then began a slow lap, lap that meant he would not wake up Mrs. Tyson after all.

She poured her own milk into a heavy blue glass and carried it silently through the living room, with its curling Oriental rugs, embroidered silk World War II pillows, the couch where Mrs. Stetwiler had tried so valiantly to defend herself, and out onto the deck. The breeze from the ocean played in her dark locks and suddenly, as she sat in the wicker chair, she felt—in an odd way—loved, or lovable. As if she was from a long way away or a long time ago, and that these pains and assaults that kept her hurting and off balance in the present moment would one day be revealed as insignificant, when fitted into the larger landscape of her existence. She filled her lungs with the sea air, sat quietly listening to distant surf, and watching occasional car lights sweep the night. She was not listening for Buck, not watching for him.

She heard a door close somewhere in the night, perhaps from across the highway. The light was on now in Bill Rose's cottage on the hillside to her left. She could barely see someone standing on the small porch. Then she heard the orange cat's low, flat growl and an answering moan from under Bill's porch. "Kitty, kitty, kitty, kitty," came Bill's voice across the canyon, a soft, coaxing call but magnified somehow by the angles of the cliffs around them. His calico cat, Hillary, streaked up the front stairs and slipped inside the door he opened at just the right moment. Bill must have gone inside too.

The shade on the window nearest was drawn down but glowed from the light behind, making her feel she could almost see, could if she tried hard enough, if her mind could come and go like a ghost through the world's partitions. She liked it that Bill made his world for himself, of cat's getting fed, being sheltered. She felt a simplicity glowing out of his house like light itself.

That house, the one Mrs. Stetwiler had showed her, she might herself be able to make such a life there. Walking slowly across the living room that day, listening to the soft creak of the wood floor under her feet, her cheek warmed by the ray of sun through the tangles of roses at the windows as she paused, she felt then almost as if this might all be possible, the simple business of living, without intrigue, without lies, without the once dear face turned aside and hardened. As this dream grew inside her tired mind she saw the solitariness of it, that although she could see easily enough her daughter playing beside her in the blowing carnations, she could not see Buck.

And really, there was nothing very frightful about solitude. She had lived alone that year she taught in Iowa. There was a solitude even in being with her mother that illness had thrown up between them. A fence with a small gate that opened at certain hours, then less and less often.

But afterward, after her death, the funeral, the casseroles from family and friends, it was worse than plain solitude, beyond aloneness. It was if the body snatchers had finally taken Marcie. She had fallen asleep and the vine in a glass by her bed had grown and climbed into her ear. Without her knowing it, a cocoon had begun to spin about her, fine as angel hair, obscuring her eyes, her nose, stopping her mouth.

That's how she was when Buck had found her. Like Donald Sutherland he had yanked her awake and yelled in her ear and got her moving again. But was the catastrophe merely deferred?

The first time she saw him she had been sitting alone outside on her mother's little patio adjoining the tenant's pool. Just sitting behind the screen of ornamental block. Doing nothing. When he came out to the pool and clattered down his pool-cleaning equipment she had felt mildly annoyed. But he had gone about his business quietly and with great purpose, as if when he ran the brush down the wall of the pool, sending clouds of sediment streaming toward the surface, that his mind was exactly there, was in fact the brush following a hard path down concrete walls.

At the very moment when he most struck her as self-sufficient, he asked her for something: a glass of water. She saw his golden fingers curved around the cold, sweating glass, his head thrown back so that his gulping throat looked like some curious creature, a thing alive. Afterwards she had not questioned herself about him. He had simply gone, with his empty chlorine jugs.

She could scarcely remember now the space between the drink of water and his pacing her living room, her mother's living room, telling her she must get rid of this junk: the sagging sofa, the tea cart with the chipped tile, the rosewood curio cabinet with unmatched china leaning, the dressers and drawers where her parents had stored their unmatched lives for forty years. It was time, he said, to face facts.

Ah Buck, she thought, groping under her chair for the empty glass and pulling Mr. Tyson's bathrobe closer about her, if facts were all we had to face.

CHAPTER 27: SPECIAL DELIVERY

The fog had not burned off yet. Mrs. Tyson stood in front of the range, burning the bottom of Marcie's egg. Marcie sat at the breakfast table, looking hard out the kitchen window, ignoring the surge of nausea, promising herself Mrs. Tyson would soon be gone to the A & P and she would have the house to herself for a full, glorious morning. The pink Fiestaware plate was poised over her head.

"Now you know what the doctor said. You got to eat and get your protein and your calcium and your whatever so the boy will be healthy. Tysons have always liked to eat." She set the plate in front of Marcie, the bright orange yolk swimming in a ring of loose albumen, the egg both raw and cooked at the same time. "I'm off to the bank and the market. Anything you want?" She grabbed her red plastic pocketbook down from the fridge and began toiling toward the door. "If not, forever hold your peace. I'm gone as yesterday." The screen door banged shut.

The egg stared at Marcie. She stabbed it into little pieces and set the pink plate on the floor for the cats. The two pieces of Wonderbread toast she snapped into fours and flung out the kitchen window for the jays. She stood looking at the crescent of sea and sand. No one on the beach yet. Sun said nine o'clock. Morning traffic beginning to thin out. A light breeze moved a dark strand against her cheek. She tucked it back behind her ear, folded her arms, breathed deep, let her mind travel on water.

She could just see the outline of Catalina. Another tourist trap, her mother-in-law called it, when she caught Marcie in the kitchen gazing seaward out the window. Still, to Marcie there was something about it, something that receded the moment her mind advanced, something that moved off the way a dream did when you tried to remember in the morning. It was like the outline of the island reminded you of something you used to know, that you had known in sharp detail, as familiar as the peeling window ledge under her elbow now. She ran her fingers deliberately over the bubbling paint to help her remember this moment, when she had stood exactly here, November 3, 1966, in the fourth month of her pregnancy, eyes scanning the rise and fall of a faraway island, island the shape of a reclining woman.

Looking at the sleeping island made her want to sleep again. Lately, a fog would seep into her mind. She crossed the scarred linoleum floor to the stove and lifted the lid on Mrs. Tyson's stout percolator. A pool of oily coffee swam at the bottom. RIGHT FRONT: she turned the greasy stove knob and the ring of gas ignited. This lethargy. It had started when her mother died (her mother resting in the bronze coffin on slate blue satin, lying like an island), had broken when she married (garlands of daisies against the sharp, blue sky), then drifted back several months later so that—in a group of people—she would suddenly excuse herself and five minutes later be asleep like the dead on a strange bed, adrift among party coats.

Sometimes she felt she was a way station where others might rest for a time from their travels. She was a bench, a couch, a footstool (Bucky coming in at two last night, colliding with his mother's credenza, swearing softly); to feel no more on impact than Mrs. Tyson's credenza, not to cry out in the night.

Marcie poured scorched coffee into a blue, chipped mug. The screen door rattled hard; behind a curled fist the mailman loomed aluminum. Inside the screened frame his red face craned right, then left, trying to see through into Mrs. Tyson's world.

"Coming," called Marcie.

"Special Delivery," he complained.

"Mrs. Tyson's out shopping."

"Ain't for Peg Tyson. It's for Marcie Tyson, says here. That be you?"

Marcie opened the door, leaning against the edge as she signed her name into his book. He handed her a long white envelope, and another packet of the regular mail rolled up in a *Newsweek*. "Thank you so much."

He turned to go. "It isn't like I got anything against you, honey. It's these goddamned stairs." Then he turned back, eyes suddenly alive: "Must be a sight to see Peg Tyson going up these stairs." He let out a sustained elephant trumpet and started down. Then, as if remembering himself, muttered back at Marcie, "No offense, I hope. None intended."

"None taken," said Marcie with a wave. Then she crossed to her favorite wicker chair on the deck, tucked Mr. Tyson's robe around her knees, and sat Indian fashion to open her letter.

The address was written in David's hand, but her brother seldom wrote and certainly had never sent anything Special Delivery. She tore off the end of the envelope and pulled out a thick check with a typewritten sentence stapled to it:

"This is not a lot of money. Love, Dave."

The check was for $12,562.13. She drew her breath in sharply. She did not like to think money meant anything to her. Yet her breath stopped in her lungs now and her fingertips went dead. It was her mother's estate, finally settled. She knew she was to get money, but she had never asked her brother how much, or even when.

In the five months between her mother's death and her own marriage she had lived quietly in her mother's Barrington Street apartment on what was left in their joint checking account, though she could not really remember having written out checks. But she had done so for her mother, in the year of her illness, and must have continued, just as her heart had continued to beat. She did remember closing out the account by writing a check to Mrs. Tyson for the balance, but she could not remember what the balance had been, whether it was great or small. She was only glad not to be involved in any more transactions with the world, to leave it to Buck or to his mother.

Since February she had not held so much as a twenty dollar bill in her hand, or even wanted to. Why were her hands shaking now?

CHAPTER 28: AN EVENING AT HOME

Mrs. Tyson dealt five pink five dollar bills onto Bill Rose's pile of currency and said with an explosion of relief, "Mercy, what a responsiblity. I can't think why I volunteered to be banker."

"You're the logical choice, Peg, what with your gift for finance," said Sarah Kimble, patting her pile of one hundreds straight and securing them under the tip of the board.

"Son, you be the realtor." Mrs. Tyson extended dog-eared deeds of title across the coffee table toward her son, leaning dangerously back in a dining room chair.

"Marcie'll do that," he said, passing the deeds to his wife. "She knows all about property."

"That's right," said Sarah Kimble, pushing an ash blonde lock away from her high and gleaming forehead, "Luwanda Stetwiler told me you young people are going to buy the old Simon house."

Buck Tyson screaked his chair back and said he would

get some firewood.

"I say something?" Sarah Kimble asked, addressing the front door that banged behind Buck Tyson.

"Lord no. If life stopped every time Buck Tyson got his back up we'd all be long in the grave," remarked Buck's mother, glancing through the stack of yellow Community Chest cards. "It's me he's mad at, because Fridays lately he's been going out and I just thought it might be fun to all stay home together, have a regular family night at home for a change. Marcie's not much for running around, in her condition. Ask me, folks should stay home more with family and friends" (here she drew her Revlon Honey Dew lips into a bow and looked meaningfully at Bill Rose) "the way we used to when I was a girl. In the 'olden days,' as my Bucky used to say."

"And what do you do, Bill?" Sarah Kimble asked, tossing playfully the red plastic teacups dangling by golden wires from her earlobes.

"Why Bill's a bartender," answered Mrs. Tyson amiably. "Isn't that right, honey? Now where is that Buck? We're ready to start."

"I'm the little scottie dog. Can I be that? I always was the scottie dog when I was a girl. What will you be, Bill?" asked Sarah Kimble, examining her lead token.

"I'll be scissors," said Mrs. Tyson, rocking forward in her ponderous chair, "and you get the chips and dip, Marcie. Back isn't hurting you today, is it?"

Feet shook the deck, and Buck shouldered his way in with oak logs. Marcie could smell the faint aroma of chlorine he always gave off as she passed behind him where he squatted on the hearth, weaving kindling in a pattern around three empty milk cartons. Chlorine, and oak slivers, and new Levis. She had wanted to touch him lightly on the neck, but he was coiled tight. In the kitchen she leaned her forehead against the dark window.

"Marcie, Marcie," Mrs. Tyson was calling. "Buck's going to be the cowboy on the horse. What are you going to be?"

"I was getting the chips."

"Yes, but who are you going to be? We got a shoe and a thimble left. Bill Rose is the top hat. Is it going to be shoe or thimble?"

"Shoe," she called into the open refrigerator.

"Well, hurry on then," said Mrs. Tyson, settling a pair of pearl pink half-glasses on her bulging nose, "you and Buck both."

Buck threw an oak log on top the flaring kindling, sending sparks out onto the floor. Then he rattled the blackened fire screen into place. "I wish to God you wouldn't put milk cartons in the fireplace. It just makes a stink."

"Milk cartons are good kindling," said Mrs. Tyson, sampling the Lipton onion soup dip Marcie set before her.

"Well now, who starts and what are these little orange cards here? I haven't played this game since God was a boy." Sarah Kimble set the Chance cards into a neat stack on the board.

"I need a beer," said Buck, jumping up from the chair he had just sat down in. "You want one, Bill?"

"You might offer the ladies too, Buck. You'd think I never taught you the least manners."

"I'll have a Dubonnet on the rocks, if you got any," said Sarah Kimble.

"We're fresh out, Sarah. You want a beer or not?"

"It doesn't matter to me," said Sarah, studying the scottie dog in her hand, "what I drink, long's the company's congenial."

"Let's go ahead and roll to see who goes first while Buck gets the beer. Whoever rolls the highest starts the game. Top Hat," said Mrs. Tyson, "you roll first."

Bill Rose rolled a six and passed the dice to Sarah, sitting to his left on Mrs. Tyson's ample couch.

"Seven," said Sarah thoughtfully. "That's what I'll need to beat. Think I'll roll eleven, just to be on the safe side."

"What in blazes are you talking about, Sarah Lee Kimble?" said Mrs. Tyson, rocking forward to snare a beer out of her son's hand and fix Sarah Kimble with a fish stare over her reading glasses. "What do you mean, you 'think' you'll roll eleven!"

Sarah Kimble rolled a six and a five. "It's a gift," she said in the direction of the bowl of Fritos, "that I got through my mother, my deceased mother. But I don't like to talk about it before the unbelieving. Just play—all of you—like I never said anything about it." She sipped her Hamms with lowered lids.

In the silence Marcie took up the dice and rolled two sixes.

"You do that on purpose, darling?" asked Sarah Kimble admiringly.

"Marcie doesn't do anything 'on purpose,' " snorted Mrs. Tyson. "Do you, honey? Not to look at her anyway."

Buck rolled a five. His mother rolled snake-eyes.

"Marcie goes first. Marcie wins," said Sarah Kimble, picking up the dice from Mrs. Tyson's roll and handing them to Marcie. "Just when are you due, darling?"

Marcie rolled a six and landed on Oriental Avenue, which she bought, handing her paper money over to Mrs. Tyson. "April 11," she said to Sarah Kimble, who began counting on her hands and studying the ceiling.

Buck landed on St. Charles Place but did not want to buy it.

"An Aries," said Sarah Kimble, completing her computations. That baby's going to be an Aries. Depend on it."

"I'm an Aries," confessed Bill Rose.

"You're quiet for an Aries," noted Sarah. "You got

small hands and feet like a Libra."

"Are we playing this game or aren't we?" said Mrs. Tyson, shaking the two dice in both her hands. She bought the Reading Railroad.

Bill Rose rolled a ten and landed on the JUST VISITING part of JAIL.

"You sure you're an Aries?" the Scottie to his left asked.

"Just roll the dice, Sarah," cautioned Mrs. Tyson.

Sarah rolled a three and landed on INCOME TAX, which cost her $175. Marcie bought New York Avenue, and Buck remarked that at that rate she would run out of money. Then he rolled an eight, landed on his wife's property and had to pay her $14.

"Small potatoes," he muttered, rising to get more beer. His mother landed on Community Chest where she learned she had won second place in a beauty contest and been awarded a $10 prize.

"Money seeks me out," she announced, slipping a pale yellow bill out of the bank and letting it fall on top a dissheveled pile of money. "I've always been that way."

Bucky set a beer down hard in front of his mother and another in front of Bill Rose. From the third he took a long pull, his Adam's apple moving in a way you could hear.

"Why, it just doesn't seem possible that you all are needing a new beer already. Marcie and I are just getting started," observed Sarah Kimble, delicately shaking her Hamms can.

Buck jabbed the fire with his dead father's old golf club, looked at his watch, then dragged his chair around backwards and straddled it.

"Whose turn is it, anyhow?" asked Mrs. Tyson, gouging a Frito through the onion dip.

Bill Rose scooped up the dice and threw a six, landing on St. James Place, which he bought. Mrs. Tyson made change for him and fixed Marcie with a stare. "Well?"

"Did I miss something?" said Sarah Kimble, rattling the dice in the cage of her hand.

"Somebody's forgot she's Realtor," said Mrs. Tyson, arching her faint brows into half-moons on her full moon face.

"No problem," said Bill Rose, taking the deed from Marcie.

Sarah Kimble held the dice up to her forehead, closed her silver eyelids, and moved her Coral Magic lips. Then she rolled a ten and marched the Scottie around to the Pennsylvania Railroad, which she bought for $200.

"Somebody's got your railroad," said Buck to his mother, who was busily tidying up the bank's money.

"Free country, I hope," she said to the twenties.

"My turn," said Marcie, handing the railroad deed to her neighbor and shaking the dice. She rolled a ten.

"Hold on a minute," said Buck, "that's me. I'm the Cowboy, you're the shoe."

"On New York Avenue," said Bill Rose, seeing the pink spreading up her throat. "You're both on New York now."

Marcie returned the Cowboy, and marched the Shoe to Marvin Gardens.

"I've always had a special fondness for Marvin Gardens," said Bill Rose.

"One's as good as another," said the Cowboy.

"Not really, Buck," said Bill Rose, passing Marcie's money to the Banker. "Usually whoever gets the orange properties wins, all things being equal."

"Are you speaking as the owner of an orange property?" asked Cowboy.

"Marcie's got one too," observed Top Hat.

"Then according to your logic, nobody's going to win."

"Someone always wins, if you play long enough," said Top Hat.

"It's your turn, son," interrupted the Banker.

Buck rolled a three and declined to buy the Electric Company.

"You got to," said his mother.

"Free country," said Buck. "It was you that said so. One minute ago."

"You got about as much business sense as my orange cat," said Mrs. Tyson, searching the board for her Scissors.

"Community Chest," said Sarah Kimble, extending her Coral Magic index finger in the direction of Mrs. Tyson's token.

"Exactly," said Mrs. Tyson, rattling the dice till her upper arms shook. She landed on Community Chest. "ADVANCE TOKEN TO THE NEAREST RAILROAD. IF UNOWNED YOU MAY BUY IT FROM THE BANK. I took your advice, Sarah," she explained, placing $200 into the Bank and holding out her hand for the deed to the B & O Railroad. "Just thought my number and next thing, there it was. I certainly do thank you for that piece of advice." She slid the new deed behind the Reading Railroad and settled back into her mammoth rocking chair.

Bill rolled an eleven and bought Atlantic Avenue.

"Peg, honey," said Sarah Kimble, picking up the dice, "is it alright if your big white cat plays with that little chest set up there by the moose's head?"

"Course not!" said Mrs. Tyson, struggling out of her chair. "That is a hand-carved chess set that Mr. Tyson brought back from Paris, France after the war."

"He thinks they're cat chow," said Bucky.

"I'll play like you didn't say that disrespectful thing about your father, Buck." Mrs. Tyson balanced on her toes, snapping her hankie at the white cat crouched in front of her dead husband's chess set.

"I guess it's my roll," said Sarah, studying the backs of Mrs. Tyson's knees where tight elastic bands cut off the circulation.

"Land on my porperty and you TELL me," warned her hostess, swiping again at the white cat.

Sarah Kimble rolled a four and landed on Tennessee Street. "My people came from Tennessee, you know," said the Scottie, counting out her money for the absent Banker. "I'm really a southerner at heart."

"You're from Burbank, far as I know," said Scissors.

"My people, Peg, I said MY PEOPLE came from Tennessee."

"I like southerners," said Marcie. "They seem more . . . gentle."

"Gentle won't pay the bills," said the Banker, holding the white cat suspended by the scruff of his neck. "And whose turn is it, anyhow?"

Sarah Kimble was staring at the dice with her eyes closed. Then she passed them to Marcie.

Marcie rolled six and landed on the Short Line Railroad. Mrs. Tyson eyed Sarah Kimble, who was smiling at Bill Rose. Marcie counted out two hundred dollars and paid them over to her mother-in-law. Buck snorted and looked at his watch. Marcie took the deed and set it next to Oriental, New York, and Marvin Gardens.

"It's about time we did a little business," said Bill Rose.

"What do you mean?" asked his hostess, glowering over her pink frames.

"Just a little preliminary trading," said Bill.

"Got to wait for your turn to do trading and it's not your turn. It's Buck's turn."

"It's getting late," said Buck. "I told Small I'd meet him at eleven."

"You got time," said his mother easily, as if dispensing time itself. "Small can wait. Roll the dice."

Buck rolled five and landed on his mother's railroad.

"That's an even fifty, son."

"Fifty!"

"I got two, if you recall. Two railroads comes to $50."
She let the tossed bill float down near her pile of currency,
then threw the dice.

"Short Line," said the Cowboy with a whoop. "That puts
you on Short Line!"

"James Fenimore Tyson, I hate it when people call out
before a person gets to walk and know themselves where they
might be landing. Now you should have sat quiet while I did
it myself. Marcie might not have noticed, and now I got to
pay her $25 just because you had to be yelling out."

Bill Rose quietly picked up the dice. "Marcie, you and I
each have a yellow and an orange. I propose a three-way
trade. You give me Marvin Gardens, for which I've already
confessed a fondness; and I'll give you St. James. Then you
give Sarah the Short Line Railroad so she can have two, and
she'll give you Tennessee."

"But she'll have a monopoly. That'd give Marcie a
monopoly! Sarah, don't you do it! There's nothing in it
for you. You'd have to be crazy to make a deal like that.
It wouldn't be fair to the rest of us. You got more live sense
in you than that, I know," said Mrs. Tyson, leaning across
Bill Rose to rest a hand on Sarah's knee.

"I always did like railroads," said Sarah gently. "My
mother's family all were in railroading. In Tennessee." She
handed the deed for the orange property to Marcie, and accepted title to the Short Line. Marcie and Bill exchanged
deeds.

"Well, son, you got to make some plans if you intend
to stay in the game with these folks. I can see that. I can
see we got beyond a friendly, family kind of game and are
playing something else now. Marcie, I hope your new status
as landowner does not prevent you from bringing us another
round of beers from the fridge. Bill, honey, I believe it's
your turn."

Bill rolled five, landed on Pacific Avenue, and bought it.

Marcie brought the beer. Buck jabbed the fire with his golf club. The white cat stared at a spot on the paisley rug, his back to the game, his ears laid flat.

"They say white cats are deaf," said Sarah Kimble to Mrs. Tyson's profile.

"No cat of mine is deaf," said Mrs. Tyson. "Take my word for it."

"See how he does his ears flat?" said Sarah.

"That's what cats do when they are sick to death of human company," said her hostess.

"I was just expressing friendly concern," said Sarah, with a flick of her red teacups.

"Is it my turn?" interrupted Marcie. She put two houses on St. James and Tennessee, and three houses on New York Avenue. Then she rolled six, passed GO, collected $200, and bought Mediterranean Avenue.

Mrs. Tyson said it was a cheap property, not worth even its tiny price, that nobody ever won who thought they had to buy everything they landed on.

"Where am I?" asked Sarah. "Is it my turn?"

"I believe you're visiting kin in Tennessee," said Mrs. Tyson, heaving herself up out of her chair and heading for the bathroom.

"It must be all that beer," said Sarah, holding the dice a moment, eyes closed, then releasing them like doves onto a piazza.

The Scottie rounded FREE PARKING and stopped on CHANCE.

There was the sound of flushing and before it ended Mrs. Tyson was standing in the doorway scanning Sarah's face for signs of tyranny. But Sarah's face was bent over the CHANCE cards. Slowly she lifted the top one. "TAKE A WALK ON THE BOARDWALK."

"Nobody owns it," said Bill Rose. "You can buy it, if you want."

"And I'm almost to GO, so it's practically free," said Sarah, handing Mrs. Tyson her money. Her Banker gave her a brief look of pity.

Buck landed on Community Chest and paid a doctor's fee of $50.

Then his mother rolled two three's and landed on Mediterranean Avenue. She collected two hundred for passing GO, then with a smile handed to Marcie one pink five-dollar bill and one white one-dollar bill.

Bill hastily picked up the dice, only to find moist fingers curled around his wrist. "Doubles rolls twice, honey. Remember?" Mrs. Tyson took back the dice and rolled again, landing on the Reading Railroad, looking pleased with the foresight of her purchase.

"Christ, this is a long night," breathed her son, crossing his arms across his chest.

"I told you," said Scissors, "that Short can wait. Matter of fact, that young man might be a sight better off than he is to look for something permanent out of life and quit riding around in a pick-up, well into his thirties as he is. And then bothering around folks that have the God-given sense to start their own families." She darted her eyes in the direction of Marcie's swollen stomach.

"Short is MY business," said the Cowboy. "You leave him out of this."

"Short," said Mrs. Tyson, inclining her moon face in the direction of Bill Rose, "is a very sad case of arrested development."

"That did it," said the Cowboy, rising so abruptly he sent his chair tumbling into the game board.

CHANCE and COMMUNITY CHEST slid across streets, knocking scotties, scissors, cowboys, shoes, green plastic houses flying.

CHAPTER 29: COUNTERPOINT (hers)

It was hard to choose a drink from the Sea Lion's long drink menu, with the waiter standing there next to the table, standing there between her and Buck, the waiter waiting. A simple decision and yet hard. Hard because Marcie had never really had much to drink. Living with her brother and his wife, almost two years, in Iowa, they had sat in the back yard late afternoons drinking beer. Or sometimes they had gone to neighborhood pubs and had tap beer from mugs so cold ice fell in sheets into the beer like glaciers slipping into Arctic waters. Cold as Alaska. But here she did not want beer. That was a life ago. Green beer on St. Patrick's day, and when Marcie finished college and got a job teaching in Dubuque they had all cried, even her brother, though he would not admit it, still she had seen his eyes shining by pub light, whatever he might say. So not beer but something else. The waiter stood off center as if his underwear were creeping, waiting for her to decide, glancing sideways at Buck in that conspiratorial way of looking men had, some men. With Bill Rose she did not feel a look pass through her from man to man. Bill Rose looked at her, did not seek around her. But now these men waiting while she tried to think through to remember what all these drinks meant: daiquiri, gin and tonic, rum and Coke, Old Fashioned. Any of these would do, would dispel this waiting air that squeezed her head like a bathing cap.

134

CHAPTER 29: COUNTERPOINT (his)

When Buck tried to swallow, his necktie held his Adam's Apple in a tight band. He remembered Gregory Peck in *The Hanging Tree* when the mob was getting ready to lynch him and a few smooth words stopped everything and eased the rope around his neck. Life was different than movies. He slid his finger up to his collar and tried to ease the strain, while Marcie read the menu for the thousandth time. A simple question like that: what did she want to drink? Could not answer it to save her soul. Probably would order . . . a Pink Squirrel. The waiter looked at him. Buck crossed his legs and drank ice water. It was not his fault Marcie could not make up her mind. Women were like that. At first, Marcie had let him decide. But more and more now she had to say, even if it took her hours. What Buck liked was things being simple. People knowing what they wanted and saying so. Or else keeping quiet about it and letting others decide. Beer was simple enough. Why couldn't she have a beer? It was good for you and simple. That's why Marcie would never choose it. Everything had to be worried to death. He looked at her now bent over the menu, watched her gaze float up and pass through the darkened window down to the beach, like the beachcomber she was, not a wife. And his mother thinking a candlelight dinner would bring back that sweet time! A few smooth words. Marcie. Bent over the menu again, her dark hair fallen forward on either side. If he reached out now to touch it . . .

134a

"A beer," she said. Then he wanted to know what kind and she could see a smile stirring at the corner of his mouth, hitching his narrow, black mustache up ever so slightly, like a French accent. She felt old enough to be his mother, anybody's mother. "Michelob." She slid the linen napkin off the table and into her lap. She would like to put the napkin to her nose and breathe in until she could see heavy ladies in soft clothes running napkins through mangle irons. A smell almost like Buck's, chlorine and new Levis. But not tonight. Shirt and tie tonight, the tie drawing him in at all points. She ran her hand across the napkin again. He smiled and took his own napkin off the table. Then he picked up the menu and studied it, tugging absently at his collar, the collar his mother had ironed that afternoon, talking at Marcie through the bathroom door while she soaked in bubbles and steam, her stomach a rosy island in the warm sea. The menu. She would read the menu, before the young man could come back. "Turf and Surf." Somehow the entrees sounded more like epigrams than food: "A stitch in time." She felt her hunger withdraw down a long corridor. If she did not eat, Buck would be mad. The food would seem to cost more if she did not eat it. She felt a stitch of fear. But she HAD liked to eat, she remembered liking to eat, could see herself, David, and Ginger sitting at a long Amish table gobbling bowls of German food, then waddling out to sit in the Iowa sunshine, hardly able to speak, laughing, full.

That was the thing about women: unpredictable. With a man you always knew where you stood. Small, for example. If he got pissed he said so and yelled a little and then was o.k. He worked hard all day and played hard all night. And once he liked you, he always would. These clothes, for example. Small never wanted him to wear anything in particular, probably never even noticed. But tonight, when he got home from work, and dead tired too, there was his suit laid out and a dress shirt, and a tie. His mother's doing, he knew, but he could tell now by the way Marcie looked at him that she liked him better in a tie, as if wearing a tie made him into a different person. Her brother probably always wore a tie, David. Probably slept in a tie. Buck could tell, too, that Marcie was worrying that he'd forget to put his napkin in his lap, like he didn't know how to act in public. Christ, the waiter was long about bringing the beers. In a place like this you had to pay for what you did not get. Service, for one. But he was not going to leave here feeling still hungry the way he always did before they got married and had to eat out so often. Marcie was not even looking at the menu but he was not going to start anything with her. His eyes went hunting through the menu. He wanted meat. Meat tonight. Prime rib? Top sirloin? FOR THE HEARTY APPETITE, Turf and Surf. Steak and lobster. Ah, beer at last. The waiter spoiled the head by dribbling the beer into the glass, but that did not matter. Buck threw back his head and gulped.

"Flounder," she said. You could see but not hear waves washing ashore, there where the Sea Lion floodlight struck the rocks below like a false moon. Pacific. It was truly pacific, the curling waves, unquestioning and constant. Almost she could smell . . . "Yes, broiled," she said. The potato baked. With chives, sour cream. Roquefort dressing on the salad. Buck would have the Turf and Surf with fries, the meat should be done, he said. And they would have another beer, he said. Not wine, he said. Her hand across the clean napkin. Buck turning his fork over and over. He could eat a horse, he said. And smiled. He turned his head in the direction of the bar, where voices came from. Unpacific voices, in waves. She watched him dig his finger between his collar and his neck, his mind gone into the next room for a beer, his ghost self settling at the bar, elbows sculpting his place, leaving her feeling suddenly alone, as if the earth were suddenly uninhabited, and she a wandering survivor. Blinking fast she looked past Buck's head to the table behind, where two men laughed and talked, neglecting their dinner. When the waiter refilled their wine glasses they seemed not to notice. What could they be saying to one another? Their necks curved gently, curved together almost like flowers in the sun, she thought, or like exotic birds in a dance. The one with his back to her reached forward, pulling the small loaf of bread on its board toward him. He sawed with the small bread knife and held the slice, balanced on the blade, toward his companion. Pacific.

Buck really wanted Marcie to have anything she wanted.
But flounder! What a nothing thing to order. Why couldn't
she have the Seafood Platter? Something with guts to.it.
At least they were not going to have wine. Wine gave him a
headache. Wine was for schoolgirls and winos. He could
feel now the steady pressure of his dress shoes against the
pinkie on each foot. He did not know why clothes should
hurt. He did not know why women should tell men how
to dress. Men did not tell women how to dress. Marcie could
wear whatever she wanted. It made no difference to him.
That dress she had on now: that was fine. But her stomach
was starting to show a little. Might be better to wear something that did not stick to her so much, something that
would float out from her. That dress Becky had on last
night at the Saddlepeak, for instance. The blue one. Polished
cotton, she had called it. Simple and cool under his rough
hand. Like a girl's dress. Becky. He had meant no harm
that night he bought her a beer, not knowing where a simple
beer might lead. His eye traveled now in the direction of
the tavern. You could tell people were having a good time
in there. Laughing a lot. Easing up to the bar, eating something out of little baskets. Being themselves. Probably their
feet did not even hurt. He tested his collar, then saw Marcie
watching him, no, not watching him but looking past him
as if he did not exist, as if her life depended on this looking,
and she had no need of him whatsoever.

"Ah, salad," said Marcie, leaning back in her chair. She nodded for ground pepper. Inside a silhouette of bell pepper slept an anchovy. She had never eaten one before. The man at the table behind theirs had lifted his on the tines of his fork and borne it momentarily aloft, then taken it lovingly into his mouth, a communion wafer. His companion had laughed softly. Marcie wanted to eat this anchovy. Buck had slung his onto the bread dish where it slumped against an abandoned bread stick. She ate the anchovy. It made her eyes water. Its taste went on and on, changing as it went, like a story. Marcie wished she had some wine. A glass of white wine would give a fitting end to the anchovy tale. Buck would be mad if she asked for wine, thinking she could not make up her mind. It seemed to Marcie that what she actually did was make up her mind more times than Buck did, that what she wanted changed. People sometimes were frightened by that. Maybe they thought if you changed your mind about what you wanted to drink, then you might as easily change your mind about them and would not love them anymore. Marcie could not remember having stopped loving anybody. You might not want to sleep with them, but that did not mean you did not love them anymore. No, love went on, longer than the taste of anchovies. She looked again at the two men balancing toward each other, and suddenly she knew they were lovers, and that what she'd been watching was a love feast.

Buck Tyson, under cover of the salad's arrival, craned his neck around hard inside the starched collar to see what had so taken Marcie's attention. Two men having dinner, that was all. He stared into his dinner salad. He had wanted Thousand Island and they had given him Roquefort because that's what Marcie had ordered. As if he had no mind of his own. He forked up the anchovy with distaste and swung it onto an empty plate near his water glass. Problem was anchovies left a trail across your salad, contamination. Taking them away was not enough. Smelled like rotten fish. Marcie hated them too, but now somehow she was willing to eat one for the pure style of it. At least she had always SAID she hated anchovies, same as he did. But Marcie was a different woman from the one he married last March. Quiet, she had been, and kind of shy, like Becky, listening to his words, nodding. Somebody to let a man be himself and be comfortable about it. But here he was instead, surrounded by Roquefort and anchovies. It was enough to take away a man's appetite. He should have asked for another beer (Marcie's glass still half full) before the waiter left. But he had been trying to see behind him. There it was again: Marcie staring past his ears, like he was some tree or lamp post, at those two men. Buck turned in warning. The man facing him looked up with food in his mouth. His hair was curly and too long for a man. Nothing to worry about there. The man was queer.

"The fish," said Marcie in appreciation. "I'll have a glass of Chablis, when you get a chance." Buck turned suddenly and faced her, his mouth ajar like the bent door on Mrs. Tyson's bread box. Then he picked up his empty glass and asked for a beer. The fish had no head. Parsley fanned around its body. Marcie squeezed a fine spray of lemon. Gently she lifted out the bones. She thought of the bones inside her, the fine bones of her child, a growing that no one could see or feel except Marcie herself, a child growing to some prodigious height, arriving with a fondness for anchovies and freighters and cello music, for running wild in the sun like a colt. She watched Buck sawing at his overcooked steak, and suddenly she did not want this child to have a father at all. All children lived for evenings when fathers worked late and, liberated, they could cavort with their mothers in disheveled kitchens. The kitchen in her mind became the kitchen in the house Lu Stetwiler had showed her, its window opening onto the garden, the island beyond like a seal dozing. Marcie and her daughter in the kitchen, waiting for no one. She drank her Chablis. The men at the next table finished their dinner, counted out bills onto the table, replaced napkins and slid chairs in. The one with his back to her turned slowly, his profile sliding into full-face: Bill Rose. His hand extended, his smile easy, shaking Buck's hand, introducing his friend Brian. Then gone, these men, these men who were nobody's father.

Buck hitched up closer to the table. About time. Red claws reached up from the plate the waiter set in front of him. No, he would not wear a bib but he damn sure would have another beer. A bib on top a tie, bound a hundred ways, hemmed in like that old sea lion in the parking lot near the entrance, a prisoner in a stinking, leaky old tank he could hardly turn around in. Buck tossed aside his parsley and cracked the first red claw, spattering juice across his tie and shirt front. He sucked the white flesh out. It needed ketchup. There WAS no ketchup. He turned in his captain's chair to ask the table behind. They were getting up to leave. Suddenly Bill Rose was standing over him, seeming much taller than usual. Buck tried to get up but Bill waved him down, shook his hand, told him to meet Brian. Then they were gone. Marcie smiling, drinking her wine. Probably did not know what was what. Just as well. He was not going to upset her now, pregnant as she was, with the big news about Bill. Men like that, not one thing or the other. Not surf and not turf. Buck took up his steak knife and cut deep. Just right. No pink. Still, he just never would have guessed about Bill. Tall guy like that, good pecks, good biceps, but queer as a two-dollar bill. Buck smiled, imagining his mother's face. But he would not tell her. What Bill did was nobody's business but his own. Besides, it made him a good friend for Marcie. After the baby was born she would have to stay home all day with it. She would be safe with a man like that.

CHAPTER 30: MAKE-UP

"If you ask me," said Mrs. Tyson, circling her mouth with Fire and Ice and kissing her lips together, "you can't expect a man to stay interested if you don't fix yourself up a little now and then. A man works hard all day and has got a right to be met at the door by a woman who has put on an attractive dress and a little make-up. Now is that too much to expect?"

"Infidelity seems an exaggerated reaction to my not wearing make-up," said Marcie.

"Course, any man will claim he doesn't so much as notice. They don't notice this and they don't notice that. But let a pretty woman in a pretty dress pass by and they notice alright. Even the late Mr. Tyson noticed. Besides, honey, men are different. You can't really call it infidelity. Believe me, I know. They don't think like us, act like us, and a good thing too." She stood up from her dressing table and hiked down her dress all around her ballooned

waist, then smoothed the back down. "I look all right?"
Marcie nodded, and backed out the bedroom door,
making way for her mother-in-law.

"It's like this, honey," said Mrs. Tyson, steaming behind
her like a busy tug, "it's infidelity when a woman does it,
because she means it. A man doesn't mean a thing in God's
green world by it, and Buck would be the first one to tell
you that, if he was the kind of man to talk about his doings,
which he is not."

"Buck did tell me that."

"Why, there you are. Didn't I say so? It doesn't mean a
thing, him fooling around with some pretty young thing
from the square dancing. Only means he's got some gumption
about him. I hope any son of mine WOULD have gumption." She opened the coat closet and took out a heavy
peach-colored sweater with sequins and a fox collar.

"It bothers me more that it doesn't mean anything to
him."

"Why, Marcie," gasped Mrs. Tyson, "you are the
strangest person I've ever met. It almost sounds like you
WANT your husband to be unfaithful, and you nearly six
months pregnant." Arms like picnic hams struggled toward
the light down dark sleeves. "Honest to Trudy, if I hadn't
aboslutely PROMISED Jeanette Foster I would go to her
Tupperware party, I'd be tempted to stay home with you
tonight."

"No, you go along, Peg. Probably I need a little solitude."

"That's right. Get your perspective back. You'll be fine.
All in the world you got to do is fix yourself up a little."
She held out her arms to Marcie, crushed her to her heart,
and was gone.

Marcie wandered into the bedroom. Luminous hands on

Buck's baseball clock said 8:25. Saturday night and Buck gone. She lay down on the bed in the dark and tried not to think about where Buck was, what he was doing, but as soon as she resolved not to think about it she WAS thinking about it, again, as she had for weeks now. It was better, though, now that he had finally admitted to her Becky's existence, grudgingly, the school boy caught. It was better to know her fantasies were true, were not really fantasies at all, but ways of knowing so subtle she could not explain them, not even to herself.

But there were fantasies, pure ones. At times, during the day, she would imagine herself parking on a street a block away from Becky's, after dark, and cutting through back yards until she saw lights at the back of the house. Then she would set up Mr. Tyson's telescope next to a tree and watch them all night. The two of them. What they did lacked detail. They were mere shadows on drawn blinds. The feel of the telescope in her hands, the damp grass curling around her ankles, the shiver of dread—these were all more real to her than the ritual she had come to observe.

Something in her held her back from the actual looking. Some remaining point of pride, perhaps. Though at times, when the dread and anger took her, she felt all pride seeping out, as if through a small but fatal hole.

Was this what they called "jealousy?" She had declared herself, long ago, beyond such feelings. Actually she was not beyond them, had simply never arrived at them until now. She had committed in the last year almost every error she had ever warned herself against. What remained?

Why, self-indulgence, of course, she answered, swinging her legs across the chenille spread and standing up. Marcie stretched her body out and felt the baby give an answering stretch, moving a leg or an arm slowly across her belly, changing her belly's shape as it moved, rearranging Marcie's contours to suit herself.

"Glass of milk?" she asked out loud. The living room had gone dark. It felt like the furniture was asleep on the oriental rug, as if her sudden move might wake it. She saw Mr. Tyson's telescope silhouetted against the faint glow from the bait shop below. It rested on legs, like a crane, meditating. Quietly, so as not to wake the furniture, she crossed the room and stopped before the telescope. She waited a long time there before she heard feet coming up the wooden stairs, starting from a long way away, and coming closer, like an image in a telescope coming slowly into focus.

"Marcie!" called the voice that was not Buck's. "You there?"

"Bill, come in. I was about to have a beer. Join me?"

"Actually, I was about to meet Brian at the bar and thought you might like to come along."

"Thanks anyway," she said, sinking heavily into Mrs. Tyson's sofa, "but I'm not much in the mood to go out."

"Pleading your belly?" smiled Bill.

"Probably."

"But it's really Buck?"

She nodded.

"You need to get out," he said, "if I have to kidnap you."

"Does it show?"

"Afraid so. Get a jacket. We might want to sit outside."

She slipped her windbreaker out of the closet. "Where are we going, anyway?"

"Top Hat's taking you on an adventure. That is, if it's alright with you." He stopped suddenly, as if for permission. "Ever been to a gay bar?"

"No," she said, opening the front door wide. "I never have."

CHAPTER 31: THE DAILY PLANET

Thursdays were like that. Lane dusted off her overalls and slowly backed down the ladder. She had wanted this fireplace finished in time for the big Christmas party, but the boys would not leave her alone. That's why her policy was to have no male bartenders on Thursday nights, except for Wilson, of course, who always kept his head. But the others all insisted on being in the Thursday night drag shows and so were spoiled for work.

Six times tonight they had pulled her away from her brick-laying to ask her opinion about eye shadow, hair spray, one thing and another, things she did not really know about, never had and never would. Luckily Julie had stopped by to help her mix the mortar.

This time it was Miss Lulu, who could not choose between the red or the black tap shoes. Lane told her she was gorgeous and was back up the ladder with only five minutes lost. She loved the smell of cement. She finally succumbed to the temptation and stuck in her tongue.

Julie laughed. "I've been wanting to do that all night."

"You got've to be in your sweet sixties. Then you can do whatever you want."

Julie stuck her tongue into the mortar. "No you don't."

"I like you, Julie," said Lane.

"I like you too. Let's run away to Mexico." Julie pushed a brown curl behind her ear and handed Lane a new bucket of mortar.

"No. I'm too old for gazelles. It would never work. You'd need braces, a motorcycle, two degrees, and trombone lessons. I can't afford you. Besides, if I said I wanted to see *Casa Blanca,* you'd buy plane tickets. What kind of life is that?"

"I'll wait for you," said Julie. "You'll change your mind."

"Well, in the meantime, finish this up for me, will you? My sciatica just started its unscheduled flight up and down my right leg. The joys of age. Just be glad I refused your offer and you won't have to sit up all night rubbing Ben Gay on my wounded body." She smacked clouds of dried concrete from her overalls and bent to kiss Julie's cheek. Then she stepped back to study the fireplace, to calculate against the coming of Christmas. They might hang stockings, she, her bartenders, and the Salvation Crew. They might have Ted make up some stockings that said "The Daily Planet" across them. She rubbed her short gray hair, sending out a smaller cloud of dust. There was a lot more she wanted to do, here in the library. Book shelves were up and filled with donated volumes. She had wanted a small sliding ladder, like the one in the Fred Astaire movie, where he had worn a violet, silk scarf tied around his neck and danced up and down the moving ladder, singing about love. There was one small lamp on a walnut table, and a comfortable, deep chair drawn up on either side. Where the capuchino machine would one fine day be installed, a card table stood, bearing an electric percolator and two unmatched cups. Not finished, but still a retreat for people who did not want to dance or shoot pool. People who wanted to talk, people who liked to read, people who valued a voice. These, of course, were her people, librarian that she was, retired now nearly a year. But they were all her people, really. What she aimed at, what she wanted to make here was a place—a heavenhaven—where people could be safe to . . . . But there she went again with her theorizing. This was a bar and she ran it and was happy in it.

She stepped from the library into the hall. At this vantage point, near the main entrance, she always paused. She loved that bar. Cypress from the north. She had borrowed a truck and driven into timber country, picked out each board herself at the lumberyard. And of course the lumber would not fit in the truck. She had not known about board feet and had always thought a truck was a truck. But the man had agreed to ship it down at cost, making the whole thing breathtakingly expensive and she was glad with her whole heart she had done it. Because, there it was, twenty-five feet of curving cypress, opening onto the bar and dance floor inside as well as the patio outside, so that the bartenders moved through the middle of the bar as if they were canoeing down a river.

The patio, there she had saved money. On their hands and knees The Daily Planet Emergency Salvation Crew had set five thousand bricks into sand, bricks scrounged by Gaywill. The sand, of course, was free, three blocks from the beach, as they were. And then there had been the patio party and Topaz Wilson as Master of Ceremonies, six foot three in his stocking feet and wearing a white tuxedo. Everybody brought buckets of sand for the final top dressing and poured them onto the patio. Then Wilson presented Lane with a new push broom, a red ribbon tied around the handle and she had ceremoniously swept the last bucketful into the cracks. What a night that had been.

Suddenly the front door swung open against her reverie, Bill Rose, and Brian, and somebody new, a woman, with curling dark hair and a wide gaze spilling into her dream. Lane wiped her hand clean on the bandana from her back pocket and took the hand of the new woman, in welcome.

"Lois Lane, meet Marcie Tyson," said Bill Rose.

"People have got fired for calling me that, William," said Lane, searching out a quiet table for her guests. She led them to a table in the corner, away from the speakers. Jeanene was getting settled in the disk jockey booth. Lane sent her the signal that meant play something quiet and slow. Then she nodded in the direction of Wilson at the bar, who had already seen and was filling a pitcher with Michelob.

Lane did not know whether to stay or go. There was something momentous about this woman that Lane did not understand, that made her want to go and stay, all at once. What was it? She had hardly spoken and yet Lane felt herself straining to hear what she had not said. She looked at her sideways while Topaz leaned down with the beer and glasses. Marcie was struggling out of her windbreaker, her face up, her eyes on Topaz, as if she had seen him before but could not quite place him. Bill began the introductions and when Marcie half rose, Lane could see she was going to have a baby. Lane felt a sudden desire to ask Marcie if she wanted to dance.

But she was not sure, she who always KNEW, she whose antennae had functioned unerringly since seventh grade. Lane had always loved women, had always known that her life with males would be as comrades and not as lovers, had fought bitterly with her mother over her friendships with girls, and then, in library school had met her Kit, had blown it, repeatedly and then finally (Kit gone away to the island on the big white steamer. I left my love in Avalon . . .).

There was another kind of lesbian, though, another
lesbian history, where the woman did not know, or only
knew somewhere in the locked attic of her own elusive mind,
for years. This woman lived two lives in her lifetime: first
the heterosexual, then the homosexual, the second as if by
solemn choice and not by chance or by chemistry. These
women—you had to be careful with them as they made
transit. You had to evoke every ounce of loving patience.
You had to watch the metamorphosis and never, ever gain
by it, not even momentarily, or you might make a tear in
something gossamer and fine. This woman was precarious.
And Lane had learned how not to be dangerous. She felt
the panic drain out of her, but not the excitement. Her
knees quivered but her hands were still.

"You staying for the drag show at eleven?" Topaz was
asking, looking from Bill to Brian and back again.

"That'll be up to Marcie," said Bill.

"Miss Lulu's in a state tonight. Right Lane?" Topaz
had drawn himself up taller than usual. "So you might
want to make it some other night. Instead of this one, I
mean."

"What's that all about?" asked Brian, watching Topaz
moving purposefully toward the bar, tray tucked under his
arm.

"It must be about me," said Marcie. "People seem to
think pregnant women need mothering. Actually they need
to be kidnapped out of their houses and taken on nighttime
adventures at crucial moments. I'm happy right where I am.
If I were going to live in a pub it would certainly be this one.
The bar is absolutely beautiful. Is it redwood, Lane? It reminds me of those giant redwood trees you can drive
through."

"Cypress," said Lane. "And thanks. It's my pride and joy."

"Not the library?" asked Bill.

"You mean there's a library? Where?" Marcie craned her neck.

"I'll show you," said Lane, rising. "And meanwhile, you two could start dancing so others would. Get Jeanene to put on something noisy. Marcie wants the grand tour and she shall have it."

There was a crescent of soft light falling on the wood floor of the library. Marcie could see the auburn shine of hair falling to shoulder, the face half-turned toward its companion face, lowered under golden hair, two women bound in conversation. A third woman at the top of a ladder, carefully setting one brick on top another. All turning now toward the rush of music through the open door, toward the triangle of sound in which she and Lane momentarily stood.

"Julie, come down and meet a friend."

"I see you're getting the tour," said Julie, dropping a trowel into a bucket and wiping her hands on her Levis. "I'm Julie, part of the Emergency Salvation Crew."

"Marcie Tyson," she said, accepting the hand extended.

"Julie, you must be getting tired. Let's call it a night. Come out on the patio and we'll have a beer."

"Give me a minute to clean up. You go on ahead. I'll find you." Julie began making scraping sounds with her tools. Lane and Marcie moved slowly back toward the door, Marcie admiring, the books, the carpentry of the bookcases; walking behind the two women, listening to their murmuring as a desert dweller listens for sounds of underground water.

In the noisy hall Lane leaned close and said, "Pisses the hell out of me."

Marcie shrugged, not understanding.

Lane motioned her to follow. They struggled past men leaning against the wall, wound in talk, in two's and three's, then turned into a second room off the hall.

"The Billiard Room," announced Lane.

Women with their sleeves rolled up leaned over spotted green felt, sighted down bent cue sticks, laughed, rubbed chalk on their hands, drank beer. On the wall hung a mottled moose head with a huge flea collar circling its neck. In the corner a rusty fan on a tall, black iron post rattled its blades and tried to rotate. Along the ceiling wooden beads kept score.

They left, this time through a side door that opened onto a narrow corridor. "Thought you might need to use the facilities," said Lane, gesturing toward a white door that said "Women." At the end of the corridor men stood, tightly packed, laughing and smoking.

"Ah," said Marcie. "How did you know?"

"I'll be out on the patio. Like Queen Elizabeth I have an epic bladder. Turn right as you come out and right again when you get to the hall. The patio's straight ahead from there."

The broken doorknob turned senselessly in Marcie's hand but the door itself gave under a push. Inside this first small room jackets and backpacks hung from hooks. Against the right hand wall there was a chintz-covered love seat where a woman in red corduroy overalls sat with her stocking feet curled under her, reading a textbook of some kind. She looked up and smiled, then back at her book, as Marcie entered the second room. Next to the sink a woman of about twenty sat in a white wicker chair crying softly. A toilet flushed. The wood door of the compartment flung open and a woman strode out wearing tails, a red velvet bow tie, and a pair of faded Levis. Where the cummerbund might have appeared she wore instead a carved Western belt studded with red, blue, and green plastic jewels.

"Hi," she said, holding the door open for Marcie. From inside Marcie could hear the woman in tails talking to the crying woman. Marcie relaxed on the seat, feeling the relief of her bladder. Over the roll of toilet paper was mounted a small green chalk board on which someone had written, "Today Rigg turned thirty. And proud of it." Marcie picked up the chalk stub and wrote, "Happy Birthday." Outside the stall the woman in tails was crouched down beside the crying woman, still talking. Marcie washed her hands. The woman in tails craned her head around and looked up at Marcie.

"You pregnant?" she asked.

"Six months," Marcie said. The other woman had stopped crying and was watching Marcie dry her hands.

"I'd like to have a baby one day," said the woman in tails. "How old are you?"

"Twenty-nine," said Marcie.

"At some point you got to start thinking about time, I guess. I'm thirty today."

"You must be Rigg. I sent you a birthday card."

The woman in tails rose quickly and stuck her head through the compartment door, then put her arm around Marcie and drew her close. "Thanks," she said, "I needed that." Then she was gone.

The other woman got up and blew her nose on a paper towel. "You're Lane's friend, aren't you?"

"Actually I just met her tonight. In fact she's waiting for me on the patio."

"I'll show you the way," she said, glancing at her red eyes in the spotted mirror.

The noise in the hall had grown; people were packed in tighter. The woman from the restroom gestured toward a pair of French doors on their right and then disappeared. Marcie pushed through the doors, parting momentarily a pair of dolphins etched on the glass. Lane waved from a redwood table in the far corner.

"Ah, there you are. It seemed like you were gone three hours. Julie left apologies but had to go study for a French exam tomorrow."

"It FELT like I was gone three days," said Marcie, pouring herself a glass of beer from the icy pitcher. "Whenever I go into a public toilet women are carrying on intense conversations with perfect strangers. I wonder why?"

"It's like they drop their guard," Lane agreed. "Maybe it's the absence of the alien sex. Maybe women, and men too, feel safer with their own. I know I always have. Always."

"You haven't met my mother-in-law," laughed Marcie.

"Maybe you haven't met her either," said Lane. "But you may, in time."

"In time, in time, in time. I wish time were a place we could all meet each other."

"My dear Marcie," said Lane, "do I detect a utopian in you? My friends all accuse me of utopian tendencies. They recognize, quite rightly, that I've tried to build my own little world here. But where's the harm in that?"

Thoughtfully she poured herself another beer, watching the foam slip down the inclines of the glass she held, as if the answer to her problem might slip over the edge like a leaf over the lip of a dam. "Actually I know exactly where the harm lies," Lane admitted. "I used to be a compulsive reader of utopias. Ideal communities hit snags when they demand that everybody be happy with the way things are, when they don't make a place for ordinary, daily pain."

"You'll be delighted to know," said Marcie after a deep swallow of beer, "that there's a woman weeping in your bathroom."

"I AM delighted." She laughed. "Actually," she confessed, "I do have to struggle against a terrible impulse to try and make people happy. I've tried to push that impulse aside and simply provide them with four walls within which they'll be safe from society. And from me. I can't concern myself with providing safety from themselves or from each other. That's THEIR affair and not mine.

"Inside the four walls I've tried to make available privacy and company, music and silence, fresh air and smoke, companionship and competition, thought and vacuity, inebriation and sobriety—the whole parade of opposites among which, for our own health, we choose to march." She took a deep breath here and shook her head. "I do so hate it when I begin to speak in iambic pentameter. Besides, the show's starting and I've broken my own rule about leaving people alone to play in their own dialectics."

She emptied the last of the pitcher into their mugs and propelled Marcie toward the French doors. But the twin doors opened unexpectedly against them and two women, the two women from the library, earlier, all but ran into them. Lane stood staring, waiting for the couple to navigate around her, not speaking. Once inside the hall, Marcie pulled Lane toward her, competing against the music from the drag show.

"You said they pissed you. What did you mean?"

"I meant their disgusting self-absorption, that's what. They give to each other—one hopes—but they don't give back to the community that sustains them."

Marcie turned to look at them once more through the glass doors, saw the woman with the auburn hair open her arms to the other, saw their two bodies move together with such a grace that something like physical pain flashed through her chest.

CHAPTER 32: THE OTHER WOMAN

"If you ask me," said Mr. Small, leaning back dangerously in his porch rocker and studying the ceiling through his cataracts, "people ought to live alone and be done with it."

"But you and Small seem to get along together," said Marcie, raising her voice above Loretta Lynn's, drifting through the open front door.

"Nobody could live with Thomas but me, and there are times when I can't hardly stand it."

April Gunner patted Mr. Small's gnarled and spotted hand resting on the rocker arm, and spoke to Marcie, across Mr. Small's line of vision, as if the cataracts had impaired his hearing, if not his senses. "Mr. Small here is just worrying how we are all going to get along after Small and I get married next month, but we'll manage. There are just lots of ways to fix up this cute little house. He's forgotten what a woman's touch can do, he and Small have been living so

153

long as old bachelors, since Mrs. Small passed away."

"It's not that I have anything against you, April. But I wouldn't live with Jesus Christ himself, if I had anything to say about it. I just want to sit here on my front porch and let this old house fall down around me. Now where's the harm in that?"

April lowered her voice, leaned close to Mr. Small, but addressed Marcie: "It's not Christian. That's the harm."

Mr. Small closed his eyes and worked his jaws silently a moment, his gaunt face tinted in dim red and green by the string of Christmas lights Small had strung across the porch for his engagement party. "And what does this young lady have to say?"

"I lived alone for awhile when I taught school in Iowa. I liked it."

"Those days are over, honey," laughed April. "Why Mr. Small, Marcie's PREGNANT."

Mr. Small let out a low groan and waved his bony right hand before his eyes.

"Isn't he a hoot," said April.

"I think I'll get a drink," Marcie said, rising up out of her green porch chair and heading for the front door.

"Well, get Small to help you," advised April.

In the kitchen a woman Marcie did not know was removing everything from the Smalls' utensil drawer and heaping it in a miniature junk pile on the drainboard.

"Any civilized house, any minimally civilized house would have a corkscrew. But not Small's." Then she turned to Marcie: "You're not related, are you?"

"A friend," said Marcie.

"Haven't found anything I've needed all night. No toilet paper in the bathroom (be warned), no ashtrays, no napkins, no glasses, and now no corkscrew."

"He's getting married," said Marcie.

"I KNOW," said the woman, her eyebrows going up like executive elevators. "Can you believe it!" She gouged at her wine cork with a paring knife. "I think I'm going to scream."

"Want a beer?" asked Marcie, nodding in the direction of a keg sitting in a washtub.

"He WOULD have beer. Yes, thanks."

Marcie found plastic cups floating in the melting washtub ice and filled them slowly with thick foam.

"You think that's really beer?" she asked the woman.

"Any port in a storm," the other woman said, taking the cup from Marcie.

"You girls finding everything you need?" asked April, suddenly hanging in the door jamb.

"Corkscrew," said the woman through beer foam.

"You mean he didn't set out the bar tools!" said April in disbelief. "Men—you can't live with them and you can't live without them."

"April," said the woman, "that hardly deserves a reply."

Marcie breathed her beer backwards and snorted.

"Elaine," said April, lowering her arms slowly in disbelief. "You went to school with Small! Where's your loyalty!"

"I am a very loyal person, April. But I am not an idiot. Small can be very trying, and I can't believe you haven't noticed it."

"Certainly Small and I have had our little problems in the past. But I think when two people decide to get married it means they've agreed to work things out. I believe in commitment. Hey, Marcie, now where's Buck? I haven't laid eyes on him all evening."

"Neither have I," said Marcie, sipping her beer. "He went to a swimming pool convention in San Diego for the weekend."

"Now he didn't tell Small he was going to miss this party.

Small is going to be disappointed."

"It came up at the last minute."

"Men!" said Elaine in broad imitation. "You can't live with them and you can't live without them."

"Anyway," said the retreating April, "Small WILL be disappointed."

The two women watched the empty door frame for a moment.

"I wish I'd brought my Swiss Army knife," Marcie said absently.

"You mean for April?"

"For your bottle of wine."

"Um. The beer's not bad." Elaine held her cup out for more.

"Foam's quieting down," observed Marcie. "We seem to have this keg to ourselves."

"That's because there's another one in the living room where Loretta Lynn hangs out."

"I like kitchens," said Marcie, hoisting herself up on the counter next to the pile of utensils.

"Lifeblood of the house," agreed Elaine, hoisting herself up on the other side of the sink.

"I'm thinking of buying a kitchen."

"They seldom come detached."

"Oh, a house comes with this one. But when I see myself in it, we're in the kitchen."

"You and your husband?"

"No. I see just myself and my daughter. And a white kitchen table."

"I have those failures of imagination with my husband too. Once we were planning a guest list together, for a party. While he was writing I made up my own private imaginary list, because Gordon can't abide most of the obnoxious people I truly love. Do you know Gordon's name wasn't on the list! Don't look shocked. He's the same way. Do you see him here tonight? I don't really mind, though. If he were here I'd have to protect him from the reality that is Small and his intended, not to mention Loretta Lynn. This way I'm free to indulge my own idiosyncrasies."

"Sounds like what used to be called 'a marriage of convenience,' " Marcie said, holding out her hand for Elaine's empty cup.

"There's no such thing. Only marriages of inconvenience. I think I'm cultivating a taste for cheap beer." She took the filled cup from Marcie.

A tall, thin man with long hair stuck his head in the door and said, "Oh, excuse me."

Marcie shrugged.

Then April was back, saying, "Marcie, I told Small that woman was not welcome in my house, and it practically is my house, but it's not like she's here as a guest. What Buck does or does not do is none of my business, as Small keeps telling me. But I know there's a higher authority than mine that will judge Buck Tyson. I'm just here to tell you she's been to the front door, crying and wanting to see you. Why do these things have to happen at my party? I told her to go away, that anybody with such disrespect for the institution of marriage didn't have any right showing up at an engagement party. But she's out there in that old rusty car of hers and she says she's got to see you. Now what do you want me to do?"

"I'll take care of it," said Marcie, sliding down from the kitchen counter.

Small caught her, squeezing along the side of the living room toward the front door. "You don't have to go out there, Marcie."

"Thanks, Small." His thick arms circled her waist and held her tight a moment. "I'm o.k."

"Good girl," he said, releasing her. "Things'll come right." His eyes glistened with beer and good will. "Seems like Buck's dragged me out of a thousand messes, and now it's him in trouble, and I just don't know how to fix it."

"It'll work out," she said.

"I know it will," he smiled suddenly. "Look at April and me. Who would have figured that one? After all that shittin' around, here I am, about to be a married man."

"I'm glad for you," she said, squeezing his thick hands and letting go, making her way once more toward the front door.

Sea air smote her, as if she were moving into a new element, breathing, instead of air, water. She crossed Small's ragged lawn, the wet grass blades curling around her ankles as they had in her vision of this moment when events, as in a telescope focused, would abruptly jump into reality, becoming twice their size. In the black Volkswagen she saw a dark shape watching from behind the wheel. She crossed over slowly and bent down to see past the fogged windows. The passenger door opened slightly.

"Marcie?" said the pale voice.

Marcie's hand closed over the cold handle and she swung it open. "Becky?"

She was twenty at best. She might have been Marcie at that age, if Marcie had ever been that age. "Sit down," she said. "Please."

Marcie sat down in the broken seat and slammed the door closed.

"Thanks," she said. "There's something I want you to know. Buck," she stopped, as if that word cracked her heart in two, "Buck . . . . He never told me . . . about . . . the baby. I mean . . . I knew he was married. It was wrong, I know, that much was already wrong. But I never knew . . . until last night."

"Does he know you're here, talking to me?"

"Oh, no. I told him last night . . . and I mean it . . . I'm not ever seeing him again. If I'd known . . . ." Her head rocked back and the breath sucked out of her; then she plunged forward and cracked her head on the steering wheel, unnoticed, moaning, "Oh, oh, oh, if I'd known, oh, oh, oh . . . ."

"It isn't you. It isn't really you." And Marcie was gathering the younger woman in her arms, holding her, rocking her. "It's us, not you."

They sat then in the quiet, time marked only by the rhythmic shudders of the one held. Marcie leaned her head back and relaxed into the seat, the silken head on her shoulder.

CHAPTER 33: CLOSING COSTS

Mrs. Stetwiler had not wanted to surrender her key to the lock box. "This key can open over two hundred houses in the Palisades alone. Why they could take my license away for this." Her painted nails had run up the back of her hair, making little nervous tucking gestures at the stiffened strands. Marcie had simply waited, smiling, until Mrs. Stetwiler's desire to sell the Simon house had eventually vanquished her professional ethics.

She stepped inside now, alone. Oblongs of sunlight fell on the hardwood floor. In the center of the living room were stacked some cardboard boxes. Mrs. Simon's things, probably, that her heirs had not come to collect yet. Mrs. Stetwiler had confided in her some of the family history, what she called "the dreadful secret," not that she would say precisely what it was. Something to do with Mrs. Simon's private nurse "insinuating" herself into the ailing woman's life, getting herself named heir to the house by "unnatural" means. Marcie knew well enough what Mrs. Stetwiler was talking about; she only hoped it was true. She liked the idea of living in a house warmed by the kind of love that warmed Bill Rose's house and The Daily Planet. She would feel safe in a house like that, as if some beneficent goddess would peek in at the window now and again to see that Marcie and her daughter were all right.

She crossed to the windows, turned the crank hard. She would flood the musty house with fresh air, while she was here. Far out on the horizon she could just make out the southern tip of Catalina, the dip that marked Avalon. She wanted to live in the presence of that island. Wanting to know about it had sent her last week to the public library, where a kind lady in a Madras skirt had found her books on the island, its history, and had even brought her a delicate book on King Arthur and flipped the gilt-edged pages to the last chapter where King Arthur was stepping into the boat that would take him to his final resting place: Avalon.

Somehow these two Avalons were one in her mind, the mythic igniting the real, giving it a pastel glow, and the present one, the one Mrs. Tyson called a tourist trap, lending the sharp edge of actuality to the mythic. Marcie pressed her face against the window, visiting in her mind the tiny cottages with decades of sand ground into their floorboards, their walls still reverberating from jazz age tourists calling from room to room, wondering where their bathing costumes had gone, wondering what big band was playing at the Casino that night.

Twice a day twin white steamers crossed the twenty-six miles, carrying dancing, tipsy couples back to the cottages, the sand sifting through the wooden floorboards, throughout the decades forming archaeological layers, layers waiting to be explored, waiting while Arthur slept. Somewhere at sea there must be a place where two white steamers met, one traveling east and one west, a point at sea where waves ceased their movement and time stopped. This, perhaps was death, the exact point where two white steamers met, one facing east and one facing west.

The rapping sound was so rhythmic that Marcie did not move at first. Then she realized someone wanted something. She stepped across the bars of light and into the kitchen. A pale face hovered briefly in the window and then disappeared. In a moment rapping began at the back door, quieter this time. Marcie opened the door on a small woman of about fifty, wearing jeans and a faded yellow t-shirt.

"You're not Mrs. Stetwiler," she said.

Marcie laughed. "Absolutely not," she agreed. "I'm Marcie Tyson. I'm thinking of buying this house, but I'm not supposed to be here."

"I'm not supposed to be here either," said the other woman. "I'm Susan Finley. The *infamous* Susan Finley."

Marcie looked blank but opened the door wide. "I'd ask you to sit down but there's nothing to sit on. Except those boxes." She gestured toward the next room.

"Actually, it's the boxes I've come about. They're May's things and I'd really like to have them. But Mrs. Stetwiler's been so paranoid." She took a cigarette out of the pack in her back pocket, offered one to Marcie, then lit it. "Sometimes I've felt like the villain in a gothic romance, honestly."

"Then you must be part of the 'dreadful secret.' I'm so pleased to meet you. Really. But this is your house, it seems to me. May Simon wanted you to have it. Even Mrs. Stetwiler admits that much."

"But I'm not going to have it. That's very clear. It's simple enough to prove somebody is not sound of mind if they've made the mistake of preferring a woman over a man. Especially if they've done so rather late in life. It looks like a mad afterthought.

"Who is that prowling around by the pool?" She stood on tiptoe to see around the roses at the window.

"That's my husband," said Marcie, watching the square male form stoop before the pool motor, watching the square male hand rest knowingly on the machinery.

"Husband?"

"A mad afterthought," said Marcie, surprising herself. The two women watched Buck Tyson straighten himself up and jam his hands down into his Levis. Then he shook his head. He was coming up the walk toward the house.

"Take the boxes," said Marcie.

Susan Finley nodded, picked up the first box, turned to Marcie and said, "Take the house."

"Yes, I will." Then she crossed over to the front door and opened it on her husband.

"Marcie, you've got to face facts: this house is impossible. That whole filtration system's got to be replaced. The water's moving through at about 30% capacity and there's black algae all over the shallow end. You're looking at a minimum of $1500."

"Who's that?" he asked, watching Susan Finley picking up a box from the dwindling pile.

"I'm Susan Finley," she said, disappearing through the kitchen door.

"Mrs. Stetwiler say she could do that?" Buck asked his wife.

"The boxes belong to her."

"Marcie, you don't want to get mixed up in a thing like that," he warned.

They both watched as Susan returned and left with the next box.

"Let's get out of here," said Buck quietly. "We don't need this."

Susan carried out another box.

"Come on. I'll take you to dinner."

"I'm having dinner with Elaine."

"You're always doing something with Elaine."

"Yes," she said, "I am."

"I'm home every night now. If you want this to work . . . ." He stopped while Susan carried out the last box. "If you want this to work you've got to do your share. You can't expect me to stay home alone forever. I'll start going out again. The whole thing will start over again. And the time . . . the baby. We've only got . . . ."

"A month," she said.

"A month to get all this straightened out. Marcie, I really want this. I was wrong before. I know that now. Please, baby, I really want this."

"Yes," she said. "I know you do."

CHAPTER 34: BACKWASH

Mrs. Tyson sat across the kitchen table from Marcie, the plump fingers of her left hand splayed out, resting on a Kleenex, while her right hand painted the short nails in Morocco Dawn.

"It's more than clear to me," she was saying to her index finger, "that Luwanda Stetwiler is behind all this mix-up. She never could keep her nose out of other people's business."

"It was important to me to buy a house," Marcie said.

"You *have* a house, here, with me and Buck. You know that. It's not like I'm going to live forever."

"I hope you *will* live forever, Peg. But I need my own house."

"It's that women's liberation has put such fool notions into your head. You can't raise a child by yourself. That child's got to have a father. That child's *got* a father, and all your moving off by yourself's not going to change that." She looked up, the tiny pearl pink glasses grasping at the end of her nose.

"Well," said Marcie, easing herself up, "I'll just get these last few boxes. Where's Buck?"

"Gone. Left the minute you called to say you were coming over. What did you expect? A man's got some pride. You don't seem to know letter-A when it comes to men, Marcie. Lord knows I've tried to teach you." She drew a crooked line across the next nail. "Seems like your mother'd of taught you something before dying on you like that. Lucky thing Buck and me came along when we did. You looked like something the cat dragged in, and that's the truth."

"Don't get up," said Marcie. "I can manage." She stacked the three boxes up, not wanting to make more than one trip. Then she set them down on the couch, bent to kiss her mother-in-law's damp cheek, hoisted the boxes to her shoulder and started down the wooden stairs.

"Marcie Tyson."

She paused, balancing the weight, turning her head slightly toward the deck overhead where Mrs. Tyson's house dress billowed around her thick legs, half-covered by her dead husband's lisle socks.

"Marcie Tyson, just you remember this. We're the only family you got." Then she turned abruptly, as if obeying an invisible drill sergeant, and disappeared back into the dark interior.

Marcie's trunk would not open. Yesterday she and Bill must have made a dozen trips and the trunk worked every time. But today it would not open. She yanked open the passenger door, flipped the seat forward, and threw the boxes into the back seat. A muscle in her lower back ripped. She slammed the door shut and got into the driver's seat, immediately starting up the engine in case Mrs. Tyson was watching. When she stepped on the clutch a pain telegraphed down to her foot. The car would not go into reverse. She gunned the engine and tried for the gear again. Metal on metal. Her back, the clutch. Relax, she told herself, then lurched suddenly backwards, too far, into Mrs. Tyson's ice plant, and forward, at last, out onto the highway, toward home.

There was a rusty white truck in her driveway when she pulled up to the house. Then she remembered the pool man was coming at three. She looked at her watch and turned off the engine. It was 3:15. Marcie found him around back, sitting cross-legged on the concrete, next to the filter system, smoking a cigar.

He looked up. "If it was mine, lady, I'd start from scratch. Ain't a square inch in it worth saving."

"What would it take to fix it?"

"That's what I'm saying, lady, it ain't worth fixing. If it was mine I'd replace the whole enchilada."

"What would it cost?"

"Well, we're looking at somewhere right around $900, not counting the acid wash and paint job. That'd bring it in at say $1500."

"I don't have $1500. It will just have to stay like that for the time being."

"Can't stay like that, lady. You got black algae. See them dark spots all around the drain? Health menace. You got no choice lady. You *got* to fix this pool. Specially," he qualified, "considering the condition you're in and all." He nodded politely in the direction of her belly.

Marcie turned away and stared into the pool. It was almost as if he had put his hand on her. "I won't be needing your help," she said.

"Suit yourself, lady."

She listened to the tools slipping into his pocket, the heavy work shoes across the pool decking, the gate clink into place behind him. Then silence. She could imagine him

. . sitting briefly in the cab of his truck writing on a smudgy clipboard: "This lady is crazy." Then the engine cranked and she was alone.

In the afternoon sunshine she could tell the water was not right. There was no shimmer to it. Instead a kind of yellow-green dust lay suspended, like sage. Like urine. Marcie became aware of the pressure on her bladder she had been ignoring for the last half hour. The baby pressed on her bladder these days and these nights.

Nights in the new house found her blindly careening down the hallway toward the bathroom five or six times. Then, awake, she would wander through the empty house, past the unpacked boxes yawning open where Marcie had angrily probed them for missing objects: forks, sheets, her blue corduroy shorts, the toaster. The toaster, once found, burned up the first time she used it. That had begun the cycle of break-down to which the pool was merely the final insult. Her hair dryer smoked, the small black and white television blew a tube, the can opener had rusted fast in its box under Mrs. Tyson's house, the clutch was ailing, all her belongings seemed to have become infested with her own human ailments.

She must pee. Quickly she strode around the pool, catching—she thought—a whiff of decay, then up the steps to the back porch, reaching in her back pocket as she went for the keys. The keys not there. Perhaps by the pool. She retraced her steps, the pressure building, her bladder a balloon about to burst. Not there, the keys. Retracing her steps, her missteps, back through the gate, a film run backwards in jerky motion, back to the car, its windows rolled up, her keys sprawled on the driver's seat, the doors locked.

Against what? That's what it came down to. All these doors she had locked against herself these past few months until, narrowing down her life like a series of Chinese nesting boxes, she found herself standing here, now, alone, nine months pregnant, with no one to offer her so much as a bent coat hanger.

Of course! You opened car doors with bent coat hangers. Marcie had seen people struggling this way in parking lots. She made her way back through the gate, moving slower now, clamping her muscles down tight but making steady progress through the yard, up the porch steps to the back door. The locked door. A sob escaped.

If there was no one to help, there was also no one to see. She would pee in her own back yard. Behind a camellia bush she yanked her elastic waistband down and peeled pants and underpants to just below her knees. Then she squatted, wavering, thigh muscles laboring to balance the extra weight of the child, the pleasure of release offsetting the pain, crying at last.

She heard a truck door slam. He was back. The pool man. Back to tell her she had no choice. Quickly she pulled her pants up, wiped her eyes on her sleeve and turned to face the gate.

But it was Bill Rose and not the pool man who flung the gate open. And just behind him was Lane, wearing a lavender t-shirt that said Daily Planet Salvation Crew on it, and behind her was Miss Lulu in bright green overalls and purple eyeshadow, carrying, with evident distaste, two jugs of pool acid, and Julie with her wooden toolbox, and Topaz Wilson carrying under one arm a sump pump and under the other a gleaming keg of beer.

BOOK THREE

EQUINOX

CHAPTER 35: THE LAST SUNDAY IN APRIL

Aside from the fact that two of the guests arrived at 3:00 instead of at 2:00, and that one little girl arrived at 1:00, when Jennifer was still in the bathtub, things—Marcie thought—had really gone quite well. Spring forward. Marcie remembered Mrs. Tyson's dictum about daylight savings, remembered herself dutifully setting all the clocks, except one, the wrong way. Long ago.

"Penny for your thoughts," said Lane, watching with evident delight while her godchild and her four birthday guests rioted in the sparkling pool.

Marcie laughed and sipped champagne out of a blue plastic glass. "Time, actually. I was thinking about time and how time isn't really time but something else altogether."

"Wait till you get arthritis, Marcie. That'll convince you time is real."

"I'm almost forty, Lane. You still think of me as the

child I was when I first walked into The Daily Planet with
Bill and . . . . Who was that young man with the curls?"

"Brian. Brian Peters. He moved up north, I think."

"Yes. Brian. Well, I'm nearly forty. I have bursitis and a
ten-year-old daughter. I know time exists, but it doesn't
have to do with clocks. Whether you set them back or set
them forward we all act in our own good time."

"That's what Emerson said."

"You going to quote Emerson at me?"

"That's the prerogative of a very old lady," said Lane,
finishing up her champagne. "Emerson said, 'Time is just the
stream I go a-fishin' in.' "

"True, though a trifle pompous."

"If you imagine Emerson bent double, looking through
his legs at an upside-down universe, he will never again seem
pompous. What are chances of more champagne?"

Marcie pulled the green bottle out of an ice-filled sand
bucket next to her lawn chair. "I wish this was Mumms."

Lane held up to Marcie her blue plastic glass for filling.
"Never mind that. You truly give the best baby parties I've
ever been to. When's this one over?"

"Marcie looked at her watch. "By clock time, half an
hour. By Emersonian time it may never end."

"God forbid," said Lane. "They're good, but they're
not *that* good."

"Drink your champagne, crotchety old godmother."

"Then Buck comes, I suppose."

"Of course."

"Then Elaine comes and takes the exhausted mother
to dinner."

"Not this time." Marcie watched her daughter lift her
tadpole body out of the water, run around to the diving
board and flip off backwards. "But then you knew that,
didn't you?"

"Are you alright?"

"I will be."

"Is it Rigg?"

"This has nothing to do with Rigg. It has to do with Elaine and me."

"Well, you know I'm not Elaine's biggest fan."

"You've always made that very clear. You've all made that very clear. From the start."

"Are you angry with me, Marcie?" The older woman leaned forward and put her hand on her friend's.

"I'll be angry if you make me cry at my daughter's birthday party. I don't want to do that."

"It isn't as if we didn't give Elaine a chance, Marcie. And you know I've never said anything directly against her. I've respected your relationship, I hope."

"Yes. You have done that." Marcie blew her nose hard on a bandana and filled both their glasses up. "I'm just trying to spread the blame around a little to ease up on myself. I feel terribly, terribly guilty. And it isn't true that Rigg's not involved. She *is* involved. Up to her eyebrows. We're very happy when we're not miserable. It even feels wrong to be miserable, we're that happy. But it seems like we can't ask anyone to be happy for us."

"I might manage it," said Lane. "At least Rigg accepts who she is, accepts it, and even on occasion celebrates it. You've never had that. I suspect—and you can correct me if I'm wrong—that Elaine doesn't think she's a lesbian, that she says she *happens* to be in love with someone who *happens* to be a woman."

"Did she *tell* you that?"

"She didn't have to."

"I used to think she was right."

"It's an attractive idea. Makes you feel high-minded. Most women get tired of that in a hurry, though. Because eventually anything that's not the truth isn't enough. I'm surprised you stuck it out as long as you did, to be perfectly frank."

"I've always stuck things out too long. I feel behind in

life. Like I'm coming to things at forty that everybody else got to at thirty."

"I'd hate to quote Emerson twice in one day," cautioned her friend. "And besides"—she tilted Marcie's chin up with her cool, rough fingertips—"just look."

Across the lawn, thin knees flying, swim suit stuck to her body by sheer momentum came Jennifer, Jennifer, cool as water, to crouch shivering between the two women, to hold them fast.

CHAPTER 36: WINGS

They almost missed the plane. The little travel alarm that Elizabeth and Grace had dragged for seven months from Italy to Greece and back again failed them, finally, the night before they were to catch the seaplane to Catalina. They found the minute hand hanging down, limp, obeying no law except gravity's. Elizabeth had thrown her raincoat over her pajamas and made her way to the tiny office where a young man with bad complexion was watching a blinking television, his back to the counter.

They did not give wake-up calls at the San Pedro Motor Court. They closed the office at midnight. For eighteen dollars a night they could not expect wake-up calls. But he would lend them, for that night only, a wind-up clock the hotel kept for desperate cases. Set it back, he said, at midnight, when daylight savings time would begin. Leave the clock in the room when they left. And the key.

Elizabeth carried the clock, ticking like a bomb, back

to the room. "Gabriel" it said across its face. The minutes were white squares, making time look orderly, manageable. "But what time is it really?" Grace had asked, winding the brass key on the back.

Elizabeth pulled her pocket watch out of the Levis she had thrown across the bed. "Twenty past nine," she said, clicking the lid gently shut.

"But I thought," said Grace, that in spring you set clocks ahead. In winter you set them back."

"Spring forward/fall back," recited Elizabeth, holding her hand out for the big clock. "You're dead right."

Carefully she had set the time ahead. Carefully she had taken her lover into her arms. But she had not set the alarm.

Next morning she woke suddenly, listening in the stillness for Gabriel, her mind working quickly, catching then slipping, gears turning senselessly, searching ribbons of sleep for the correct time. She sat up and groped for the switch on the lamp. Nothing turned. She ran her hand down the cord until she found the little plastic wheel. Grace moaned in the sudden light. It was 6:15. Their plane left in half an hour.

"Oh, Christ, I hate doing things this way," Elizabeth said, throwing off the covers. "It has a cosmic tackiness."

"I could live with that," Grace said. "It's not having a shower I mind. And missing coffee."

"We'll find coffee," said Elizabeth, tossing Grace her blue backpack and spilling her underwear across the bed. "Have we ever not had coffee?"

"Yes. Venice."

"We were broke in Venice," Elizabeth said, pulling on her last clean shirt.

"And why were we broke?" asked Grace through toothpaste foam.

"We were broke lots of places."

"We were broke in Venice," she said, "because you had to ride in a gondola."

"True enough," said Elizabeth, appearing at the sink, "but I love you anyway, even now, looking like a mad dog." She kissed her on her foaming mouth.

Fifteen minutes later they were jogging down a San Pedro hill toward the Catalina Airlines hanger, duffle bags banging their hips.

Grace slept now, her head resting on Elizabeth's shoulder, the single engine drone vibrating through their tired bodies. But Elizabeth could not sleep. She watched the silver thread of sea spinning out of the plane's body. They flew low over the water. Three porpoises played alongside a sailboat. There was a woman at the tiller, standing, feet spread like the feet of a triangle. She waved, head back. Her hand traced slow loops in the air, as if she were waving sparklers onto the night, or skywriting a message for passengers in the tiny plane.

Things would be different, Elizabeth knew. They had not been back to the island for nearly five years, not since she and Grace had graduated from the university. She had not gone to see Juno, deliberately not gone, feeling apologetic, unready. Explaining her relationship with Grace to her mother had seemed more than she could handle in one visit.

And she had not explained. Instead, Grace had gone to stay with her mother, and she had stayed with hers. She and Grace had both followed the lead of their mother's expectations, had scarcely seen one another in the ten days they spent.

Together at last, steaming away toward the mainland on the white ship, clutching and tearful, they resolved angrily that the next visit would be on their own terms.

The tiny plane began to bank its wings now, making an arc. Its shadow ran before it now, chasing up into the wind, the engine laboring, pontoons closing on the light waves,

Grace awake now, her hand stealing into Elizabeth's, a wave breaking over the windshield seen through the cockpit door, then closed hastily, as the frail plane lunged in spray, once, twice, and then grew quiet on the sea.

Through the splattered window on her left Elizabeth could see three people standing on the seaplane dock, waiting. One must be Leon. She shuddered.

"You tell me," Elizabeth's mother had written, "who's worth more. A step-father who worries over you day and night for ten years and more, or this 'natural' father you go on about, this dreaming sailor Eddie, disappeared without so much as a look at you."

Well, she preferred this dreaming sailor, who—whatever else he was—had never planted his mouth down hard on hers. She could see Leon more clearly, now, in their approach, remembered him years ago standing on the Pleasure Pier with his saxophone hanging by a black cord around his neck. He stood here now on a different pier, a small man with a protruding belly in a powder blue leisure suit. Her mother's husband.

The passenger in front of Grace stood suddenly and smacked his head hard against the bulwark. Elizabeth reached into her jacket pocket for the baggage claim stubs. Her hand ran against something cold and hard. It was the key from the San Pedro Motor Court.

CHAPTER 37: UNDER THE UMBRELLA

Mrs. Tyson flung her weight against the beach umbrella and twisted hard, keeping one practiced eye on her granddaughter, playing near the surf. She pivoted until she felt the sand yield under her swinging flesh. Then she opened out the red canvas, waving to Jennifer, establishing their place on the beach.

The wind gave a playful snap to the blanket as she settled under the umbrella's shade. Out of a shopping bag she extracted her novel, Mr. Tyson's binoculars, her reading glasses, and a tube of zinc oxide. Then she unfolded her canvas backrest and leaned against it, breathing heavily. The long trip down her stairs, across the Pacific Coast Highway, and across the sand had left her winded, more tired than she ever remembered being. She felt like a balloon that the air was rushing out of.

Seventy-four now. She would not live forever. At least she could thank Jesus for giving her a grandchild, even if she could only see her on Sundays.

Mrs. Tyson fitted the binoculars to her eyes and scanned the beach for Jennifer. On her knees in a moat. How that child loved to get dirty. Sand had dried on her arms up to the elbows.

Later Mrs. Tyson would put her in the bathtub with mountains of bubbles, where she would sail her boats, leaving behind an invisible layer of sand that Mrs. Tyson would inadvertently sit on that night, after Jennifer was gone from her house, gone for another long week. Sand scraping her bottom, Mrs. Tyson would sit in the cooling water, feeling water rolling to the edges of her eyes, bulging like a sea of tears held back.

A pelican circled, out at sea, then folded its wings and dropped like a cannonball. Mrs. Tyson remembered to put zinc oxide on her nose. Her nose had always been tender. Jennifer had zinc oxide on her nose, her lips, and the tips of her ears. Sun screen was on every remaining square inch. Children burned easily. When you rubbed them you were always surprised at how warm they were and how there was a light hum of energy coming out of them like out of a refrigerator at night when everything was quiet.

Buck had been like that once, but to tell the truth she sometimes got tired of him now, after all these years. Tired of his moods and his ways. Somehow he had not turned out the way he was supposed to and it really did no good to keep trying with him. Jennifer was different. She had a spunk in her that Mrs. Tyson left alone. Buck said she spoiled Jennifer. But it was not spoiling. It was more like respect.

She reached her hand into the shopping bag and explored its recesses until she found the bag of fig newtons. She extracted three and ate them, one after the other. Lu Stetwiler would join them for lunch soon, bringing fried chicken and a cooler of lemonade.

Lu Stetwiler was a sad case. She had to retire from the

real estate business before earning diamond class because of her endometriosis. Mrs. Tyson had asked her doctor what endometriosis was and he had said little parachutes going through your body and sticking wherever they landed. Mrs. Tyson wondered how Lu could sleep with all those little parachutes waving in the current of her blood.

And she did, for a fact, look tired now as Mrs. Tyson fixed her in the binoculars, a worn figure, thin now as a celery stalk, a bag of fried chicken in one hand and a picnic jug in the other as her feet struggled to keep her moving diagonally across the sand instead of sinking down and being swallowed alive.

Survival of the fittest, thought Mrs. Tyson. Not a pretty fact, but then she had not invented life; God had done that. She had only lived it. Now here she was at seventy-four, having outlived her husband and nine friends, most younger than she, at that. Luwanda Stetwiler, young as she was, would be next. Margaret Tyson held up her heavy arms to relieve her friend of the fried chicken.

"Luwanda, honey, you look sick as a dog. You should've stayed home today instead of roving all over God's sand and making yourself exhausted like that."

"You always did know when my endometriosis was acting up, Peg."

Mrs. Tyson saw new parachutes opening in Luwanda's bloodstream, tiny figures swaying from them, special forces troops on a mission. Search and destroy.

"How about a fig newton?" she said.

Her friend shook her head. "Not hungry." She rolled her slacks up to her knees, revealing blue-white ankles and calves.

"Zinc oxide?" offered Margaret Tyson, extending the pink tube.

"I never burn," Luwanda said.

"You look like you'd go up like rotten timber in a windstorm."

"It's my pigmentation," explained Mrs. Stetwiler. "My grandmother was one sixty-fourth pure-blooded Indian.

"Suit yourself, then," said Mrs. Tyson, searching for her binoculars.

Luwanda Stetwiler snorted and said, "Remember, Peg, that time Bucky smeared two different kinds of suntan oil on him and came out striped?"

"You're thinking about somebody else," said Mrs. Tyson. "Here comes Jennifer."

"Good. I wasn't sure she'd be here, but I brought plenty of chicken. Because she usually is with you Sundays on account of Buck being so busy and all that he doesn't have much time to see his little daughter."

"Buck didn't want to get divorced, Luwanda. That was Marcie's idea, if you remember correctly. And I won't have this discussed in front of that child."

Jennifer fell on her knees on the edge of the blanket, greeting Lu, reaching for a drumstick, shaking sand onto the paper plates, shivering like a wet dog. Mrs. Tyson pressed an experimental index finger on her shoulder, testing for sunburn.

"You'd better put your shirt on now, Jenna."

"I'm fine. Don't worry, Gram. Did you see my castle? King Arthur lives there. He keeps pirahnas in the moat. Anybody gets in the moat and the pirahnas strip them to the bone."

Luwanda Stetwiler shuddered.

"Then Morgan lays a curse on their bones." Jennifer took the t-shirt her grandmother held out at the exact moment she rose, spun around, and streaked back to her castle.

The two women sat in silence for a moment.

"She's the light of my life," confessed Peg Tyson.

"I can believe that," agreed Luwanda Stetwiler. "Still, I can't help wondering."

"Wondering what?"

"Where she gets her strange ideas."

"What's strange about man-eating fish?" asked Mrs. Tyson. "I saw them myself in *National Geographic*. Fish do eat people. That's the God's own truth."

"Seems morbid to me, is all. Dwelling on it like that."

"Jennifer was just trying to be polite to you, Lu, because she could see you don't know how to talk to children on account of you never could have any yourself."

"Man-eating fish, though. I can't help thinking about that morbid house she's growing up in and those strange goings on there."

"What strange goings on?" Mrs. Tyson studied the gaunt face before her, the swollen arthritic joints like knobs on table legs. Not a decent meal for a fish there, truth to tell. And there was more at work in Luwanda Stetwiler's body than mere parachutes. She looked just like Sarah Kimble did when the cancer went from her left breast into her whole body. The doctor told Sarah her body was just eating itself alive.

Her own body would never do this. Her hand reached out for the thigh of chicken.

"You know, the goings on when Mrs. Simon was so sick and that nurse that looked like a man moving in and then getting left the house, with the children having to go to court to get back their own property."

"Yes, yes. I know all that. But get to the point."

"It's like that house—don't laugh at me Peg Tyson—it's like that house has an evil influence."

Mrs. Tyson threw back her head and saw the blue, blue sky with wheeling white gulls spinning out, it seemed, from her own red beach umbrella. "There is no such thing, Luwanda Stetwiler, no such thing as evil influence in God's universe." She felt strong and fit in the presence of this foolish, ailing woman.

"Say what you want," said Luwanda Stetwiler to the

drumstick resting, alone and untouched, on the desert of her yellow paper plate, "now your daughter-in-law's got it and is living with a woman looks like a man."

Mrs. Tyson paused, the chicken thigh balanced precariously between her thumb and index finger.

CHAPTER 38: TICK-TALKING

Olive Rivers, sitting under a yellow umbrella on the deck of her golf-course home, spread a shimmering line of Plumb Crazy nail polish down her index nail, stopping just short of the cuticle.

"I'm only twenty-nine," said Elizabeth. "I don't know why you go on about this. You were nearly forty when you married Leon."

"I had a daughter to finish raising," said her mother over her slipping eyeglasses. "I had responsibilities. I don't see you having any responsibilities. I don't see you having to work eight, nine hours a day to put meat on the table. Not for anybody but yourself."

"My responsibility is to Grace and myself. I did put meat on the table, as you so colorfully describe it. For five years I put meat on the table while Grace went to graduate school. And what really pisses me now is I never once thought of it that way, in those old, contractual terms of debt and repayment. I don't like to think in those terms. Life doesn't need to be that way."

"Dreamers don't think so, but others know different. Life's an account book with debits and credits. Those that don't know it are bound to be life's bankrupts, you ask me." Olive blew quickly on her nail.

Elizabeth rose from her yellow deck chair, stretched, and walked over to the railing. She spread her hands wide on the warm wood. Breathed deep. The touch of light was growing gentle, shadows deepening. From her mother's new house she could see all of Avalon spread out beneath her, from the bell tower on her left to the Wrigley mansion on her right. There was a scent of brush and animals on the air.

"Let's not argue," said Elizabeth.

"Libras don't argue," observed her mother, screwing the lid down tight on the polish. "They observe." She picked up the wads of streaked tissues from the table, then looked at her watch, holding her arm farther and farther away. "It's this new watch, Elizabeth. Can you see it? Leon bought it for me. Pretty, but it's got no numbers."

Elizabeth studied the face of the large, gold coin under a bulging crystal. "Almost five," she said, giving her mother's hand a squeeze.

"Then we can have a drink," Olive said. "If you drink before five you might be an alcoholic."

"Nonsense," said Elizabeth with a laugh. "You read that somewhere. One of those magazines you were always reading. I had a friend at college that called it 'tick-talking' when you started talking like a ladies' magazine."

"You can learn a lot from magazines, Elizabeth. As you get older you got to keep yourself up, or life will pass you by. God put us here to improve ourselves and leave this life just a little bit better than how we found it. I don't care if you laugh at that. Now fix us a drink. Leon'll be home in an hour and then he's taking us som place nice for dinner."

Elizabeth, behind the bar, reached out the bottle of rum, then turning toward the squares of mirror, opened the small refrigerator, took out a can of Coke and a tray of ice, looked up unexpectedly into her own divided face looking back, looking amused, looking superior. She smacked the tray of ice down. Why, in three days with her mother, must she become all over again a gloating adolescent? Why couldn't they simply sit down as equals and share together the crumbs of their experience?

She dropped an ice cube into the crystal glass and heard a clear tone. She would try, she resolved, to become that tone. She would try . . . .

A key was turning in the deadbolt, the front door opening, gum soled shoes moving soundless across the parquet entry and down the Aztec Gold hall. "Honey, I'm home!"

Olive left her chair, paused by Elizabeth at the bar to indicate another glass would be needed, and went to greet her husband. "You're early," she accused.

Elizabeth could see his hairy right arm steal down her mother's back to rest on her rump as they kissed in the hallway.

"You're home early," Olive said more quietly, yet pushing him away. "Elizabeth and I were about to have a drink."

"I'm fixing one for you," Elizabeth said through clenched teeth.

"Couldn't stay away from my two lovely ladies," said Leon, strolling into the living room, looking first at Elizabeth and then at his Rolex. "Grace here?"

"Visiting her mother today. But she should be back any time now," said Elizabeth, setting three glasses up on the bar.

"Well, I like a girl cares for her mother that way," said Olive. "Wrote once a week and sent a check every blessed month. Shame about her mother, though, letting herself go like that. They say she can't get herself to the porch and back if Yolanda Jamison next door doesn't lend a hand. Three hundred pounds. Hard to believe she ever was a bank teller making a good living. But cheerful. I give her that. And raised Grace to be a hard worker. Always did like working with Grace. Kept the salt and sugar filled up. Ketchup too. Without being asked. Not a penny short in four years. I like Grace."

"Too bad about that jaw of hers, though." Leon gulped rum and Coke, then slid out of his sports jacket, loosened his tie.

"Let's sit outside," said Olive, picking up her glass and looking at Elizabeth.

"What do you mean, her jaw?"

"Looks like a prize fighter with that jaw." Leon laughed.

Elizabeth studied the dark lines around his bridgework. Rhino mouth.

"Grace is beautiful inside and out and that's final," said Olive.

"More than final," said Elizabeth, following her mother toward the deck.

The bell tower chimed the half hour. "That hasn't changed," said Elizabeth.

"The Baron passed away three weeks ago," said Olive. "You were in Turkey. He was only sixty-seven. Not very old at all. He was a fine figure of a man. And successful."

"Old boozer," said Leon.

Olive fixed him with a stare.

The phone rang, and Elizabeth jumped up. "I'll get it. Probably it's Grace." She escaped into the kitchen.

The voice on the line said, "Am I going to get to see you this time?" It was Juno.

The doorbell rang. In the hall she heard Grace greeting Leon, and Leon's loud laugh. Then their voices traveled through the dining room to the deck.

"Yes, of course. I was going to call you."

"Were you?"

"Yes. I was. How are you?"

"Very well, really."

"How's Diana?"

"She died last winter. Crawled off to the tool shed. She was twelve, you know. Old for a cat."

"Have you thought about getting a new one?"

"I don't want a new one."

"Shall I come over tomorrow?"

"Is Grace with you?"

"Yes. She'll be at her mother's in the afternoon. Besides, she understands."

"I wish I did," said Juno.

"I love you," Elizabeth said unexpectedly. Then she saw Leon watching from the dining room.

"Din din," he said.

"Look, we've got to leave for dinner. I'll see you tomorrow." She hung up the wall phone.

Olive came in with her arm around Grace.

"Seems like Elizabeth's got herself a boyfriend stashed away on this island," Leon said, rocking forward on his gum shoes.

"That reminds me," said Olive. "Charles Gem wants to see you before you leave."

"Well we know it isn't Gem," said Leon. "He's queerer than a two-dollar bill."

"How do you know things like that?" demanded Olive. "Honestly, the things you come home with."

"Everybody knows there's a network of them here. Some of them, like Gem, you can spot a mile away. Other's aren't so easy. You could be standing right next to one and never now it."

"Really?" said Elizabeth.

CHAPTER 39: THE KITCHEN TABLE

Marcie looked up from her paper-grading to watch Rigg across the kitchen table from her, setting a minute anchor into place on the deck of her model sailboat. The smell of glue was in the air, pleasant, really. She might be high on it, she felt so unaccountably content. Part of the joy of loving was being able to look up like this and savor the other person and go right back to what was daily and plain.

With Elaine, she had never had that. However they disguised their time together it felt somehow like a date. Minutes had to be ransacked for their pleasures, or else elaborately planned and garbed.

This was different. Marcie wrote "A" in red at the top of Buzzy McClure's spelling test. When she looked up, Rigg, a tiny crow's nest resting between her thumb and index finger, was looking at her.

"You caught me," she said.

"Yes, said Marcie, "I certainly did." She got up and

bent across the table to kiss her love. Then she stretched and yawned. "Do you think if we had coffee this late it would keep us awake?"

Rigg held her arms out. Marcie slipped inside the circle. The pounding was at the front door and not inside her. They looked at each other. Shrugged.

"I'll go," said Marcie.

"Yell first," cautioned Rigg.

Marcie nodded. At the door she bent down to look through the peephole. Mrs. Simon had had installed at her own eye level. The walkway was elongated and the porch light threw shadows in strange patterns. There was a man standing, his head seeming too large for his body, like a face in a spoon. The face turned away. "Who is it?" she called.

The face turned suddenly to answer the door, annoyed perhaps at the challenge. It was Buck.

She unlocked the deadbolt and opened the door to him. The air smelled suddenly of Acacia blossoms and chlorine. His Levis and cotton shirt were both faded as if some intense inner conflict had drained his clothes of their color.

"I had to warn you," he said.

"About what?" asked Marcie, gesturing him over to the living room couch.

"She found out," he said, his eyes fixed now on Rigg hesitating in the doorway. "My mother."

"Found out?" said Marcie. "Found out what?"

"You know what. About you. You and Rigg." He took out a cigarette and lit it with a small wooden match from a box. His hands shook very slightly.

The three sat in silence, Marcie and Buck on the couch, Rigg at the other end of the coffee table, perched on an ottoman.

"What about us?" asked Rigg.

"Look, I'm not the one to be grilled here," He sunk

farther into the corner and smoked with apparent concentration, as if he'd come here for that specific purpose.

"What does your mother want? Of what interest can Rigg and I possibly be to her?"

"She wants Jenna," said Buck.

"Aren't you enough?" said Rigg with a curl of the lip.

"What's that supposed to mean?"

"Forget it," said Rigg. "Forget I said it." She stretched her legs out in front of her, examined the toes of her cowboy boots.

"Does she have to be here?" demanded Buck. "This doesn't concern her. This is between you and me."

"What concerns me, concerns her."

"Buck's right," said Rigg standing, slapping her pockets for keys, wallet. "This is between you two. I'll be at the Planet if you need me."

The door closed behind her. An engine cranked at the second try, then faded on the evening air. The two parents sat.

"What's she going to do?" Marcie asked at last.

"She's hired a detective. Some old local geezer sitting outside your house in a black, '58 Pontiac."

"She has a vast will, your mother. That much we know."

"That we know," Buck agreed. "What will you do?"

"Whatever it takes. Just that."

"You got a beer?" he asked.

They stood up, relieved. He followed her into the kitchen. She handed him a beer from the refrigerator and took one herself. They leaned against the counters, drinking thirstily.

"Is Elaine one too?"

"Not fair," cautioned Marcie. "But the answer's no. Not really."

"I figured she wasn't, being married and all."

"Exactly," she said.

"Well, when did you know you were one?"

"Grammar school."

"No!"

"I was desperately in love with Mary Lou Elton."

"Were you desperately in love with me?"

She thought. "I was in love with you but not desperately."

"I can't compete with Rigg. You know that."

"You're not supposed to."

"It makes me mad. It made me so mad that I almost didn't come to warn you. I felt like that was the reason you left me."

"That wasn't it."

"No," he said. "That wasn't it."

"And I feel mad that I haven't successfully divorced your mother."

"She should never get Jenna. And I'm not much good at being a father."

"You have your moments," she smiled.

He looked through the keyhole of his empty beer can. "Well, I'd better get, before Sherlock wakes up and recognizes my car."

She put out her hand. He squeezed it hard, then slipped out the kitchen door, leaving behind the mingling scent of chlorine, flowers, and airplane glue.

CHAPTER 40: COURIER

Elizabeth's glass of chablis sent a beam of light across the glass-topped table. Shadows came from the afternoon sun through eucalyptus leaves. Everything seemed transparent, made of fibers and filaments.

Juno had gone to get the quiche. Elizabeth looked through the kitchen window, obliquely, the very sideways drift of her eyes reminding her of her senior year, the year she had spent watching Juno's refracted image.

The French door swung open, glinting, propelled by Juno's foot. "Seems funny not to have Diana underfoot. Still, you may be right. I probably should get a kitten." She set the quiche down on the glass. "You *do* like spinach."

"Yes," said Elizabeth, pulling a cotton napkin into her lap.

"There's so much about you I didn't have time to find out. Sometimes I'm struck with that. Other times it feels to me as if we had a complete life together, you and I. As if we had been together twenty years."

"At least," said Elizabeth.

"How long was it really?" Juno asked.

"It was really twenty years."

"No, really."

"Three weeks," said Elizabeth, watching Juno plunge the shining knife into the quiche. "Remember, I missed registration, and Grace had to pretend she was me and forge my name. She thought she'd be arrested."

Juno balanced the first triangle of quiche on her knife and gestured for Elizabeth to pass her plate. Elizabeth picked up both plates and held them out. Juno set a triangle down on each.

"Penny for your thoughts," said Juno, reaching now for the walnut salad bowl.

Elizabeth laughed. "Actually I was thinking about Mr. Cochran and how I almost failed tenth grade geometry because I could never find the area of a triangle. Pi always made me think of blueberry pie."

"I was thinking," said Juno, heaping salad into Elizabeth's plate, "about that crazy fourth of July picnic we had out at the Point. We had quiche then and that garish cake Charles baked and all that sangria. It's a wonder we weren't all violently ill."

"I need to go see Charles," said Elizabeth, cutting a triangle off her quiche with the side of her fork and spearing it.

"I think he wants to offer you a job."

"What doing?"

"Something with Indians, I think." Juno filled their wine glasses.

"I'll probably go back to school. To study writing. Now that Grace has a real job, we'll have the money. I couldn't write while I was working. Probably didn't have the discipline. Or the craft. I'm almost thirty, and all I have to show for my time is a filing cabinet filled with unfinished stories."

"Thirty, my goodness," said Juno in mock-astonishment, "and no masterpiece yet? Defoe wrote his first novel after he was sixty."

"Time is just a stream," began Elizabeth with a smile.

"Exactly," said Juno. "Speaking of which, do you find the island much changed?"

"Well, I *thought* it would be changed. Actually, that's partly why I stayed away."

"Partly," Juno repeated.

"I was pretty convinced by the you-can't-go-home-again argument. But it really hasn't changed. Not that much. I miss the steamer, of course."

"That's right," said Juno, offering Elizabeth a second piece of quiche. "You used to dive for coins. I saw you once. I held my breath."

"So did my mother."

"That's a fair analogy."

Elizabeth put her fork down. "What do you mean by that?"

"Just a self-conscious remark about my age. Sorry. I was about to tell you, before vanity intruded, why the island is unchanged. And then I was going to take credit for it."

"We're really the same age, you know."

"How do you mean?"

"Some people think every time we're reborn we choose the same people we've chosen before but that we come back in different relationships. Grace might have been my father in a previous incarnation. I might have been your mother."

"Do you believe that?"

"Yes I do. With my whole heart. Trouble is I can't figure out why I keep choosing my mother." Elizabeth laughed and drank more wine.

"Maybe she keeps choosing you. I remember once you

said you were raised by Indians. When you were nineteen that explanation seemed more plausible than a cosmic one."

"Actually, I have made a little headway with the problem of my mother. I do see little gossamer lines of connection.

"But you were about to take credit for keeping Catalina in a time warp."

"Well," said Juno, "you remember old Mr. Loomis. When he died he left all his money to a group called Sanctuary. You'll be interested in this. The group organized initially to resist your step-father and some other realtors who want, among other things, to sweep the flats away and replace the old beach cottages with condominiums. Chris, Charles Gem, and I are the founders, but the ranks have grown in numbers and in strength. Mr. Smallwood from the bank joined, and Tula, the baker, Estelle Nolin from the Elbow Room, Sally Bates, even Helen Valentine. A curious collection of people. But we've all agreed to resist demolition and to provide a workable alternative through low-interest loans for repairs and improvements.

"And in the meantime we're working on other projects: bike trails, campgrounds, museum expansion, child care. We have a finger in every island pie."

"And all of this," said her guest, "so that when Elizabeth Rivers returned home she should not be disappointed."

"Yes," said Juno, pouring the last of the wine into their two glasses. "That was our motive. And our only motive."

"But you couldn't save Mr. Loomis. I liked him."

"Yes, I know. And we let the Baron die too. Ours must really be a second-rate utopia since we haven't managed to conquer death, disease, and general unhappiness."

"*Are* you unhappy, Juno?"

"No. Not really. Are you?"

"Do you want to go for a walk? It's so gorgeous today and I've eaten too much."

The two women gathered the dishes up and carried them

into the kitchen.

"Should we do these now?" asked Elizabeth.

"No, it's too beautiful a day for that and I see you so seldom." Juno put her arms out for Elizabeth, held her tight for a moment, let her go. "There, that was alright," she said, almost to herself.

They passed out of the kitchen, through the French doors, across the patio, and struck off down the drive that lead away from the house. There was a May hum in the air, and late afternoon sun struck at a slant the stand of eucalyptus lining the drive.

Elizabeth breathed in. "Ah."

"Does that mean you *are* happy?" asked Juno.

"I know I didn't answer you. And I want to. But it's a hard question for me, whether I'm happy or not. I know that I feel deeply restless. I feel . . . . It's like this. If life were a novel, with chapters in it . . . . Say life *is* a novel. Well, nobody knows how many chapters their novel has. No, that's not really the problem. It's more basic than that. I don't know where I am in the particular chapter I'm in. Am I at the beginning, or am I at the end? Or worse yet, am I wallowing somewhere in the middle?"

"I think," said Juno, stooping to slide a weed from its shaft and slip it into her mouth for better contemplation, "I think you've begun Book Three."

"Really? How do you know that?"

"I just know it," said Juno. "Don't ask me how."

"Is it Chapter One of Book Three?"

"More like Chapter Six, but it threatens to be a very long book. Longer even than *Middlemarch.*"

Elizabeth laughed. Then she stopped to look at the western corner of Chris Broadwin's house. Sun striking the windows made them look like sheets of copper against the gray, weathered wood. "I guess she got her screens up."

"We would stop in to see her, but she's over town for

a few days. She's *in love.*"

"How nice," said Elizabeth.

"Yes," said Juno, turning back to the house, "it is nice. We did try, after you left, to see if there was anything left of our old relationship. But that kind of thing usually doesn't work. I don't know why. Actually I think we were both a little relieved."

"I guess everything depends on which chapter you're in, and which chapter the other person's in."

"You did know that Chris and I were lovers. Before Kit."

"Yes, she told me the night you came back."

Juno nodded.

"Do you mind?" Elizabeth asked softly.

Juno shook her head. "There has never been anything, dear, that I did not want you to know."

"Among other things, I was intrigued with the fact that you all three stayed friends."

"Yes," smiled Juno, "women are like that."

"And then you and Katherine took care of Mary Broadwin while Chris went back to school. Raised her. I saw some pictures, yes, snooped," she confessed, "in Katherine's things, because until I did I *couldn't* understand. It was a picture of Mary as a baby, running toward Katherine. You could almost *see* a line joining one to the other, it was that real. I called you then, in my mind, 'the pioneer family.' And somewhere inside me I carry around that snapshot, an idea called 'the pioneer family.' "

"Maybe that will be Book Four," said Juno, leading the way up the brick steps toward the French doors. "*The Pioneer Family: A Feminist Utopia* by E. A. Rivers."

"More like *A Novel Fragment* by E. A. Rivers," laughed Elizabeth.

"Why do we all know you will do something with your life? And we do. Charles knows it. Chris still refers to you as 'the Island Historian.' Even Kit knew it. I think she believed you would rescue the library from Helen Valentine one day. Want some coffee?"

"Thanks," said Elizabeth, checking her watch, "but I've got to pick Grace up at her mother's soon, and I do want to see Charles first. We're leaving day after tomorrow, Grace and I. Not much time left."

"And then where?"

"We're going to try and find a cheap old house in an unfashionable canyon somewhere off Pacific Coast Highway."

"Could you, would you and Grace do me a big favor?"

"Of course," said Elizabeth, taking her hand as they stood in the living room.

"Wait here," said Juno, squeezing then releasing her friend's hand. "I've got something for you to take to someone. It shouldn't be much out of your way." Her voice trailed down the hall. There were thumping sounds from Kit's study, then Juno returned carrying a tin spool box tied shut with faded red thread.

"Letters," said Juno, a little out of breath. "These letters were Kit's. Lois, her old lover, wrote them years and years ago. Kit saved them. I want Lois to have them back, to know she saved them."

"Where can I find Lois?" asked Elizabeth, taking the box.

"She owns a bar in the Palisades, a gay bar. Everybody in Santa Monica knows the place. It's called The Daily Planet."

"Count on it," said Elizabeth. She gave Juno a strong hug and a gentle kiss, then disappeared through the French doors and into the afternoon sunlight.

CHAPTER 41: LONG DISTANCE

"It's just that I don't understand," said Rigg, scouring the frying pan from breakfast, "why that old bat can't pick her up if he can't."

Marcie leaned against the kitchen wall next to the phone. "He's in Miami and she's not well. Something about her liver. Jennifer says her eyes are yellow."

"Well what the hell's he doing in Miami when his mother's got yellow eyes and why didn't he tell us all this before we had made plans? We get out of here seldom enough, for Christ's sake!"

"Please, Rigg, she'll hear you."

Rigg slammed the pan into the sink. "That's what it comes down to, isn't it? Isn't it? Every damn time. 'She'll hear you.' And I shut up." A tear slid down her face and dropped on her silk shirt. "Shit."

"She'll be disappointed too. I'm disappointed. Mrs. Tyson's disappointed. . . ."

"I guess I'm supposed to feel sorry for Mrs. Tyson now. I'm not supposed to mind being followed to work every morning and home every night and that I can't even wipe my ass without being observed. Frankly, I don't care if Mrs. Tyson's eyes are yellow. I don't care if they're lime green. She's supposed to get that kid on Saturday night. Let her do it. Let her goddamned detective do it." She wiped her hands on the kitchen towel, threw it into a corner, yanked the back door open, and slammed it behind her.

"Mom, Mom!"

Marcie pushed herself off from the kitchen wall, slowly, as if moving through water. Her knees seemed to be bending wrong as she turned into the hall and made her way toward the bathroom.

Jenna sat in the bathtub heaping bubbles onto her leg and scraping them off with an ice cream stick. "I'm shaving," she said.

Marcie flipped down the toilet lid and sat.

"What's the matter, Mom?"

"Afraid I've got bad news."

"What?"

"Your Daddy can't pick you up and Gram is sick."

"You can drive me."

"But Gram can't take care of you."

"Daddy can."

"He's in Miami."

"Shit," said Jennifer.

"Yes, exactly," said her mother.

"I don't really *need* anybody to take care of me. I'm ten."

"True. But Gram doesn't understand that."

"She must feel pretty awful. Who's taking care of her?"

"I don't know, Jen. Buck didn't say."

"What's he doing in Miami?"

"He didn't say that either."

"We were going to Disneyland."

"Another time."

"I guess," she said, standing suddenly, bubbles gliding down her shining body.

Marcie handed her a towel. "Maybe you'd like to have dinner with Rigg and me."

"Maybe," said Jenna. "Or maybe I'll just stay home alone."

"Alone?"

"I'm old enough now. I feel silly with a babysitter."

"You'd like it if Lane could come, wouldn't you?"

"Can she?"

"I could call."

"But if she can't, then I get to stay alone."

"That's not what I said."

"But I'm old enough."

"We'll see," said Marcie, rising heavily from the toilet.

"I hate it when you say that."

"Me too. I'll go call Lane."

In the kitchen she picked up the receiver, held it to her ear, and put it down. She could not remember for a moment what she was supposed to do. There was no way to please everybody. Not even a way to please anybody. The evening began to feel like a credit card debt. She stared down at the gentle folds of the velvet trousers, the toes of her best shoes just peeking out.

Time to change plans, retrench. Easy enough when she lived alone with Jenna. She had known how to make decisions around the needs of her daughter, to change direction abruptly, to live with her in the moment, like apes in the jungle.

Elaine's needs could always be kept separate. Elaine even preferred it that way. It was a compact where each had silently agreed to allow room for a life that excluded the other.

But Rigg wanted more. That was the joy of her. And the pain of her. Now there were two in her life, two people pulling in opposite directions, wanting—in a way—the same thing, her total commitment. She felt sometimes her mind was the center of a tractor pull. Or that she was a trapeze artist balancing a pyramid of people.

Somewhere, she knew, she had the capacity to do this, but in the clamor of their demands she could not think how, or remember how to achieve that balance of mind that can mete out with almost divine unconsciousness equal love.

And anyway, was that what she really wanted? She put her hand up to the phone, absently, as if she could call Information and ask what alternatives there were. Then she remembered she had been going to call Lane. Lane would know. Might know, anyway.

And then suddenly it was as if she were in an airplane looking down on the geographical patchwork that represented her problem. She was looking at the Daily Planet, as if the roof were cut away, as if it were a stage setting where instead of the fourth wall being removed, the roof was. Inside people moved from place to place—library, billiard room, hall, dance floor, patio, rest rooms, the bar—freely and at will, both identifying and fulfilling their own needs, walking around solidly on their own two feet.

She felt a longing strong as thirst or hunger or passion itself to live inside that world where community and independence were joint tenants. Her hand reached up for the receiver, every movement of every muscle feeling strangely purposeful, her finger entering the circle that said 9 W X Y, when suddenly, the scrape of key in lock, the door opening on a contrite Rigg.

"Hey, I've got a great idea!"

CHAPTER 42: TEN PERCENT

"Well, this certainly wasn't my idea," said Olive Rivers, settling the fox collar of her jacket. "It's not like we didn't have sense enough to cook our own dinner."

"Don't worry, hon. Old Leon will take care of his ladies."

Elizabeth watched her stepfather elbowing his way through clusters of hungry people in expensive clothes toward the Maitre 'D. He would press a rolled-up bill into the man's hand and then they would be seated.

"I wish we *had* cooked our own dinner," Elizabeth said, looking uneasily into the glass eyes of one of the foxes.

"Leon wanted to take you and Grace someplace nice on your last night. Can't fault him for that."

"It's really very nice of him, Mrs. Rivers," said Grace, staring absently into the main dining room of the Zane Grey Hotel.

There were enormous wagon wheels suspended over the tables where people bent over their plates or gazed through plate glass windows onto the brilliantly lighted golf course. Silver clinked beneath a tide of voices. The maitre 'd approached them with two fingers raised as if he were calling a cab. Leon followed, nodding to associates in tight collars, proudly leading his ladies through the traffic of tables.

Elizabeth felt as if she were riding a float in the Rose Parade. Surely her mother did not enjoy spectacles like this, Olive Rivers of the Sea Gull Cafe, empress of the business lunch.

The maitre 'd pulled out fat chairs from a table near a large, stone fireplace. While the busboy filled their goblets with ice water, he handed them tall menus with golden tassels hanging down the spines. Leon stared about the room. Olive held the menu away from her face, then rummaged in her purse for her glasses. From a turquoise vinyl case she extracted a pair of tortoise shell glasses and fitted them carefully onto her nose.

Staring into the large circumference of reflecting glass, Elizabeth said to herself, "Pi r square," and instantly smelled warm blueberries.

"I haven't seen those," said Elizabeth. "They're very nice."

"You always hated my others."

"Time for a change."

"I suppose so," said her mother, "but I never had much use for change." She looked down at the menu and her heavy glasses slid down her nose until, reflecting in the candlelight they revealed their secret, Olive's initials engraved into the lower corner of the right lens: OR. She slid them up absently with a freckled index finger.

"Now Olive, you don't mean that about not liking change," said Leon to his menu. "You can't tell me you'd like to go back to that shanty in the flats instead of being on the golf course like you are now."

"Shanty! That shanty was home to me and Elizabeth.

And to you too, Leon Feeney, before you made your way
in the real estate business. I still remember that night you sat
on the front porch, dead drunk on champagne, dead afraid
you were never going to amount to anything."

"And I'm saying you ought to sell that house while you
can still get two nickels out of it."

"Keep your voice down, Leon. He gets worked up over
the simple idea of real estate," Olive explained to Grace.
"You'll have to excuse him."

"Nothing simple about real estate," said Leon, looking
for the waiter. "I need a drink."

"I'll have a daiquiri," said Olive, pulling her fox collar
back into place. "How about you girls?"

Leon raised a finger for the waiter, who stopped in
flight. It was Louis Heydon from high school.

He greeted his old classmates and took Elizabeth's hand
for a moment. "Charles told me you were in town. Maybe
we can have lunch." He had little feathery smile lines around
his eyes, gray eyes.

"I wish we could, but Grace and I are leaving tomorrow.
She's starting a job."

"One of the daring ones," he sighed. "I don't seem to
be able to leave the island myself. Charles says I'm en-
chanted. But let me get you something. You obviously
didn't come here for my life story, interesting as that may
be."

"Scotch and water," said Leon in a flat tone.

"And three daiquiries, Louis," said Olive.

Elizabeth smiled.

"Oh they're not all for me," said Olive.

"He knows that," growled Leon.

"Three daiquiries and one Scotch and water. I'll be
right back," said Louis.

"Fag," said Leon into the silence that followed.

"What?" said Olive.

210

"I said 'fag.' You heard me."

"They don't like to be called that. I read in a magazine they don't like to be called that."

"Overrunning the whole Goddamned island."

"Ten percent," said Olive. "That's what the magazine—*Readers Digest* I think it was—said. Ten percent."

"Ten percent of what?"

"Ten percent of everybody."

"Is queer you mean?" Leon's eyes stared straight into Olive's glasses. "No. You must of got that wrong."

"Ask anybody," Olive said.

Leon looked at Elizabeth. In the distance the chimes sounded faintly but could not be counted.

"I've got to take a leak," said Leon.

Olive watched him out of sight. "He's not so bad really."

Louis set icy glasses in front of the three women.

"No comment," said Elizabeth.

Grace stared out the window at the deserted golf course.

"I mean," said Olive, "there's worse."

"He's not going to make you sell the house, is he?"

"That's what I wanted to tell you. I had the house put in your name. Leon and Ned Carter want to plow everything under, all the houses in the flats, and build fancy condominiums for rich people over town to buy."

"Can they do that?" Elizabeth asked.

"Remember old man Loomis?" said Olive, leaning close now, her foxes fallen off one shoulder. "He left money. Mr. Gem and Miss Reed, they know what to do." She looked up, scanning the horizon for her husband, eyes big behind lenses, the periscope of her intention. "The house is in your name," she said once more, then folded her hands on the pink linen napkin in her lap.

CHAPTER 43: BIFOCAL

"The child is purely insane for reading," said Mrs. Tyson approvingly. She and her daughter-in-law watched Jenna settle into a beanbag chair under Mr. Tyson's bookcases. "Would you like me to wheel you outside?" asked Marcie. "It's a gorgeous afternoon."

Mrs. Tyson removed her glasses and placed them face down on the June issue of *Life* magazine, the bifocal casting an electric line across the "i." "Marcie," she said in a voice of patience, "it is not like I am helpless. I thank God I have still got the strength to wheel myself out on the deck in nice weather. It's people like Luwanda Stetwiler you have got to be concerned about. You knew the hospital sent her home to die. Like putting out the trash, you ask me. You'd think Arthur Stetwiler didn't make a decent living and couldn't afford to keep his wife in a nice hospital where she could die in peace.

"I never did expect to outlast her," conceded Mrs. Tyson,

resting her yellow eyes for a moment. "Young as she is too. But always having female problems, ever since I've known her. Endometriosis, they say. But I know cancer when I see it. I give her three weeks. Four at the outside.

"Thing that upsets me, though, is I'll never get to the funeral of my best friend. I'll never get down those stairs again, except feet first."

Jenna looked up at her grandmother, then down at the page again.

"Doesn't miss a thing, that Jennifer Tyson. The light of my life and that's the God's truth. She's worth twenty-five Buck Tyson's, you ask me."

"Maybe we should go outside, Peg."

"I guess I know what she can hear and what she can't hear. Soon as she knows her daddy's a zero on the face of this earth the better off she'll be. Took me more than forty years to get to the simple truth of that."

She looked at Marcie's blank expression. "Defending him, are you," she said in a voice so low it hardly seemed to come out of Mrs. Tyson at all. "He's my own flesh and blood. I guess I got a right to say if he's a low thing or not. Know where he is right now? Know where he is instead of taking care of his daughter or his mother? Riding motorcycles with that crazy man, Small, that's where. In Mexico, where they are apt to kill Americans soon as look at them. I showed him magazine pictures of Americans in Mexican jails, living like gorillas.

"It's not," she said, pushing her sparse bangs out of her glowing eyes, "like I was going to live forever. Bucky knows that. I told him enough times."

Marcie put her hand palm up on the table between them. Mrs. Tyson did not move.

"We got hot dogs for dinner," she said toward her granddaughter.

"Shall I pick her up tomorrow afternoon?" asked Marcie, rising.

"Bill Rose will take her," said Mrs. Tyson, putting on her glasses and pivoting her chair so she faced Marcie now. "Marcie," she whispered, "I don't like being stuck up here where I can't ever put my feet down on dirt. I feel exactly like those chickens in *Life Magazine,* the ones raised on chicken wire instead of on the ground. They say the meat from them tastes funny, and I know why.

"Listen Marcie, I had a dream. You and Jenna and I, all living in a little house. Why, the ocean was right outside our front door. I was sitting in the sand, waving to Jenna down the beach a ways. And you came to the door and said, 'I made you something.'

"And I woke up then, but there was still the smell from the ocean, and some other smell too. It might have been zinc oxide." She looked down at her feet, tight old lady shoes with fluffed-out laces.

Marcie bent down quickly, hugging her way through layers of girdle and flannel, pulling toward her this resisting, longing woman.

CHAPTER 44: CANON IN D

"I can't help it," said Grace's voice over the line. "I'm not in a position to tell them no. I won't *be* in a position to tell them no for seven years."

"You make it sound like you're an indentured servant," said Elizabeth, walking the phone out into the tiny patio and sitting on a plank bench.

"You go," said Grace. "Jules has got to get the fall assignments ready for the catalogue by morning and it's nice of him to ask me to help, green as I am."

"Well, I kind of hate to put this off any longer. It's something I promised Juno. And I'd rather go on a week night. Less crowded."

"Please go."

"I love you," said Elizabeth, then waited. "Did somebody come into your office?"

"Yes, that's exactly right," said Grace in her public voice.

"But do you love me?"

"Of course."

"I don't think I'm going to like respectability, Grace."
She set the receiver on the phone and lowered it to the
moss-covered bricks at her feet. Ferns curled in on her. A
lone bug light shone near the door, and beyond at the round
wooden dining table another light shone, an angled blue
architect's lamp next to her typewriter, making the blank
paper glow in expectation.

Elizabeth rose and stretched. She had not eaten. She
stepped inside and closed the glass door against the mos-
quitos. Probably some had already gotten inside. A moth
fluttered around her desk lamp.

A small, rusty refrigerator hunched in the tiny kitchen,
making a buzzing sound that at irregular intervals would
lapse into a hum, then a shudder, then total silence, as if
it never meant to revive itself. Elizabeth had named it
Phoenix because it always did revive itself, rose from its
ashes like the mythic bird.

People were like that too. They survived disaster. They
shook themselves back into their essential hum, into
serviceability, cycles of resurrection, self-creation, self-
deception (Elizabeth stared into the dim maw of Phoenix,
extracted a package of salami, Swiss cheese, baby Kosher
dills, a bright jar of mustard, a head of lettuce.)

Life was essentially shaped like a circle where pi r square
could be of no help (she had forgotten the mayonnaise).
For you could never find its circumference. Not through
geometry (Elizabeth squeezed a circle of mustard onto the
slice of sourdough bread, then ran a horizontal bar through
it to represent death). But possibly through fiction, if you
wrote long enough (A layer of Swiss cheese, salami, lettuce,
an enclosing slice of bread and the sandwich was complete).

Beer, she thought; crouched again, searching, yes Coors.
She poured the beer straight into a tall glass with blue flowers

around the top and sipped off the foam just in time (Was
life an extravagant sandwich; time, beer flowing into a
celestial glass?).

Carrying sandwich and beer and paper towel she sat
down at a chair opposite her typewriter. "Be ever thus,"
she said to her Smith-Corona, and lifting her glass in tribute,
drank deep. Then she leaned forward and yanked the blank
sheet out of the typewriter, wadded it up, and tossed it
lightly onto the topmost box of their unpacked belongings.

Then she put on the tape of Pachelbel and finished her
sandwich. Circles, she thought, is the whole idea with him,
this writer of one glorious piece. The melodic line that
danced with itself, that was pregnant of itself, that cele-
brated itself, that magnified itself, that threatened suicide,
and then jumped out at you, self-amused, self-regenerated,
complete. A master of slow fireworks, Pachelbel.

She rewound the tape to play the Canon again, then
crossed to the mountain of unpacked boxes, scanning their
surfaces for messages in red. "Grace's Sweaters," said one.
"Kitchen Crap," said another. She turned to a third:
"Memorabilia; attn. Courier."

That was it. She poured the rest of her beer into the
glass, drank, then ran her pocket knife through the strips of
package tape. On top of the opened package was a framed
picture wrapped in moss green tissue paper. She sat down
cross-legged with it on the braided rug and unwrapped her
prize. It was a photograph of Florence Chadwick walking
out of the surf, her broad mouth smiling, big-hipped figure
in her lucky, black jersey swimsuit. Underneath, the caption
read, "I don't know yet exactly how far I can swim." Charles
Gem had given it to her for high school graduation, together
with the same desk dictionary that rested by her typewriter
now.

She felt the room filling up with these gentle but in-
sistent shades—Pachelbel, Florence Chadwick, George Eliot,

and even Dorothea Brook—asking her to build cottages, write novels, swim channels, and compose canons! Thirty now and she had not begun to know how far she could swim; empress of blank paper, philosopher of refrigerators. Why wasn't Grace here, now, when she needed her, needed someone.

She looked at the photograph again, stared hard into the squinting, dark eyes of Chadwick. What did she know, this woman covered in bear grease, slender eyebrows raised in apparent surprise?

Elizabeth looked at her watch. Almost ten. She had nearly forgotten the errand for Juno. Under another layer of tissue paper her hands closed around a faded blue tin box with pale roses garlanding the top, so lifelike you could almost smell them, and red thread wrapped around to hold the top on. There was a little rust on one corner, from the salt air, no doubt. For an instant Elizabeth almost looked inside to make sure the letters were not damaged. But she was determined never to violate Kit, this curious woman whom she had scarcely known, never liked, but always honored, loving her in that special way reserved for lovers of lovers.

Elizabeth set the framed picture on the table next to her typewriter, then she took down her book bag from the coat rack by the door and placed the tin box inside. If she could love Juno's lover, then what would this new woman be to her, the lover of her lover's lover?

She slipped into her windbreaker, dropping the keys inside her pocket. Then she turned out the lights and locked the door behind her, the book bag light on her shoulder.

CHAPTER 45: MERCURY

"She says I'm not spiritual enough," replied Marcie, biting a pretzel in two.

Lane whooped. "Nancy Rigg spiritual? My grandmother's ass."

"Your grandmother's ass, notwithstanding."

"Last person in the world," said Lane, sipping her beer and settling back into her armchair in the Daily Planet's library.

"She's on a two-week Buddhist retreat somewhere near Big Sur. They don't talk for seven days."

"She'll be back in two days."

"They eat seeds and chant."

"What's really going on?"

"She's tired of living with a child and a detective, is my guess. She says she needs more space." Marcie sipped her beer.

"I have trouble with all this desire for space, Marcie.

There seems so much of it in my own life. At night the wind howls through it. My house echoes. My very bones echo."

"I know what you mean. But I also know what Rigg means. I'm used to it, Lane. Used to having my room invaded, my refrigerator ransacked, my living room sacked and littered, my brainwaves scattered. But I haven't lost my pleasure in living with an untamed creature; she reminds me of my old, free, naked self, hunched before a fire. I've got to tame her, I know, but I'm doing it reluctantly and very, very slowly.

"That's my choice. And in return I get Jennifer's wild love, her trust. Rigg never made that choice, not really. She had thought of having a child, even before I met her. But beyond the dreaming, the fantasy of having a child, she had never taken one step in that direction. I think what she wants is for Jenna to love her right now. That's number one. Number two is her presence should hardly be felt. That she should be seen and not heard, like a Victorian child.

"Really, Lane, it's a terribly hard thing to do, raise somebody else's child."

"You seem more understanding than anybody in your position could possibly be. I think Rigg is selfish and childish. If I were you I'd be in a rage."

"Oh but I *am* in a rage. A towering one."

"Oh, good," said Bill Rose, slipping through the library doors, "I've never seen you in a rage before."

"It's rather disappointing actually," said Lane, leaning forward for her kiss. "It's taken me half an hour to even discover she is in a rage. No animation, just talk."

"But in my mind," said Marcie, "I'm in the bar right now, breaking Lane's furniture to smithereens. A chair sails into the mirror behind the bar. Patrons dive under the tables."

"No! Not the mirror!" Lane exclaimed, covering her eyes with her hands.

"Yes, Goddamn it, the mirror!" Marcie rose suddenly and Bill pushed her gently into her chair.

"Let me get us a pitcher. I've got news that should cheer you, Marcie."

"Just you try."

The door closed behind him.

"I wish we could have a fire," said Marcie, glancing longingly at the fireplace.

"In June?"

"Why not in June?"

"Anything you like. When you're in a rage I can do nothing with you."

"True."

"I've never seen you eat so many pretzels in my life."

"They calm me," said Marcie, picking up another.

Bill came in with a pitcher and a mug. He poured the beer very slowly, encouraging foam. "I'm building suspense," he said.

"Get on with it," said Lane. "I can't handle her much longer."

"I come from the Lady Tyson," he said, drawing up a third chair with evident relish. "About six o'clock I went over to see if she and Jenna needed any help with dinner. They were boiling hot dogs. Can you imagine? Boiling them!" He shuddered. "Well, anyway, she called me aside and told me to tell you she had called off her detective."

"She can't do that," said Marcie.

"I thought you'd be pleased," said Bill, looking from Marcie to Lane.

"She is pleased," said Lane. She's doing the mad scene from *Hamlet* tonight."

"She does look a little like Sir Lawrence Olivier," said

Bill, picking up a handful of pretzels. "Now that you mention it."

Marcie looked at him ruefully over the top of her glass. "That detective was the one bright spot in an otherwise dark existence, Bill Rose. You know what they used to do to bearers of bad tidings?"

"What?".

"Cut off their heads."

"Occupational hazard," he said. "But they don't still do that, do they?"

Marcie smiled. Then she reached behind her neck and fumbled at the clasp of her necklace. Leaning forward she fastened it around her friend's neck. "There, Bill. They gave gold chains to the bearers of good tidings."

Bill kissed her and touched the chain lightly. When the library door opened, he said, "Sorry, only family tonight."

A woman in a windbreaker stood hesitating, dark curly hair falling nearly to her shoulders, a book bag slung over her shoulder. "I'm looking for Lane," she said, patting the bag. "I have something for her."

CHAPTER 46: THE FOURTH OF JULY

They could see Miss Lulu from a long way off, balancing a large tray in his left hand, hips swaying in white summer pants, red suspenders traversing his deep brown chest. Behind stood a row of palm trees, then the highway running beyond, then hills rising under brown chaparral, dots of green yucca, blue sky turning a dusty rose. He waved.

"Who's that?" said Jennifer Tyson, her yellow shovel dangling from her hand.

"It's Miss Lulu with the rest of our dinner," Lane said from behind her faded green beach umbrella.

"Who's bringing the fireworks then?" Jennifer fell to her knees in the sand. "Have you got any?" she asked Elizabeth.

"We're not supposed to have any. It's against the law," said Elizabeth, hearing her own grown-up voice, her mother's voice. "I mean," she said, "we get to see the big fireworks from across the bay."

222

"We'll never see them from here," Jennifer said flatly. "It's silly to think we could see them from here." She began slapping the sand with the flat of her shovel.

"I'm afraid that's my fault," said Lane, leaning around her umbrella again. "I wanted us to come here so we could have a fire on the beach. You can't do that anywhere but here."

"Why not?" said Jennifer.

"What are you complaining about now?" said a tall woman in her forties, throwing down a huge log with one end burned.

"Rigg, you haven't met Elizabeth and Grace," said Marcie Tyson, crawling forward from beneath Lane's umbrella. You remember I met Elizabeth a couple of weeks ago at the Planet, when you were at Big Sur. Grace and Elizabeth, meet Nancy Rigg."

Rigg extended a long, substantial hand. "Glad to meet you. Marcie said you found a house in Topanga. You like it there?"

"Aren't any of you good people civilized enough to help," wailed Miss Lulu.

"Over here," said Lane, "out of the wind."

"Wind," said Miss Lulu gaining the blanket, "tornado is more like it. No place for Lollipop Kids."

"Give me that nasty little dog," cackled Bill Rose, taking the tray from the exhausted Miss Lulu and depositing it under the umbrella next to Lane.

"This doesn't look like Kansas," said Miss Lulu, "that's for sure." He planted a kiss on Jennifer's head. "Hi kid. You look like a piece of sand sculpture."

"We haven't got any fireworks," Jennifer told him.

"All you got to do is close your eyes," said Miss Lulu, extracting a piece of celery from beneath the cellophane. Course it helps if you've got a pair of ruby slippers."

"That's not real fireworks," said Jennifer.

"Have we got anything to drink?" asked Miss Lulu.

"Over here," said Jennifer. "I'll show you how." She took a blue cup out of a bag. "Now, do you want the one with pineapples or the one with strawberries?"

"I'll take the one with liquor."

"They both have liquor," said Bill Rose.

"Then I'll take them both," said Miss Lulu.

Jennifer pushed the tap on the piña coladas and filled the cup half full, then the tap on the strawberry daiquiries.

"I won't be responsible," said Bill Rose.

"You're never responsible," said Miss Lulu. "When have you ever been responsible?"

"I hate that word," said Rigg, wadding up newspapers and stuffing them under the arch of her log.

"I used to," said Lane. "But think about it: response-able. It really means capable of response."

"What it really means," said Rigg, "is being fettered."

"What's fettered?" asked Jennifer, licking strawberry daiquiri off the back of her hand.

"Fettered," said Grace, accepting a piña colada from Bill Rose, "is not having tenure."

"What's ten-year?" asked Jenna.

"It's when you can be fired from your teaching job," explained Marcie. "Remember when Elaine used to talk about tenure all the time?"

"And the Commotion Committee," added Jenna. "Commotion and Ten-Year."

"Anybody got a match?" asked Rigg, slapping her front pockets.

"You might want to meet my friend Elaine," Marcie said to Grace. "She's been through that ordeal and survived it."

"That's a matter of opinion," said Rigg, taking a book of matches from Bill's outstretched hand.

"Really," said Marcie, "she's very nice. And it does help

to talk to people about it, people who've been through it."

"I'd like to. Sometimes I think I'm losing my mind," said Grace. "I'm developing paranoia."

"What's paranoia?" asked Jennifer.

"It's when you feel like people are out to get you," said Rigg, holding the match to newspaper.

"And they usually are," sighed Miss Lulu. "Ask one who knows."

"You're too young to be so cynical," said Lane.

"Why thank you, dear," said Miss Lulu, giving his hair a pat. "Have we met?" he said turning toward Grace.

"Grace Medina," she said.

"David White," he said, "but you can call me Miss Lulu. Unless it grosses you out."

"Why should it gross me out?"

"I guess I'm just paranoid," he said.

"So am I," said Grace.

"I don't have tenure either, Grace. We're meant for each other. Let's run away to the Azores and get married."

"Elizabeth wouldn't like it," said Grace, smiling.

"I don't want to stand in your way," said Elizabeth solemnly.

"Can I be in the wedding?" asked Jennifer.

"Why not," said Miss Lulu. "You can be my best man."

"I'm not a man," said Jennifer.

"That makes two of us," said Miss Lulu. "Want to run away with me to the Azores, kid?"

"I like it here," said Jennifer.

"That's the most sensible thing I've heard all afternoon," said Lane rising slowly from her low beach chair. "Let's go down to the water, Jennifer, and see if we can find anything the tide's washed in."

"I'll join you," said Elizabeth. "Want to come, Grace?"

"No thanks. I'm feeling indolent right now."

The three started off across the shadowed sand, Jennifer

in the lead, pulling the shifting triangle seaward. Spray from the breakers blew across their faces. Lane pulled the hood up on her sweatshirt.

"Catalina," she said, pointing. "But you know that already, my messenger-friend."

"Yes. Home."

"Do you miss it very much?"

"Lately I do."

"I was very glad to have the letters." They sat down on the sand together, the child digging at a small distance. "Did you know Kit?"

"Not very well," admitted Elizabeth.

"We went to library school together. We fell in love over the Dewey Decimal System. She was quite, quite wonderful. Nobody like her. Ever. My fault, of course. Major stupidity of my life. Compulsive fooling around until she just climbed aboard that white steamer and put a large body of water between us, between my claim on her and her own precious sanity. They don't have them anymore, do they?"

"What's that?"

"The steamers. They don't have them anymore."

"No," said Elizabeth. "Just two fat cutters and a sea-plane."

"Well," said Lane, looking out to sea, toward the outline of the island, "things change." She cleared her throat. "I suppose I had to sow my wild oats. We don't start out response-able. At least, I didn't. Though I hope to God I am now. You are, aren't you?" she asked, turning toward Elizabeth.

"Lane. Lane." Marcie's voice struggled against the surf. The two women turned in her direction. She came, leaning against the wind, breathless. "Bill's hungry and so is Grace. Shall we go ahead and eat, or wait until sundown?" She sat in the sand next to Lane. "You hungry, Elizabeth?"

"I'm always hungry," said Elizabeth.

"Marcie, said Lane, "why don't you stay here with Elizabeth and enjoy the sunset. I'll take Jennifer back with me."

"You're a sainted angel," said Marcie gratefully.

They watched Lane and Jennifer, hand in hand, dragging their shadows back up the beach, the older woman's loose clothes flapping about her like sails coming up into the wind.

Marcie leaned back on her hands and breathed deep.

CHAPTER 47: TIME OUT OF MIND

Elizabeth heard a wave break and then the chimes from the bell tower strike: one, two, three, four, five. She sat up suddenly, the waterbed rising and falling under her, making a gentle sloshing sound like water lapping the pilings at the Pleasure Pier. A bar of afternoon sun fell across her bare ankles. She picked up the alarm clock Grace had stolen from the San Pedro Motor Court that morning when they had almost missed the plane. Five o'clock. There was still time. Marcie had told Elizabeth to come at six, but she had to pick up Lane from the Planet on her way.

She stripped off her jeans and t-shirt, tossed them into the straw hamper in the corner, then walked quickly across the cool white tiles of the bathroom. The hot water heater never got the water quite hot. Elizabeth stepped under the spray of warm water, turning her body slowly. Time enough. Time is just the stream. Rivulets of water braided across her breasts and across her brown belly. Carefully she washed.

Carefully not thinking of the woman on the beach pointing across the channel to her island, Elizabeth's island. The island that this woman called Marcie had watched out her kitchen window, this sleeping island on which Elizabeth had wandered, a sleepwalking child, a voyeur, an island historian, Chris Broadwin had called her, ten years ago, almost to the day.

But what was the difference between a snoop and an historian? And she had never wanted to be an historian anyway, but a writer, a novelist, a magician of time. She toweled herself off, wandering into the bedroom and pulling open each drawer in her chest, then every drawer in Grace's, feeling somehow that she wanted to shine like a gladiator tonight.

In the mirror on Grace's chest she caught sight of herself, asked the shining profile, "And what do you have in mind, Elizabeth Austen Rivers?"

That stopped her. No one ever used her middle name, except her mother, in warning. Her mother's voice had entered somehow into her central nervous system, passing into her as easily as the chimes from the hill, tolling the hour, the half hour, the quarter hour, even in her sleep, her deepest sleep. Dear God!

She pulled Grace's new blue shirt out of the open drawer and strode into the living room, struggling arms into sleeves. There it was, her typewriter, dormant, as ever, on the dining room table. The light from the desk lamp threw a harsh light, a light not needed in the bright afternoon sunshine, a light hot and useless in the dark of her own failed inspiration.

It has been her mother all the time, her voice tick-tocking through Elizabeth's mind and snaring her typewriter keys. If her heroine planned a trip to Mexico, her mother would warn of diseases in foreign countries. Better pack a lunch, her mother would caution. Don't drink the water. Be back before dark. Money doesn't grow on trees. Her internalized waitress mother had simply cleared the table before anybody could get so much as a morsel.

Elizabeth sank down onto the chair. She had always thought of her characters as living in a trunk. She could take them out, one or two at a time, and let them prance about on the lid of the trunk. And all the time there had been a duplicate key!

Well, two could play at that game. She would open the trunk and let them all run free. She would no longer pay their bills or worry over their digestive tracts or advise them in matters of the heart. She would look at them as through a telescope, from great distances, and with the aloof rapture of a voyeur.

CHAPTER 48: GEOGRAPHY

"She says she needs more space," said Elizabeth, leaning back in her chair.

The three women sat around the dining room table, silent for a moment, the relics of their meal outlined sharply, like shells at low tide. Lane glanced at Marcie.

"What?" said Elizabeth.

"Nothing really," said Lane, reaching for her wine glass. "There's just a familiarity about those words."

"Yes," agreed Marcie. "I heard them very recently myself."

"Well, I believe in space," said Elizabeth. "I believe in giving it and taking it. Both. I wouldn't want to be the one to breathe up all the air, God knows."

"I'm for space if that's what we're really talking about," said Marcie. "What I object to is people saying that's the issue when what they really want is no responsibilities. I'm sick to death of that kind of 'space.' It's a Goddamned childish way of saying you're moving on and you don't give a shit what happens to the other person."

"Marcie's upset," explained Lane.

"You bet your sweet life I'm upset."

"Actually she's in a rage," said Lane smiling, reaching her hand across the table toward Marcie.

"Don't patronize me," said Marcie, giving the offered hand a squeeze.

Elizabeth sat staring at her empty plate.

"I'm sorry," said Marcie. "You probably don't know about Rigg."

"Lane told me on the way over," said Elizabeth, looking up, her forehead feeling suddenly damp.

"I did so want some company tonight and to feel my life was going on. But Jesus, every time somebody says 'space' I run amuck. Actually, it's very funny to think your lover has run off with a Buddhist priestess."

"Especially if you know Rigg," snorted Lane.

"The woman actually balances on a prayer pillow." Marcie stood up, her hand curved around the wine bottle, tears standing in her eyes. "It's very funny, really."

Her two friends rose quietly and followed her into the living room. "We've forgotten our wine glasses. But we'll use my mother's liqueur glasses and pretend there's liqueur in them. Look, they have little indentations in the glass and you can see rainbows if you look just right."

Elizabeth held the tiny glass before the candle. Toward the top she could see a circle of color.

"How's the novel coming?" asked Lane, settling into a corner of the couch. "Or shouldn't I ask?"

"Well," said Elizabeth, "we had a very important meeting this afternoon."

"We?"

"Yes, my characters called a meeting. They want more space," she said, looking suddenly at Marcie.

"That word. You said that word."

"Marcie, repress yourself, for our sakes," said Lane.

"What kind of novel are you writing?" asked Marcie. "You must hate it when people ask you that. Forget I said it. I'm better off in my rage."

"It was a feminist utopia as late as a week ago Thursday," said Lane, sipping from the tiny glass.

"How can you know," asked Marcie, "what's ideal? I mean I can't figure it out for myself, let alone for other people."

"That's just what my characters say. I've been pushing them around, not letting them decide. They tell me, But Lane doesn't push people around in the Daily Planet. She lets people move freely from room to room."

"Matter of opinion," said Marcie, with a satiric wink.

"That's right," said Lane. "I've been accused more than once of pushing them around. I think the charge is false myself. But I do confess to creating the rooms in the first place. That means I decided what their legitimate needs were."

"But you asked them first," said Marcie.

"I asked, but I didn't always choose to listen."

"You're not pretending you're sorry you didn't put in the steam room."

"No," said Lane. "I'm not sorry about that at all. I'm a benevolent dictator and I suspect that's what Elizabeth is going to have to be for her subjects."

"I'm not going to mother them," said Elizabeth, "even if they plead."

"You won't spoil them, if that's what you mean," said Marcie. "The surest way to make them independent is to offer to mother them. And to mean it. Look at Jenna. I really like her and try to do for her. Because she feels that, she seldom needs it. When she does, she simply comes and asks: a kiss on the knee, a story at night, a loan, a hug. Then there are people like Rigg, whose mother mostly didn't mother her at all, except for random, guilt-ridden excesses. So now, at forty, Rigg is a starving person. I hope it's obvious that Rigg is not on my mind tonight."

Lane smiled. "You know the enemy would say you just admittted lesbians are looking for mothering, that it's a neurosis."

"Not at all, my dear devil's advocate. The whole world needs mothering at times, especially the enemy. And if everybody was mothered more, they would require it less. Quite simply. And you may put that in your feminist utopia, everybody. You have my permission."

"Who mothers the mother?" asked Elizabeth.

"Well in *my* utopia," said Marcie, "everybody would mother. Mothering is just an expression of tender regard and respect that grows out of liking someone, quite apart from what they can do for you."

"How is that different from love?" asked Lane.

"It's less selfish," said Marcie. "By half."

"My dear cynic," said Lane struggling up from the couch, "you won't say so in six months. And now, Elizabeth, please drive an old lady home. I'm tired, and your utopian sensibility has been through the wringer tonight."

CHAPTER 49: CHINATOWN

Through the rearview mirror Elizabeth could see Jenna in the back seat, her nose pressed to the triangle of window, her dark curls blowing, curls like her mother's. Elizabeth eased her VW around the hairpin curve at the Self-Realization Fellowship Society, taking the opportunity to glance sideways at Marcie beside her.

"I don't really want to go see Gram," said Jennifer. "She's too yellow."

"Bill will be there," said Marcie.

"Why can't Daddy be there?"

"He's in Miami on business."

"Daddy's always in Miami. He must have a girlfriend there."

"I wouldn't be a bit surprised," said Marcie.

"Seems like everybody wants a girlfriend except Gram."

"Who is too yellow."

"Yes," Jenna agreed.

"Is Elizabeth going to be your girlfriend now that Rigg's gone?"

"Elizabeth and I are friends, Jenn."

"That's what I said. You're girls and you're friends. Girlfriends. See."

"There's a difference," said Marcie.

"You're being patronizing," said Jennifer.

"Sorry," said Marcie. "I guess this conversation is embarrassing me a little."

"It isn't embarrassing Elizabeth," said Jennifer.

Elizabeth made a wide turn from Sunset onto Pacific Coast Highway. "Not at all," she said.

"We're almost there," said Marcie. "Just past the bait shop on the right."

Gravel crunched in the drive. Elizabeth parked the car and turned off the ignition. A heavy yellow face rolled into view at the porch railing. Bill Rose appeared, smiling. Elizabeth stood up in the August heat and pulled the seat forward for Jennifer, who was half-way up the steep stairs a moment later.

"Come on up," called Bill.

"Sorry. Can't," Marcie said. "We have a movie to catch. Thanks anyway."

The yellow face nodded above, like a helium balloon tied to the railing. Marcie blew two kisses and sat down in the passenger seat. Elizabeth backed through gravel, paused at the highway, and pulled into the southbound lane.

"Ahhhh!" breathed Marcie.

"What does 'ahhhh!' mean?"

"Relief."

"From?"

"From being a mommy. For just a little while. It means you've slipped off your pack and can rest against a tree."

"Like when I put my characters back into their box?"

"Not exactly," laughed Marcie. "You won't get a call

saying they've come down with measles, but *I* might."
"Oh I get calls like that all the time," said Elizabeth.
"But I have an excellent answering service." She turned
back up Sunset, asking, "Right way?"
"Yes. We're going to the Bruin. Not far."
"You're being very mysterious about this movie."
"A hint," she said. "The setting will be of great and
momentous importance to you."
"Chinatown? I've only been there twice and the food
wasn't particularly good."
"Chinatown is a metaphor," she said, "but I can't tell
you any more. You'll have to be your own detective and
follow the clues. You and Jack Nicholson will be the de-
tectives. Private detectives."
"Very private," said Elizabeth, pulling into a pay lot
and taking an orange ticket from a man in baggy pinstriped
pants.
"Going to the movie?"
"Yes," said Elizabeth.
"It'll still cost you," he said.
"That's fine," said Elizabeth, "I'll take it off my expense
account."
They parked against a brick building and walked across
the lot toward the theater. The sign posted in the cashier's
window said: "Chinatown," 3, 5:15, 7:25.
Elizabeth looked at her watch: 4:10.
"I'm sorry," said Marcie. "I must have got the time
wrong. I thought it started at 4:15."
"Don't worry. Detectives are very inventive at moments
like this. Let's go to the Hamlet and have a beer."
"Ah wonderful," said Marcie. "I feel more than ever like
I'm on a holiday."
"Do you?" asked Elizabeth. "I do too. Even though I've
been out of work since . . . February." She led off in the
direction of the Hamlet.

"Not really 'out of work.' Your writing counts. Seeing the world counts."

"There's something kind of invisible about writing, though. I mean, *you* can say by five o'clock, 'I taught twenty children their four tables today.' But sometimes I have to say, 'I wrote two paragraphs today and had the good sense to tear them up.' That's a difficult enough admission to make to myself. I cringe waiting for Grace to ask how things went today."

"Grace doesn't look very tyrannical to me." They stepped through thick glass doors into the cool interior of the Hamlet. There was an empty booth at the back, next to the window. They sat across from each other, a checkered tablecloth between.

"You're right, of course. Grace is not a tyrant. She's my childhood love. A horse of a different color." Elizabeth drew in her breath. "But she's with Elaine today. Elaine has something to offer her that I don't."

"Uncertainty," said Marcie.

Elizabeth smiled. "Thank you."

A young man with a disappearing chin handed them menus. "We'll just have beer," said Marcie. "Whatever you have on tap. A pitcher."

"Is that o.k.?" asked Marcie, as the man disappeared toward the bar.

"Yes, fine."

"Beer always reminds me of my ex-husband. Beer is his dearest friend next to Small."

"We could have something else," said Elizabeth.

"Oh, it's not a thoroughly unpleasant memory. He's part of my history. I wouldn't know how to regret having chosen him for that piece of time. Besides," she smiled, "I wouldn't have Jennifer."

"What do you think time is?" asked Elizabeth, pouring from the pitcher into Marcie's mug.

"A stream of beer," said Marcie.

"Yes," said Elizabeth. "Time is surely a stream of beer."

"All good detectives know that."

"Bill Rose said you had a detective following you and that's why Rigg left."

Marcie made a face. "People don't leave for little things like that. Besides, he was a very nice detective, clean and well-spoken if a little shabby. When Mrs. Tyson told him to stop shadowing me I felt a little lonelier than before. If we can't have guardian angels in this modern age, I would certainly settle for a private detective with a sense of duty."

"I wish Grace would hire one for me."

"Lonesome?" asked Marcie.

Elizabeth nodded and swallowed beer the wrong way.

"I know," said Marcie. "It helps me having Jenn around. She makes a truly satisfying depression almost impossible. You can't get completely depressed if you're interrupted every ten minutes."

"I've thought of a child," said Elizabeth, staring into her foam.

"It's different than you think," said Marcie. "People are always surprised. Rigg was. She thought it would be uplifting to have a child. She didn't realize how many of her own needs she would have to keep putting on hold. That's easier to do if the child has trained you since birth, but very difficult to learn on the job. Maybe impossible."

"It sounds like you're thinking of withdrawing from society."

"Not society. But maybe from love relationships. It's too complicated. I've tried twice now. For the time being I might just have a meaningless relationship or two."

"But lesbians do raise families. I know of one myself."

"I'd love to think I was wrong. I'd love to think a partnership could be that strong." Marcie looked out the window onto Westwood Boulevard. "Tell me," she said, turning to

Elizabeth, her eyes filling, liquid, "how did they turn out, this family you know of?"

"Well, actually, you almost know one of the parents. It's Kit Tebolt, Lane's former lover. The one who ran off to Catalina. I'm sure Lane told you."

Marcie nodded.

"She and a woman named Juno—my high school English teacher, actually—raised another woman's child together. For awhile. The mother was in school. A good friend of theirs."

"So this child had three mothers. Ah, I like that. If we were all raised by three mothers we'd be better off. Three mothers could spell each other, could nod agreement at night and say, 'I know. Oh I know.' That's all I've ever wanted in terms of help: someone to say, 'Oh I know.' "

"My mother raised me by herself. She probably longed for two others to share the burden. God knows I was not an easy child," said Elizabeth, draining the last of the pitcher into Marcie's glass.

"You turned out very well, though. Tell me, how did the child with three mothers turn out?"

Elizabeth laughed. "I wish I could tell you she was a channel swimmer, or a surgeon, or a social worker in Africa. Actually she married Larry Sutton, the boy whom the scaled-down version of fate that controls Catalina had destined for me. Ugh." Elizabeth gave an old shudder and drank the last of her beer. "Larry Sutton works with my step-father as a despoiler of the land."

"There goes the dream of a three-mothered utopia."

"The fact that a proposition is wrong is no argument against it. I read that somewhere. Besides, the mothers turned out well."

"Ah well," said Marcie. And then, "What time is it? I forgot my watch."

* * * * *

"My treat," said Marcie, sliding a five-dollar bill under the glass toward the gum-snapping cashier. Two purple tickets popped out together. "After all, this is my mystery afternoon. You're just the detective."

The detective bought the popcorn.

In the dark they stood, waiting for their irises to open wide, moving then cautiously, through the screen credits, arm in arm, toward seats. It was Los Angeles in the thirties. Water, said Mr. Mulray of the Department of Water and Power, belonged to the people. Mr. Mulray wore expensive suits, however, and his wife, Faye Dunnaway, drove a cream colored convertible not usually available to the people. This apparent contradiction made Jack Nicholson lift his famous eyebrow skeptically.

Chinatown was a place he had worked as a police detective back when times were even more corrupt and violent than now, notwithstanding the fact that somebody recently had sliced one of Nicholson's nostrils because they had found him snooping around the Department of Water and Power's dam.

You're better off not knowing, Nicholson was saying to a client who thought his wife was cheating on him, saying it in a way that meant this statement might be more than cheap advice to a jealous husband. You're better off not knowing.

Knowing meant caring, it seemed, and people began suffering all over the screen for caring. Then Jack Nicholson was stepping off a boat . . . onto the Tuna Club dock but calling it the Albacore Club ("Apple core," his operative had heard Faye Dunnaway's father, Noah Cross, say through the roar of traffic on Wilshire Boulevard) and listening to the chimes from the bell tower tolling the hour, and driving off through palms and sunlight in a station wagon with wooden sides. Her heart tightened as they followed along Casino Way, her hand tightened on Marcie next to her as they drove the station wagon up to the Wrigley Mansion to see Noah Cross and watch him lunch on a fish with its head on while he talked about loving his daughter (which one?) so much, making it imperative for Jack Nicholson never to have another curious thought about anybody in Noah Cross' family ever again.

The bandage on Jack Nicholson's nose emphasized this thought. The bandage said, You're better off not knowing. Still, Jack Nicholson kept on being curious, kept on demanding answers to the questions that stood up like stricken palm trees wherever he looked.

In the end it turned out that while Faye Dunnaway's father may have loved his daughter and his daughters, he loved land and water and money much more, that the water which Mr. Mulray had said belonged to the people ended up belonging to Faye Dunnaway's father and Faye Dunnaway ended up being dead. In her cream-colored convertible.

And while Elizabeth knew she was not Faye Dunnaway, alive or dead, and that Leon Feeney was not anybody's Noah Cross, she also knew a thief of land and water when she saw one, a hypocritical spoiler of daughters, and she knew as the houselights flickered on and she saw this woman, Marcie, standing smiling at her, that she, Elizabeth Austen Rivers, had been given her commission as private investigator.

CHAPTER 50: REVISION

"What does it matter to you what I do? You won't be here to see it. You made a decision, I made a decision, and that's that," said Grace.

Elizabeth looked at the insides of her folded hands. Her legs sprawled out in front of her. She felt like her insides were seeping out and becoming evident. Grace was staring at a spot on the patio as if something were about to manifest itself there.

"I just don't see," said Elizabeth, drawing her feet in and resting both hands next to her on the rough bench, "what Elaine has to do with any of this."

"What did you think I would do; sit and wait for you like your mother waited for your wandering father? The figure in the door, staring out to sea? The waiting woman? I have needs too, Elizabeth."

"Yes," said Elizabeth. "I know."

"Do you? Do you? I wonder."

"I know Elaine gives you something, something you want. But Elaine is a very closeted person. You haven't lived like that, not ever. I can't think you'll like it."

"You don't know what it's like out there for people like Elaine and me. It's like you're still living on the Island. You're cut off from reality. We're on the line. Every minute."

"What line? said Elizabeth. "What is this exclusivity, anyhow?"

"The line you stand on while people try to shoot you off. The line you walk to earn a living."

"I've earned a living," said Elizabeth quietly. "Surely you haven't forgotten already."

"This is different, Elizabeth. And you're not going to understand until you become a professional like Elaine and me."

"That's a crock of shit, Grace. And you know it. You don't even sound like yourself. It's like Elaine's really doing the talking while she pulls a string that moves your mouth up and down."

"We aren't that different, Elaine and I. Probably you can't see that."

"I see that she has no intention of ever living with you. That kind of woman won't leave her husband. She has things now the way she wants them."

"She's different now, changing. She can't live like that anymore. She wants my help. She needs me."

"She needs you alright. But not in the way you hope, Grace. The energy is going to flow in one direction only. And you and I both know who'll be the power source." Elizabeth glanced at her watch.

"And that's what I mean." Grace stood abruptly and pointed at Elizabeth's watch. "For the last month you've either been at Marcie's or on your way."

"I promised I'd stay with Jenna while Marcie visits

Mrs. Tyson in the hospital."

"And the sudden interest in children."

"I've always liked children."

"You've always liked the *idea* of children. Not the *fact* of them. It's part of your *pioneer family* idea, just a blueprint. You never intend to really go through the inconvenience of a commitment like that. Your head tells you to do things, like going back to Avalon now, after all these years. But there's no way you could ever turn those utopian dreams of yours into hard facts, even if you wanted to. You're just like your father, a wanderer."

"You don't believe that," said Elizabeth, getting to her feet. "Let's not say things we don't mean. It really won't make us feel any better."

"You're edging toward the door. I can feel it."

"I promised her."

"You promised *me*," said Grace.

CHAPTER 51: REMOTE CONTROL

Mrs. Tyson had deflated down to the girl that had always lived inside her. She lay on the hospital bed with two IVs in each arm and fluids running through tubes like some complex Japanese transportation system. The stands that held the four plastic sacks looked like traffic lights. Each one had a red light and a green light. Stop and go. All that movement going on inside Mrs. Tyson's body.

Her eyes snapped open. She had always believed you could not die if your eyes were open, even though people often died in movies with their eyes open and their friends, or even a kind stranger, would have to close them by hand.

She lifted her left arm, slowly. It was covered with bruises, as if she had been beaten. She had done nothing to deserve this abuse, unless it was to live too long. Now she was supposed to die. The bruises were part of the beating life gave you to get you to the point where you would agree to die, or even ask to die.

Same way with the food. Mrs. Tyson heard the distant tinkle of silverware. The dinners traveled on wheels with aluminum covers over their tops so visitors would not be revolted in the halls. When the nurse lifted the cover the aroma of flayed beef would reach down Mrs. Tyson's throat and yank upward on whatever was left of her innards. Then she would slowly shake her head.

They did not like it if you sent your plate back with each clump of food still in place, looking like bright countries on a map. They would not believe you had given your dinner the benefit of the doubt.

Mrs. Tyson did not want to eat any more of what used to be living creatures: cows stolen from their pastures to have their throats cut. Chickens from the henhouse. She saw her grandmother standing in front of the clothesline swinging two chickens in opposite directions over her head. Fish pulled from the sea.

Do unto others. She would have no more of it. God might feel as strong about fish as about cows. God might feel almost anything at all.

Mrs. Sinibaldi in the next bed, her curtain drawn between them, twirled the channels. Remote control. Every afternoon she watched soap operas, one after another, as if she must drip them through tubes into herself to stay alive.

The silverware advanced, grew louder. Mrs. Sinibaldi yelled for her walker. She did not understand pushing the button to call the nurse, only the button to change the channel.

Mrs. Tyson let fall her eyelids. She would rest like this for a minute. It was safe enough. She had not yet gone through enough pain to be allowed to die. In time the pain would arrive for which they could not give her quite enough morphine. After she had refused one dinner too many.

Behind black velvet eyelids she painted a picture of the seashore. She was sitting under her red umbrella, her hand resting in a bag of fig newtons, while Jennifer dug in the sand close by.

Somehow the cat had come with them and wanted a fig newton. Mrs. Tyson explained patiently to her cat about how only the fit could survive. Jamie pasted his ears flat against his head and started pulling and kneading at the blanket with his claws. "Oh, alright," said Mrs. Tyson reaching into the bag. But when she opened her clenched hand in front of the cat, she held—not a fig newton—but a tiny green house made of plastic.

"I'll take a hotel," Jamie said.

"You'll have to wait," Mrs. Tyson said irritably. "It's not like I'm going to live forever."

"Let's try another game, then," said Jamie, "if you don't like that one."

"It's not that," said Mrs. Tyson. "I'm tired, is all."

"We'll play a quiet game, then," conceded Jamie. "How about *Scissors, Rock, Paper?* That's very quiet and you don't have to think much, which is always an advantage."

"I don't know how," said Mrs. Tyson, wondering if she had remembered to put zinc oxide on Jennifer's nose.

While she looked seaward a large, sailing ship appeared very close to the playing child. Mrs. Tyson put the binoculars to her eyes. There were women on board. Women and children. They were all looking at Jenna. The child waved her red shovel at them three times.

"Pay attention," said the cat.

"It's not like I'm going to live forever."

"I know that," said Jamie. "Anybody knows that. But this game doesn't take very long. Not nearly as long as the one with green houses and red hotels."

The women on the boat were beckoning now, and the children calling to Jenna. They were going somewhere important and wanted her to come.

"Did you remember your zinc oxide," called Mrs. Tyson

to her granddaughter.

Jennifer pointed to her white nose, waved, and climbed over the side into the arms of the children.

"Well, then," said Jamie. "We can play our little game now. Do you choose scissors, rock, or paper?"

"Scissors, of course," said Mrs. Tyson, waving at the disappearing stern of the white ship.

"Wrong again," Jamie said. "Now hand over that hotel."

"Let me rest first," said Mrs. Tyson, not able to remember where she kept the red hotels.

"And I suppose you'll want to eat your dinner first. It looks disgusting."

Mrs. Tyson's eyes snapped open. The nurse was taking the aluminum cover off her dinner. "We'll eat today," she said.

"Wrong again," said Mrs. Tyson, closing her eyes.

CHAPTER 52: TIME BEING

Marcie watched until the tail lights of Lane's station wagon disappeared around the corner. She stood on the front porch in her pajamas long after, as if there might be a change of plan. A reprieve.

Mr. Kasarian's front door opened and he came out in his robe looking for the newspaper. Marcie went inside. The house was still. Jennifer would not be up for an hour. Time felt emptied out and folded up flat like a used grocery bag.

There was still coffee in the pot. Marcie poured some into Elizabeth's cup and drank. She did not want to read the paper. The letters in the words would fall apart in her mind. She thought she might go back to bed but stopped in the doorway, not wanting to feel the warmth of Elizabeth in the rumpled covers.

She would have a bath, until the sun came up and the world shook itself awake. Then she would have someplace to go. The first day of school.

Marcie put the stopper in the tub and opened both taps wide. Elizabeth had asked her if she'd bought her Big Chief tablet yet, knowing instinctively how the first day of school had—all her life—made her heart beat faster, that she was a person who marked off her life by semesters and holidays, who felt the excitement every September when twenty-five people all carried their Big Chief tablets to Room 5.

But there was none of that today. She had not bought her Big Chief tablet.

She pulled the blue stool up to the bathtub and set the coffee cup down. Then she slipped out of her pajamas and into the bath. Water lapped at the overflow drain. She turned off the taps and slid down until she floated just below the surface, belly and breasts rising slightly above, like three islands.

Elizabeth would be on the freeway now, silent against the window, Lane trying to make conversation. Elizabeth there, she here. Incomprehensible. There was time, and there was place. Incomprehensible. Really they were all figures on a board, moving by dice-throws, she, ironically, the shoe.

No. That was not true. She sat up suddenly, sloshing water almost over the rim of the tub. It was she who had said to Elizabeth that evening after the movie, Then you've got to go! It was she who had made gestures, flinging out one arm saying some nonsense about keeping the despoilers from the land, about women's houses, about giving back and not just taking. And she had meant it, really, every word.

If someone took you up on your own pronouncements, then you could not, in good conscience, rage and smash furniture. She had learned long ago, painfully, that consequences followed, as if by invitation. All this she accepted. Or would accept. Still, in her mind furniture broke. She babbled in Ophelia's voice and scattered torn flowers.

Floating again, the three islands rose, her belly looking like the island she had watched from Mrs. Tyson's kitchen window long ago. Mrs. Tyson, the folds of her chin cascading down to her breast, the breast spreading wide in turn like ripples in a lava flow, a faint smell of oppressed flesh and baby powder rising from the creases and crevices as she stood on her toes, reaching, stretching for her red plastic pocketbook on top the refrigerator, dislodging the white cat, Jamie, hitting the linoleum floor hard with his soft feet, and Mrs. Tyson gone out the screen door to the A&P for the morning, forever.

But the window remained. Mrs. Tyson's kitchen window that framed that island, island of cottages and jazz bands, island like a woman sleeping, she had thought then, feeling a longing for that woman, an ache beginning in her mind and ending in her body, satisfied only years later, by Elizabeth, Elizabeth opening to her, holding nothing back.

Elizabeth, that night when Marcie saw her for the first time, standing in the doorway to the library at the Daily Planet, uncertain, light from behind falling through her dark hair, saying, "I have something for you."

This store of love. And where did it come from? Other women had held themselves back from Marcie, held back pieces of themselves as if against impending famine. Elizabeth had not. Against her knock, Elizabeth had flung wide the door and given her welcome, spreading the table as if for a feast.

She could do this, Elizabeth, because she loved herself. Not greedily, not out of fear, or need, but out of health and strength. And Marcie loved herself the same. That was why—and she did not say this out of pride—she, of all women, could love Elizabeth the right way, near and far, from either end of the telescope. It was her best self that had decided to stand back for now, for the time being, letting time flow past her like a stiff breeze from behind while Elizabeth sailed on ahead.

CHAPTER 53: AVALON

Elizabeth ran her hand along the splintered railing of the cutter's gangplank. Beneath, in the crevices between boat and dock, debris washed: a beer bottle, a cast-off lobster trap, a sea gull, its head plunged into the foul water as if seeking a grim final supper, one leg curiously twisted, floating. Elizabet turned away, watched her own feet in faded deck shoes climbing the splintered boards, following close behind a laboring fat lady in white lace-up shoes pulling a child behind her as if he were a wagon.

On deck now, Elizabeth turned to look for Lane. She stood alone, apart from the small collection of sleepy people who had come to see their loved ones sail off-season on a rusty water taxi. Lane raised her arm and waved it in sweeping arcs of farewell. Elizabeth waved back, then crossed the narrow deck and entered the cabin.

The stink and racket of the diesels eased. A bar stood against one wall, where coffee scorched in two smeary coffee carafes, and an odd assortment of liquor bottles saw double in a foggy mirror. Fiberglass benches ran from port to starboard, both inside the cabin and outside, on the forward deck. No use going on deck until they were beyond the sea wall. The water was polluted with factory waste and oil spills; the air with greasy, rancid smells from the soap plant. Elizabeth tossed her backpack onto a bench next to the splattered plexiglass window that ran the length of the cabin on either side.

Tucking her legs up under her, Elizabeth felt another afternoon collide with this: she and Sally Bates on the *Island Queen* heading for the Isthmus with supplies, Sally asleep and Elizabeth sitting cross-legged at the wheel, her eyes sweeping the cliffs for wild goat. On a quest, she had been, searching the lost seas for Florence Chadwick, she who went before. More than ten years!

And yet, what did that mean? She could smile at that Elizabeth struggling over rocks and sliding down cliffs to wind her way to Karl, the oracle. But this was a quest too, today. And here she was, surer in some ways, less sure in others, still Elizabeth, daughter of Eddie the Sailor, voyaging out (I don't know yet how far I can swim), pressing, pressing toward the secret of the island that sleeps on the horizon.

The fat lady settled the child on her lap. Mr. Smallwood from the bank sat in the far corner reading the *Wall Street Journal*. Lines hit the deck, screws labored. They were away.

There was something, it struck Elizabeth now, as she watched the child in the fat lady's lap snuggle against the pillows of warm flesh, something undeniably solitary about this business of adventures. When she thought back to that last summer at home and saw her slim, warrior self, the virgin, clambering over rocks, standing in the shadows and peering into windows at dusk, leaping off the Pleasure Pier after treasure, whizzing down streets on her bicycle she always saw herself alone.

But there had been another self too, the one who trembled in Juno Reed's energy field, who dogged her steps around the island for two years, the one who took the glass from her sleeping mother's hand before it could slip, this caretaker self opening cans of tuna for her rival's cat.

Ah, and it was she who only three days ago had held Marcie Tyson lovingly in her arms murmuring, "Come with me, oh, come with me." She rose quickly and grabbed her backpack.

The fore deck was deserted. Against the rail she crushed her pack, heard the pencil inside snap, like something breaking inside herself. This fragile caretaker self.

She hated to be fragile. Anger grew up around her now like a stockade. Armed, she stood at every window.

Not fair, life. Marcie. Marcie showing her Leon's real danger, saying, "A woman's house, Elizabeth. This," she had said, sweeping her hand through her own house that evening, after the film, "this house is a woman's house. Two women, lovers, poured their love into the very walls." She had stood, trembling, defiant, as if she would slay single-handed any male who threatened her house. This woman, this lovely Marcie, whom time had made both gentle and strong.

And they had loved that night at a heat new to Elizabeth, their hands moving like candlelight, their wandering selves surprising each other around corners, behind doors, down canyons, across deserts, on the floor of the old sea. Adventures were no longer private, but honed and focused down to a single shared image as if through powerful binoculars.

"I'm not saying no to you," she had said. "You know that."

But it had felt like a no. It had sung through the air and hit her heart like an axe. It cleaved her. She could not breathe.

Lane looking up from paperwork at the bar, peering over magnifying specatcles, her gray hair sticking up where she had tried to pull the answers out of her brain. "She only means you should wait, that you are both just out of relationships."

Elizabeth's face appeared in the bar mirror. There was a bruised look around her eyes and mouth. She had looked down, at Lane's papers. Figures all over. Disobedient figures. Pi r square.

"And there's the child," she was saying, "Jennifer."

"But I want to help," Elizabeth had said, her hands tingling oddly, as if they were suddenly growing. Caretaker hands. She knew she was strong.

"A year won't hurt," Lane had said, taking one of Elizabeth's huge hands in her own small ones, "if this is what we all three think it is."

"I couldn't stand it if you quoted Emerson," gulped Elizabeth. "I really couldn't."

"What's that?" asked the fat lady, suddenly appearing at Elizabeth's elbow with the child tucked under her ponderous arm like a pocketbook.

"Used to be a lighthouse," said Elizabeth, squinting to port. "Abandoned," she said.

The lady nodded philosophically. "At least the water's getting cleaner. You on a holiday?"

"Moving," said Elizabeth.

"I didn't know anybody lived here," said the fat lady, nodding in the direction of the island. "Don't seem likely."

"Not likely, but true nonetheless," said Elizabeth, picking up her backpack from the deck, excusing herself, and moving away toward one of the benches on the opposite side.

The sea wall was just ahead. The wind quickened. She craned her neck around for another look at the lighthouse. There were government signs nailed all around the door and two boards nailed across. Up toward the top a large window had been broken out, and the initials WV had been spray-painted in red across another.

She could have been a lighthouse keeper and a good one. All day she would read novels, play music, or write. At night she would tend the light and watch through her telescope for ships in distress. On a table by her bed would be a journal, a book, and a small ship-to-shore radio with earphones. "This is a Mayday," she said out loud.

It might be rough today. There was some promise of it. Away to starboard she could see a ketch with its sails billowing, and she thought with a little start of excitement, how at sundown she would walk along Crescent Bay once again, listening to the sounds of dinner coming from the moored sailboats and the snatches of conversation, words walking on water. And then she would stroll home to her own house on Clarissa Street, her own house which she would snatch from the jaws of Leon Feeney's world-wrecking tractors if it was the last thing she ever did.

And in this house she would write her novel. Not the old tormented novel with its timid, harried characters, but a new novel that somehow would write itself, a novel of women.

Elizabeth looked again toward the sailboat, its railing buried now in speeding, freezing water, saw a yellow slicker, a hand raised, waving, and then, just astern, a school of porpoises, rolling and roiling, all but laughing, not knowing exactly how far they could swim.

Yes, said Elizabeth to nobody in particular. Then she pulled out her spiral notebook from her backpack and on a clean page wrote with a broken, yellow pencil:

Austen stood in the bow of the ship. Slits of light began appearing in the western sky. Behind her, groups of women and children curled together in two's and three's, surrounded by their possessions, rocked and lulled as wind and sail bore the sleeping pioneers on toward a new life. Austen lifted the binoculars to her eyes.

A few of the publications of
THE NAIAD PRESS, INC.
P.O. Box 10543 • Tallahassee, Florida 32302
Mail orders welcome. Please include 15% postage.

Spring Forward/Fall Back by Sheila Ortiz Taylor. A novel. 288 pp.
ISBN 0-930044-70-3 $7.95

For Keeps by Elisabeth C. Nonas. A novel. 144 pp.
ISBN 0-930044-71-1 $7.95

Torchlight to Valhalla by Gail Wilhelm. A novel. 128 pp.
ISBN 0-930044-68-1 $7.95

Lesbian Nuns: Breaking Silence edited by Rosemary Curb and
Nancy Manahan. Autobiographies. 432 pp.
ISBN 0-930044-62-2 $9.95
ISBN 0-930044-63-0 $16.95

The Swashbuckler by Lee Lynch. A novel. 288 pp.
ISBN 0-930044-66-5 $7.95

Misfortune's Friend by Sarah Aldridge. A novel. 320 pp.
ISBN 0-930044-67-3 $7.95

A Studio of One's Own by Ann Stokes. Edited by Dolores
Klaich. Autobiography. 128 pp. ISBN 0-930044-64-9 $7.95

Sex Variant Women in Literature by Jeannette Howard Foster.
Literary history. 448 pp. ISBN 0-930044-65-7 $8.95

A Hot-Eyed Moderate by Jane Rule. Essays. 252 pp.
ISBN 0-930044-57-6 $7.95
ISBN 0-930044-59-2 $13.95

Inland Passage and Other Stories by Jane Rule. 288 pp.
ISBN 0-930044-56-8 $7.95
ISBN 0-930044-58-4 $13.95

We Too Are Drifting by Gale Wilhelm. A novel. 128 pp.
ISBN 0-930044-61-4 $6.95

Amateur City by Katherine V. Forrest. A mystery novel. 224 pp.
ISBN 0-930044-55-X $7.95

The Sophie Horowitz Story by Sarah Schulman. A novel. 176 pp.
ISBN 0-930044-54-1 $7.95

The Young in One Another's Arms by Jane Rule. A novel.
224 pp. ISBN 0-930044-53-3 $7.95

The Burnton Widows by Vicki P. McConnell. A mystery novel.
272 pp. ISBN 0-930044-52-5 $7.95

Old Dyke Tales by Lee Lynch. Short stories. 224 pp.
ISBN 0-930044-51-7 $7.95

Daughters of a Coral Dawn by Katherine V. Forrest. Science
fiction. 240 pp. ISBN 0-930044-50-9 $7.95

The Price of Salt by Claire Morgan. A novel. 288 pp.
ISBN 0-930044-49-5 $7.95

Against the Season by Jane Rule. A novel. 224 pp.
ISBN 0-930044-48-7 $7.95

Lovers in the Present Afternoon by Kathleen Fleming. A novel.
288 pp. ISBN 0-930044-46-0 $8.50

Toothpick House by Lee Lynch. A novel. 264 pp.
ISBN 0-930044-45-2 $7.95

Madame Aurora by Sarah Aldridge. A novel. 256 pp.
ISBN 0-930044-44-4 $7.95

Curious Wine by Katherine V. Forrest. A novel. 176 pp.
ISBN 0-930044-43-6 $7.50

Black Lesbian in White America by Anita Cornwell. Short stories,
essays, autobiography. 144 pp. ISBN 0-930044-41-X $7.50

Contract with the World by Jane Rule. A novel. 340 pp.
ISBN 0-930044-28-2 $7.95

Yantras of Womanlove by Tee A. Corinne. Photographs.
64 pp. ISBN 0-930044-30-4 $6.95

Mrs. Porter's Letter by Vicki P. McConnell. A mystery novel.
224 pp. ISBN 0-930044-29-0 $6.95

To the Cleveland Station by Carol Anne Douglas. A novel.
192 pp. ISBN 0-930044-27-4 $6.95

The Nesting Place by Sarah Aldridge. A novel. 224 pp.
ISBN 0-930044-26-6 $6.95

This Is Not for You by Jane Rule. A novel. 284 pp.
ISBN 0-930044-25-8 $7.95

Faultline by Sheila Ortiz Taylor. A novel. 140 pp.
ISBN 0-930044-24-X $6.95

The Lesbian in Literature by Barbara Grier. 3d ed. Foreword by
Maida Tilchen. A comprehensive bibliography. 240 pp.
ISBN 0-930044-23-1 $7.95

Anna's Country by Elizabeth Lang. A novel. 208 pp.
ISBN 0-930044-19-3 $6.95

Prism by Valerie Taylor. A novel. 158 pp.
ISBN 0-930044-18-5 $6.95

Black Lesbians: An Annotated Bibliography compiled by
J. R. Roberts. Foreword by Barbara Smith. 112 pp.
ISBN 0-930044-21-5 .... $5.95

The Marquise and the Novice by Victoria Ramstetter. A novel.
108 pp. ISBN 0-930044-16-9 .... $4.95

Labiaflowers by Tee A. Corinne. 40 pp.
ISBN 0-930044-20-7 .... $3.95

Outlander by Jane Rule. Short stories, essays. 207 pp.
ISBN 0-930044-17-7 .... $6.95

Sapphistry: The Book of Lesbian Sexuality by Pat Califia. 2nd
edition, revised. 195 pp. ISBN 0-930044-47-9 .... $7.95

All True Lovers by Sarah Aldridge. A novel. 292 pp.
ISBN 0-930044-10-X $6.95

A Woman Appeared to Me by Renee Vivien. Translated by
Jeannette H. Foster. A novel. xxxi, 65 pp.
ISBN 0-930044-06-1 .... $5.00

Cytherea's Breath by Sarah Aldridge. A novel. 240 pp.
ISBN 0-930044-02-9 .... $6.95

Tottie by Sarah Aldridge. A novel. 181 pp.
ISBN 0-930044-01-0 .... $6.95

The Latecomer by Sarah Aldridge. A novel. 107 pp.
ISBN 0-930044-00-2 .... $5.00

VOLUTE BOOKS

Journey to Fulfillment	by Valerie Taylor	$3.95
A World without Men	by Valerie Taylor	$3.95
Return to Lesbos	by Valerie Taylor	$3.95
Desert of the Heart	by Jane Rule	$3.95
Odd Girl Out	by Ann Bannon	$3.95
I Am a Woman	by Ann Bannon	$3.95
Women in the Shadows	by Ann Bannon	$3.95
Journey to a Woman	by Ann Bannon	$3.95
Beebo Brinker	by Ann Bannon	$3.95

These are just a few of the many Naiad Press titles. Please request a
complete catalog! We encourage and welcome direct mail orders from
individuals who have limited access to bookstores carrying our publications.